**Joanna Johnson** lives in a little village with her husband and too many books. After completing an English degree at university she went on to work in publishing, although she always wished she was working on her own books rather than other people's. This dream came true in 2018 when she signed her first contract with Mills & Boon, and she hasn't looked back. She now spends her time getting lost in mainly Regency history and wishing it was acceptable to write a manuscript using a quill.

**Also by Joanna Johnson**

'Their Yuletide Reunion'
in *Snowbound Regency Christmas*
*One Secret Away from Ruin*
*A Marriage to Shock Society*
*Their Inconvenient Yuletide Wedding*
*Her Grace's Daring Proposal*
'A Kiss at the Winter Ball'
in *Regency Christmas Parties*
*The Officer's Convenient Proposal*
*The Return of Her Long-Lost Husband*

Discover more at millsandboon.co.uk.

# MARRIAGE MADE IN SCANDAL

Joanna Johnson

MILLS & BOON

All rights reserved including the right of reproduction in whole or in part in any form. This edition is published by arrangement with Harlequin Enterprises ULC.

This is a work of fiction. Names, characters, places, locations and incidents are purely fictional and bear no relationship to any real life individuals, living or dead, or to any actual places, business establishments, locations, events or incidents. Any resemblance is entirely coincidental.

Without limiting the exclusive rights of any author, contributor or the publisher of this publication, any unauthorised use of this publication to train generative artificial intelligence (AI) technologies is expressly prohibited. HarperCollins also exercise their rights under Article 4(3) of the Digital Single Market Directive 2019/790 and expressly reserve this publication from the text and data mining exception.

® and TM are trademarks owned and used by the trademark owner and/or its licensee. Trademarks marked with ® are registered with the United Kingdom Patent Office and/or the Office for Harmonisation in the Internal Market and in other countries.

First published in Great Britain 2026
by Mills & Boon, an imprint of HarperCollins*Publishers* Ltd,
1 London Bridge Street, London, SE1 9GF

www.harpercollins.co.uk

HarperCollins*Publishers*, Macken House, 39/40 Mayor Street Upper, Dublin 1, D01 C9W8, Ireland

Marriage Made in Scandal © 2026 Joanna Johnson

ISBN: 978-0-263-41874-3

03/26

Printed and Bound in the UK using 100% Renewable Electricity at CPI Group (UK) Ltd, Croydon, CR0 4YY

# Chapter One

'Sit up straight. Pull your shoulders back. Not too far! Don't thrust your bosom out—but don't hunch either. Any moment now he'll look this way and you must be ready when he does. Remember: dignity at all times.'

Mrs Burcombe's instructions issued from the side of her mouth but her daughter paid them little heed. There was no need for anyone to tell Louisa how important it was that she showed herself to her best advantage as she sat on her uncle's sofa, willing the young man on the other side of the crowded parlour to turn in her direction. Every time he moved her pulse quickened and she laced her fingers more tightly in her lap, outwardly serene but beneath her bodice her heart fluttering like a trapped bird.

*I wonder who'll break first if he doesn't turn round soon: me or Mama?*

Both women were well aware of what was at stake as they waited for him to glance over. With her twenty-fourth birthday looming time for her to find a husband was running out and Sir Christopher Stanhope's return to town after years abroad had come like a gift from above. It might be her last chance to avoid the spinsterhood that beckoned and she took a breath to steady the jangling of her nerves.

It was largely her own fault she was in such a precarious position, she had to admit. There had been a number of innocent flirtations since her debut and quite a few gentlemen who had expressed an interest in taking things further, but no proposal had ever followed and Louisa knew for that she was to blame—although it *could* have been argued that her parents should have shouldered at least some of the responsibility for her remaining so long on the shelf.

The birth of a daughter almost a decade after the last of three sons had come as a surprise for both Mr and Mrs Burcombe, who were occupied by ensuring the raising and education of their trio of fine boys. The late-coming little girl was pushed into the background, regarded with distracted fondness but trusted to the care of a succession of nannies whose affections were paid for rather than sincere.

Her basic needs were met, but she was the centre of nobody's world, left to her own devices as her older brothers took precedence in their parents' attentions. Perhaps it should have been no great shock that to feel wanted was something she came to crave more than anything else. The desire to be valued rather than overlooked, combined with unchecked hours in the library voraciously consuming her mother's collection of novels, shaped Louisa's impressionable and lonely mind. By the time her brothers had all left home and her mama remembered she had a daughter whose future also needed consideration, it was already far too late.

Her views on matrimony had been irreversibly formed. A man who truly cared for her was the only one she would entertain, she had decided when she was barely eight years old, determined that in marriage she would find what had been lacking all her life. An acquaintance formed over the course of a single ball was not enough to tell her whether such a deeper understanding was likely and so she'd hung back from her suitors rather than pushing herself towards them, preferring to take their measure first instead of blindly racing after status or wealth.

A more obliging young lady generally came along at just the wrong moment and whisked the young man away, a predictable turn of events that always made Mrs Burcombe pinch the bridge of her nose and sigh, but it only proved to Louisa that he evidently hadn't been the right choice. *Her* husband would only have eyes for her, always making her the priority she'd never been rather than an afterthought, and when she wed it would be to someone with whom she felt a connection that stood a good chance of blossoming into something more.

Love took time to grow, her books had told her, and she wasn't so foolish as to expect it to be immediately apparent, but a mutual warm regard was the first step towards it. Now Sir Christopher had arrived in Warwick, it seemed her desires might finally have the potential to come true.

Unfortunately, she wasn't the only one who had noticed his return.

'There goes Miss Jarvis again, talking his ear off,' Mrs Burcombe muttered, glowering across the room to where a young woman had drawn Sir Christopher into conversation. 'I'm amazed your uncle invited so many ladies to stay. Doesn't he care at all about his niece's prospects?'

'I imagine he cares a great deal, considering how often you've raised the subject with him,' Louisa replied wearily, privately thinking that her mama's own concern for such a thing was only a relatively recent development. 'He could hardly tell his friends to leave their daughters at home so I might have first pick of the parties' eligible men, however.'

Mama tutted. 'Your brothers wouldn't be so passive. You might put up a little more of a fight. That Jarvis girl has been putting herself in his way ever since she got here and she's determined enough to get results.'

Reluctantly Louisa followed the direction of her mother's disapproving gaze. Sir Christopher *did* seem to be enjoying the other woman's company, perhaps almost as much as he'd appeared to appreciate her own over the previous few days.

Uncle Emanuel's frequent gatherings generally lasted the best part of a week, during which time as many guests as possible were crammed into Cressex Hall, and there had been plenty of opportunities for her and Sir Christopher to take turns around the gardens and compare their favourite books. To her mind they had got on well, the accord between them growing nicely, so she couldn't deny a flicker of dismay as Miss Jarvis tapped him flirtatiously with her fan… and he didn't move away.

The unpleasant jolt was difficult to ignore, but she tried none the less. 'Would you have me fling myself at him? What happened to "dignity at all times"?'

'It would be better than just sitting and watching someone else take him as you usually do,' Mrs Burcombe countered. 'I thought you'd decided *this* one was worth your notice. Now you finally have an admirer you like, are you really content to let someone steal him from under your nose?'

'Steal him?'

Louisa frowned at her mother, glad to look away from the young lady coyly smiling up into Sir Christopher's face. 'He doesn't belong to me. As much as I like him, you know I won't beg a man to choose me if he'd prefer another.'

Her mother tutted again, this time a little more forcefully. 'Please, darling. Don't begin again with that romantic folly. And no one said anything of begging. A woman of twenty-five, however, can't afford to be too proud.'

'I'm twenty-three, Mama.'

'Well. That's hardly any better. In the blink of an eye you'll be thirty and if you're still not wed by *then*, what will you do?'

Louisa didn't have an immediate response to that nightmarish scenario, but fortunately a deep voice from behind their sofa came to her rescue.

'She'll come to visit her old uncle, or so I'd hope. Even an unmarried thirty-year-old niece would be welcome at Cressex Hall.'

Both women twisted to look up at the man now leaning over them. Uncle Emanuel stood arm in arm with his wife, first beaming down at them but then directing his attention to the other side of the busy room. Another couple of young ladies had gravitated towards Sir Christopher, who was now surrounded by beauties hanging on his every word, and their host shook his head in mild bemusement.

'They flock to him like bees to a honeypot, don't they? Poor Stanhope. I remember when he was just a boy—nobody was this interested in him *then*.'

'Keep your voice down, my dear.' Aunt Eliza patted her husband's arm, a gentle reminder that a distinguished military career spent standing directly next to a cannon had rendered him inclined to speak a little too loudly. 'That's because he hadn't yet inherited.

A man is always so much more fascinating after he's come into his fortune.'

'Is that why you married me? A wretched creature old enough to be your father?'

Aunt Eliza rolled her eyes at this oft-repeated joke. 'Of course not. Rich or not I would have loved you anyway. And the age difference isn't so very great. What's a mere two decades when a couple is otherwise so well suited?'

Mama pursed her lips at such flippancy, but Louisa slid her aunt a smile. There were less than ten years between them and as a result their relationship was friendly rather than formal, although when she saw the twinkle in Eliza's eye Louisa suddenly wondered whether a touch more formality could be a good thing.

'So, Louisa? Do you have a liking for our wealthiest bachelor yourself?' Aunt Eliza murmured discreetly, although still with that knowing gleam. 'A love match is always preferable, of course, but I suppose the Stanhope fortune would be a suitable consolation for any lack of real feeling.'

Louisa felt herself flush. How honest ought she be? Christopher was indeed a prize, but the substantial inheritance he'd recently received wasn't what had caught her attention. His smile had done that, followed swiftly by the discovery that he enjoyed Cowper's poems as much as she did. She liked him very much and crucially he seemed to think as highly of her in return, and she deliberately turned her head slightly to spare herself the sight of Miss Jarvis all but hanging off his arm.

'I admit a fortune would be useful, but his money isn't my first concern. He's pleasant and easy to talk to, and we like many of the same things. I would much rather marry a man based on a real connection instead of being led by his pocketbook, no matter how heavy it might be.'

'Bravo. Very well said.' Uncle Emanuel nodded approvingly, but then flashed an alarmingly unsubtle wink. 'Perhaps your motives aren't entirely noble, however. He's handsome as well as charming, or so many of the ladies here tell me.'

Louisa's blush deepened. 'I won't deny I'd noticed that.'

'Well. If you like him that much, I hope you're the one to secure him. It sounds as though you'd be a good match.'

Mrs Burcombe pounced. 'She'd stand a better chance if you helped her, Brother. How can you allow so many unmarried ladies into your house when your own niece is teetering on the brink of becoming an old maid?'

'An old maid?' Uncle Emanuel scoffed. 'Don't be absurd. She's only lost *some* of her bloom. I'll wager she stays handsome for at least another couple of years. It's pure bad luck that she's come close to landing a husband so many times only to be passed over at the last moment.'

Aunt Eliza's second warning tap on his arm came too late. Her uncle meant to defend her, Louisa was sure, but all the same she wished he'd kept his loud chivalry to himself. Fortunately Christopher was too far away to have heard, but all the same she preferred to avoid any more backhanded compliments and with her cheeks feeling like a pair of griddle pans she rose quickly to her feet.

'It's warm in here. I think I'll just go to step into the garden for a moment.'

Her aunt nodded in immediate understanding. 'Of course. I'm sure your mama wouldn't want you to develop a headache. A turn outside would do you good.'

Mrs Burcombe waved an assenting hand. She was watching Sir Christopher out of the corner of her eye, one that narrowed when another of his admirers lightly placed a finger on his sleeve. 'Yes, go. Then when he finally looks around he'll wonder where you went. A little mystique is no bad thing.'

With a grateful glance at Eliza Louisa turned for the door, although she paused when her aunt called after her.

'Oh. Don't be alarmed if you see a man out there. It'll only be my cousin. He arrived this morning, but as usual he'd rather skulk about on his own than come in and join everyone else.'

At Louisa's questioning look Eliza gave a wry smile. 'I don't believe you've met him. He lived in Staffordshire until very recently and took a house here in Warwick only last month. I invited him this weekend so he could meet people, but he's so unsociable I don't know how he expects to make any new acquaintance at all. If you do happen across him, he'll probably walk the other way rather than stop to talk.'

With a comical lift of an eyebrow Eliza returned her attention to her husband and sister-in-law, leaving Louisa free to make for the door that opened into the garden.

A cooling breeze hit her the moment she emerged and she lifted her face towards it, catching the scent of roses drifting up from beds beside the door. In the September sunshine every colour seemed especially vivid, from the lush green of the grass to the powder blue of hydrangeas waving in their pots, but it was difficult to fully appreciate the beauty around her as she wandered away from the house. Behind her she could still hear the buzz of conversations and laughter and hoped none of it concerned her, Uncle Emanuel's faux pas probably providing amusement for his guests whether he'd meant to or not.

She groaned inwardly. Cannon fire might have left *him* half-deaf, but that didn't mean his guests were likewise and she shrank from the thought of Christopher hearing her damned with such faint praise. If even her loved ones thought she was almost past her peak, there seemed small chance of him thinking any different and she felt a dark cloud forming above her as she turned off the lawn and down an avenue of trees.

She had no claim on him and yet seeing him enjoy his devotees' attentions stung all the same. Her dream was for a man who wanted her and no other and to instead find herself once again in some kind of queue made her steps drag. Christopher could have his pick of Warwickshire's ladies and if past experience was any guide he was unlikely to choose her, even if to her mind they had formed a connection. He was clever, well read and, yes, undeniably handsome, and it was no wonder he seemed to be relishing his popularity among the county's eligible belles.

'Perhaps Mama had a point,' she mused doubtfully. 'Maybe I should take a page from Miss Jarvis's book and throw myself in his path?'

Her nose wrinkled in automatic denial.

She had decided years ago she would never compete for a man's attention, jostling with other women like pigeons squabbling for crumbs. Her entire childhood had been spent feeling second-best, wishing she could claim more of her parents' interest, and she wouldn't countenance that again when it came to marriage. If Christopher had intentions towards her, he should make them plain instead of leaving her to guess... although such an outcome seemed more and more depressingly fanciful the further she walked.

A small courtyard lay at the end of the tree-lined avenue, in the middle of which stood a raised pond, and Louisa found herself drawing towards it. She'd sat on its edge countless times since she was a little girl frequently sent away to stay with her uncle and unthinkingly she twisted to sit and peer down into the rippling depths.

At first all she saw were the blurred outlines of fish, but as her eyes adjusted to the reflection of the sun on the water she recognised a familiar face gazing back at her. It looked weary and a little sad, and it copied her as she ruefully shook her head.

'Is it already too late?'

Her mirror image seemed to fear the same answer she did. If a marriage proposal wasn't secured after a debutante's first Season, or at the very least her second, then the chances of receiving one grew slim. Every year brought new young ladies and those that came before were pushed to the fringes, only able to watch as the cycle turned again and again. Miss Jarvis and her friends had been out barely a few months and their novel freshness drew male eyes with an ease it was impossible for more established women to compete with. That was just the way the marriage market was and would probably always be, and there was no point in railing against things that would never change.

'Christopher is probably my last chance.' She and her reflection exchanged grave looks as they acknowledged this unwanted truth. 'If he decides any connection between us isn't worth pursuing, I'll have to stay at home for ever, living with Mama and Papa until any hope of *really* meaning anything to someone has—'

'Have you dropped something?'

Louisa jumped so violently it was lucky she didn't fall into the water.

Her head jerked up. A dark-haired man was standing on the other side of the pond, watching her in vaguely guarded enquiry. She hadn't heard him approach through the opposite line of trees and his sudden appearance startled her into silence.

'Have you dropped something,' he repeated, now with a slight edge of impatience, 'into the water? Do you require assistance?'

The suggestion of irritation in his eyes helped her find her tongue. They were dark like his hair and might have been considered an appealing shade of cocoa brown had their expression been a little more friendly.

'Oh, no. Thank you. I was just…watching the fish.'

'I see. Pardon the intrusion.'

With an abruptness almost as startling as his unexpected arrival he swung around, evidently intending to leave the same way he had come. So determined was his retreat that Louisa knew there was only one person he could be and hurriedly she slipped down from the edge of the pond.

'Wait, Sir. Would I be right in thinking you are my Aunt Eliza's cousin?'

The man paused. He didn't seem pleased to be delayed, but he turned to her none the less, perhaps the mention of their hostess making him think twice. 'You would. Lord Harnham. And you are?'

'Miss Burcombe. Your cousin's husband is my uncle.'

She gave her most graceful curtsy, hoping to cover her surprise. Eliza hadn't mentioned her cousin was titled and Louisa wondered briefly what kind of lord he might be. He certainly looked well bred, she saw now as she rose and studied him more closely. He carried himself with the natural assurance of a powerful man, his broad shoulders held back and covered in a beautifully tailored coat, and his eyes showed the quick intelligence of an expensive education. From the top of his gleaming hat to the toes of his polished boots he exuded refinement and wealth, but also a cool detachment that told Louisa her smile was unlikely to be returned.

She was correct.

'That would, I suppose, account for you calling her *Aunt* Eliza.' He spoke almost rudely, although this time he at least offered her a terse nod before beginning to move off once more. 'Excuse me.'

He couldn't escape fast enough. He strode away from her with a firmness that implied he wouldn't be waylaid a second time and she was more than content to let him go, watching as he dipped back behind the line of trees and disappeared from view.

Waiting a moment to be sure he had gone, she

leaned over to address her reflection again. 'No wonder Aunt Eliza hadn't mentioned *him* before.'

Her watery twin agreed. Surely nobody would be in a rush to claim such an unfriendly relation, especially someone as hospitable as Eliza. Lord Harnham was good looking—in his early thirties, perhaps, with pleasing features and a firm jaw—but his conduct didn't match his face. A handsome countenance wasn't enough to make up for such an off-putting manner and, as Louisa seated herself again, reaching down to dabble her fingertips in the water, she hoped she wouldn't have cause to see much more of him.

'I imagine I'm safe enough there. Somehow, I don't think he'll be seeking me out for further conversation.'

She poked at a slimy wisp of pondweed, trying to recapture her train of thought. Eliza's cousin had interrupted her despondent line of thinking and perhaps for that he deserved *some* thanks. She'd been settling into gloom before he came along to distract her with his brusqueness, but even so she couldn't give him too much credit. There was only room for one man in her thoughts, after all...and soon enough she forgot about Lord Harnham completely as Sir Christopher returned to the forefront of her mind, taking hold there and refusing to let go.

Gabriel kept his head raised as he walked, scanning ahead to make sure he didn't stumble across any more young women scattered about the grounds. The one he'd just encountered had been quite attractive, with rich auburn hair and a friendly smile, and was therefore just the type he wanted to avoid. As Eliza's niece, however, that might be easier said than done and he realised he was frowning as he thought about what awaited him back at the Hall.

It had been a mistake to come in the first place and he wasn't entirely sure what had possessed him. He disliked large gatherings and this one was no different, the same sort of people as always stuffed into overheated rooms with nothing to do but gossip and play cards. It had been kind of his cousin to invite him to meet his new neighbours, but in hindsight he should have stayed at home, away from the prying eyes that would inevitably turn towards him once they learned of the reputation he was trying to outrun.

He sighed, unconsciously slowing his pace. How long would it take before the mutters that had surrounded him in Staffordshire followed him here? If it was just for his own sake, he wouldn't care what people said, but it was growing ever more important that Leah be shielded from what so many took to be the truth.

She was getting older now, able to understand more of what was whispered behind hands, and their hurried move to Warwick had felt like the closest of close shaves. He might not be able to hold back the rumours for ever, but he would for as long as he possibly could, his daughter's happiness too precious to warrant anything less.

A painful smile tugged at his lips. Doubtless she'd be having a wonderful time at that moment, currently away staying with his sister, Miriam, and her children near Oxford. She loved being with her cousins and already he'd received three letters telling him about all the adventures she'd had, along with her delight at sharing a bedroom with someone other than her stuffed bear.

He'd always tried to extend her visits there for as long as possible to shield her from the difficulties at home, but soon enough the letters would veer on to how much she missed him and he would know the time had come to fetch her back.

'Perhaps I won't need to send her away quite so much now. It might turn out I'm wrong and the lies they told won't reach us here.'

There was nobody around to contradict him, but even so he didn't have much confidence in his own muttered words. Gossip had a bad habit of travelling and his smile faded as he reminded himself just how much was at stake.

The secret that sat inside him so heavily was one he intended to keep. He could have told the truth, fighting the damning rumours with fact, but that would have left him open to something far worse. To speak out honestly would have revealed too much and so instead he'd weathered the storm of suspicion until it had come too close to touching Leah, then snatching her away before she could be swept up in a fiction it was too dangerous to deny.

The despicable falsehoods his former parents-in-law had spread about him following his wife's death had tarnished his once-respectable name, inviting murmurs and sidelong glances in the street. As the fifth Baron Harnham he had still been invited to every ball, but mothers no longer tried to steer their daughters into his path as they had before he'd been married, once the most eligible man in the county, but now looked at with a mixture of curiosity and fear.

No young ladies rushed to smile at him or tried to entice him into dancing with them, as they might have with any other wealthy widower, but of course for that he'd been grateful. He would never wed again after what had transpired with the first Lady Harnham and it was a relief that nobody seemed to want to change his mind—although he still wouldn't be taking any chances.

He kicked a stone out of the way, sending it scudding beneath a hedge. Keeping a sensible distance from single women was more difficult when his host had invited great hordes of them to stay at Cressex Hall and he grimaced to wonder which of the bevy of beauties he would be seated next to at dinner that night. Having to make conversation with any one of them was possibly the last thing he wanted, but he knew he couldn't stay in the gardens for ever and with an unwilling grunt he turned to make his way back to the house.

Eliza was on the patio when he reached it, gazing out across the lawn with a hand shading her eyes.

'Ah. The wanderer has returned. Did you happen to see Louisa on your travels? She went for a walk and has yet to come back.'

Gabriel paused. 'I met a Miss Burcombe, if that's who you mean. Auburn hair?'

'That's her. Sweet thing, isn't she? A little reserved on occasion, but good natured all the same.'

'If you say so.'

Eliza fended off his narrow glance with a perceptive one of her own. 'You needn't look at me like that. I have no hidden agenda in speaking well of her. I don't forget that you don't intend to remarry, even if you refuse to be drawn on why.'

She gestured towards the open garden door. 'Will you come inside? We'll be eating soon.'

'Yes. Thank you.'

With what he hoped was at least partially disguised reluctance he followed his cousin into the parlour. Immediately the sound of at least a dozen conversations enveloped him in a mess of raised voices, while a young lady exhibiting her prowess on the pianoforte did nothing to lessen the noise. A few interested glances flickered his way and Gabriel pretended not to see them, although he felt them on him as he leaned down to mutter into Eliza's ear, 'Dare I ask who you were thinking of seating me by this evening?'

Eliza snorted. 'I was waiting for that. I've put you next to Louisa, but you needn't suspect an attempt at matchmaking. Someone has already caught her eye, so you'll be quite safe.'

He nodded slowly, not completely reassured. This Louisa was pretty, he recalled, with hair that had glowed coppery in the sunlight and wide greenish eyes enhanced by the soft sage colour of her gown. At one time he would have been pleased to sit beside a woman with such an engaging smile, but not any more.

If she was already spoken for, however, she probably wouldn't spare him a second look—besides, he'd hardly charmed her on their first brief meeting. He'd been his usual surly self, or at least the self it seemed safest to favour these days, and even if Miss Burcombe's attentions hadn't been directed elsewhere he doubted she'd now be inclined to turn them on him.

Fortunately, Eliza didn't seem to notice his speculating. 'That's assuming she's back in time for supper, of course. I think Emanuel may have embarrassed her into hiding. He's the kindest man in the world, but also the least tactful. He knows he's given to shouting and yet saw fit to bellow details of her marital situation into a crowded room. If I were her, I think I'd have run off, too.'

She shook her head, exasperated, but Gabriel didn't

ask for further details. It was none of his concern what she meant by *marital situation* and he had no wish to know more. The world would be a much better place if more people minded their own business, he thought darkly, although his cousin's unease prodded him into making at least some reply.

'Will you send a servant for her?'

'I doubt I'll have to. If she doesn't return soon, her mama will go looking. Since her sons have left home my sister-in-law has apparently recalled she also has a daughter and there's no chance she'd let Louisa miss a dinner spent seated opposite a wealthy bachelor—especially one on an active hunt for a bride.'

That was another topic he had no wish to explore and he was glad when a maid approached to speak to Eliza.

'Excuse me. I'm needed in the kitchen. The cook is having one of her tyrannical spells and the footmen are too frightened to go in.'

She began to move away, but then turned back. 'Gabriel,' she murmured, her hand on his arm. 'Do at least *try* to speak to a few people. You might even find you like them.'

She shot him a direct look very similar to one their grandmother used to deploy to great effect, but she didn't press her point. Letting go of his arm, she followed the maid from the room and Gabriel found himself on his own, surrounded by people and yet feeling—as usual—entirely alone.

He leaned back against the wall. All around him people chatted, the pianoforte still doing its best to cut through the din, and he took in the scene with the detachment of one watching a play. He was out of place there amid such high spirits and life, and he found himself wondering how soon he could leave.

The call of his new house was almost as loud as the voices currently ringing in his ears. Sisslehurst Manor was grand and imposing and, most importantly, quiet and would remain so until Leah returned from her visit to Miriam. Once his daughter was there the house would feel more like a home instead of the empty shell it was without her presence and his mood lifted a little to think of it, although another thought soon brought it crashing back down.

He'd promised to attend Emanuel's shooting party the next day, he remembered now, gritting his teeth on a groan. Leaving before that would be an insult to his host, would it not? As Eliza said, Emanuel was a kind man, if not always particularly diplomatic, and Gabriel couldn't throw his host's generosity back in his face. There was nothing to be done but reconcile himself to staying another day and the frown that was never far away settled itself once again across his brow.

*Get tonight out of the way first. One delight at a time.*

An evening spent next to Miss Burcombe still beckoned. It was no more appealing now than when he'd first learned of his fate, but at least it seemed he had little cause for concern. Both Louisa and her mama apparently had their eyes on other prey and with any luck he might get through dinner without exchanging more than a few words with her. The man who *had* captured her attention probably considered himself fortunate to have done so, and Gabriel hoped for their sakes that their eventual experience of matrimony would turn out to be far better than his own.

## Chapter Two

Louisa could hardly keep from smiling as she wended her way through the trees. They grew so thickly in this part of Uncle Emanuel's estate that the morning sunshine barely reached the ground, leaving occasional puddles of dappled light where it managed to break through the canopy. Leaves stirred in a breeze that made her skirts cling to her legs, but she didn't mind the slight chill, the first hint that autumn was on its way far less interesting than what was already on her mind.

She'd been delighted to see Sir Christopher seated opposite her at dinner the previous night—at Aunt Eliza's insistence, she suspected—and they had talked practically all evening, the conversation between them never ceasing to flow. Miss Jarvis had looked daggers at her from the other end of the table, but Louisa had barely noticed, Sir Christopher the focus of her attention as he'd regaled her with stories from his time abroad.

He was easily the most fascinating man she'd ever met and any doubts as to his regard for her had begun to melt away at how attentively he'd listened to her thoughts on Richardson's work, opinions it had turned out he shared to the letter. The connection she'd thought might be growing had surely been confirmed and she abandoned any last attempt at stopping a smile as she waded through a patch of tall grass, allowing herself to be carried along with little regard for where she might end up.

From somewhere in the distance she heard the crack of gunshots. The men had gone out shooting straight after breakfast, Christopher among them, and she recalled how handsome he'd looked in his outdoor clothes. It would be some hours yet before he and the others returned to the Hall and she was all but counting the minutes, the real purpose of her walk to prevent her from watching the clock.

Another shot rang out. Who had fired it? Perhaps Christopher, modest if he hit his target and laughing if he didn't, or Uncle Emanuel with his keen soldier's eye? There were at least ten gentlemen out on the estate that morning and it could have been any of them, although there was one individual in particular who she doubted would be enjoying the experience.

Her mouth twisted as her thoughts turned in an unwanted direction. Had Lord Harnham *ever* enjoyed himself in his entire life? He certainly hadn't at dinner and she found herself shaking her head as she squeezed between two oaks.

He'd barely looked at her the previous evening, uttering only the most grudging of one-word answers in response to all her attempts at polite conversation. For the entirety of the meal, he had kept his eyes on his plate, ignoring everyone around him, and eventually she'd given up trying to draw him out. She hadn't been the only one to notice his poor behaviour, judging by the unimpressed mutters she'd overheard from other sources, and she was inclined to agree with the other guests.

It was amazing he and Eliza were related: he was standoffish where his cousin was approachable, brooding where she was lively and certainly their hostess would never dream of being so rude. Lord Harnham on the other hand was quite possibly the most ill-mannered man Louisa had ever met and his failings only served to make Sir Christopher shine more brightly.

*I suppose because the Baron is titled, he thought it beneath him to converse with me. How fortunate Christopher doesn't share his sentiments.*

His lordship undoubtedly had the larger fortune—and, if she was to be completely honest, a slightly handsomer face—but the young knight's good nature was far more important. Her and Christopher's connection was based on shared interests and genuine liking and all the money in the world couldn't outweigh that. A match born of affection was what she'd always longed for and at last it seemed that might be just what she was going to get. All the years of loneliness and feeling overshadowed would have been worth it if they had been leading up to something real and she felt her heart quicken at the thought.

*I wonder if he'll ask my leave to speak to Papa?*

Mr Burcombe rarely attended his brother-in-law's parties. He'd be entrenched in his library, making the most of the peace afforded by an empty house, but she was sure he'd emerge if a man came seeking her hand. He might be vaguely sorry to see her leave, attached to her in the same absentminded way her mother was, but he was certain to give his consent. The only trouble would be in stopping Mama from triumphantly inviting half of Warwickshire to the wedding breakfast, but even that would be a small price to pay if the result was a ring on the third finger of her left hand.

A volley of shots splintered the quiet whispering of the trees. They sounded louder now, as if the distance between her and the hunters had narrowed, and she fell still to listen.

What direction were they coming from?

She could have sworn the shooting party had been far to her right when she'd entered the woods, but now the guns seemed to echo from directly behind her. She'd been careful to keep out of their line of fire, but perhaps in her happy daze she'd wandered off course and when another shot split the silence, she realised she needed to move.

It was difficult to walk quickly through the low-hanging branches and clinging weeds and she winced as thorns pricked her, bristles and burrs snatching at her skirts as she pushed her way through the scrub.

'I shouldn't have left the path,' she muttered as she kicked aside a rotting log. 'It's impossible to tell which way is which.'

She stumbled on, trying to guess if she was anywhere near the edge of the woods. Unease was beginning to build and it sparked brighter when yet another bang came from somewhere unnervingly close by. Belatedly she realised the dark green of her gown camouflaged her perfectly amid the shadows of the trees and she felt a keen stab of fear at what that could mean.

Every direction looked the same and in her growing alarm she had no idea where to turn. It crossed her mind to go back the way she'd come, meeting the guns head on, but she dismissed the idea almost at once. They might hit her by accident before she reached them and so instead she pressed on, picking up her skirts so they wouldn't slow her down.

A sudden crashing sound far too near to her made her flinch back in instinctive dread.

Something was breaking through a line of shrub only a few yards away. The bushes shook and snapped and then, to her combined relief and dismay, a familiar figure came into sight.

'Oh! You gave me a fright.'

In the shade of the trees it was difficult to tell exactly what expression flitted through Lord Harnham's dark eyes. He stood looking down at her from a height she hadn't realised until then was quite so imposing and, for reasons she didn't fully understand, she felt her cheeks grow warm.

'Miss Burcombe.' He jerked one of the nods she was coming to see was as close as he came to a bow. 'You shouldn't be here. It's dangerous to stray too near the guns.'

His stating of the obvious made her bristle. Did he think that hadn't occurred to her? He didn't even have the good grace to acknowledge she might have been startled by his sudden appearance, any more than he had when he'd surprised her by the pond, and she had to take a second to remind herself to remain civil.

'Thank you. I'm aware of that. I hadn't intended to get so close—I must have lost my bearings among the trees. I'll be returning to the Hall momentarily.'

'Good. Be sure to go quickly.'

He nodded again, this time with an air of curt dismissal, and Louisa felt her annoyance build.

Be sure to go quickly? As if otherwise, if he hadn't advised her, she might have lingered in harm's way? He spoke with such authority and yet she had no need of his instructions, especially after his rudeness at dinner the previous night. Apparently having a title gave a man leave to behave however he wanted, or so Lord Harnham evidently believed, and so strong was her irritation that she let it take hold of her tongue.

'But what of yourself, Sir? As you're so alert to the dangers, surely you shouldn't be walking here either?'

Lord Harnham's face didn't change. His eyes remained trained on hers with no hint of a smile softening the hard angles of his face, his jawline alone almost sharp enough to cut anyone so foolish as to touch it…an odd thought, Louisa acknowledged, and one she wasn't sure why had crossed her mind.

He folded his arms over his chest. 'I came in to find your uncle's spaniel. The other guns have a safe awareness of my whereabouts—unlike yours.'

His bluntness was so aggravating that it took her a moment to realise he was right. The guns had indeed stopped firing since he'd come hacking his way through the undergrowth and she very nearly felt a glimmer of relief before he went on.

'You do not, I presume, desire to be shot?'

'Of course I don't!'

'Then it's time for you to leave.'

She glowered up at him. How did he mean to lecture her on her own uncle's estate? She'd been coming to Cressex Hall since she was a child, long before Eliza became its mistress, and for Lord Harnham to behave as though he owned the place was vexing in the extreme. For all his money and good looks, he was barely a gentleman at all, and she was debating whether to tell him so when she felt something brush against her skirts.

'Comet?'

A liver-and-white spaniel was sniffing at her hem, looking up with a lolling grin at the sound of his name. He was Uncle Emanuel's favourite dog and she knew at once it was him Lord Harnham had been dispatched to retrieve.

She leaned down to ruffle a silky ear. His arrival presented the perfect excuse to ignore the man watching her with his arms still folded sternly and it gave her a curious thrill to carry on as though he wasn't there.

'You're supposed to be working, not running about wherever you please. You're not a puppy any more.'

The dog licked her hand, his bobbed tail wagging. He at least was delighted by her presence, although it seemed the same couldn't be said of Lord Harnham.

A finger was tapping an impatient rhythm against one bicep. Unless she was mistaken his jaw had tightened, too, the already angular line stretched taut, and she felt a childish satisfaction. It was probably a novel experience for him not to be immediately obeyed, but he only had himself to blame. If he'd been more agreeable she would have thanked him for his intervention and then left without delay, his unfriendliness instead tempting her to answer it like for like.

All the same...

Reluctantly she straightened up. It wouldn't do to be *too* antagonistic. Lord Harnham was still Eliza's cousin and she respected her aunt too much to be rude to her relations, even if said relative seemed almost deliberately provoking. It was as if he was purposefully trying to make her dislike him and she had no idea why, only that if that *was* his plan it was having the desired effect.

'Miss Burcombe. As I said: it's time for you to leave.'

The irritation betrayed by his tapping finger didn't feature in his voice. It was as flat as ever; but deep as well, she noticed, and distinctly masculine in a way that would have been appealing had it issued from any other lips. *His* still wore no trace of a smile and she didn't bother to find one of her own as she straightened her bonnet and prepared to depart—in her own good time, of course.

'As *I* said: I was already intending to return to the Hall, Sir. You needn't worry yourself on my account.'

With all the poise she possessed she turned away, bobbing him only the shallowest of curtsies before she went. She still wasn't entirely sure which was the right direction, but she would rather have spent all night in the woods than ask Lord Harnham for help. The most sensible thing to do would be to walk straight forward, outrunning the guns he would warn of her presence, and she made sure not to look back as she stepped daintily over a thatch of weeds. She'd leave him standing there, probably watching as she went, and her retreat among the trees would be so graceful he might even reproach himself for acting like such a boor.

Much later, when the day's events were impossible to undo, Louisa would reflect that everything would have been fine if Comet hadn't disappeared into that damned bush.

Lord Harnham called out, but the dog took no notice. With his tail a blur Comet plunged into a tangle of scrub not far from Louisa's path, vanishing with a rustle of twigs and dry leaves. He didn't emerge again and Lord Harnham muttered something he probably didn't mean for her to hear.

'That dog...'

She turned around. He was standing closer to her than she'd realised and she took an involuntary step backwards, although not before she caught the faint scent of wood smoke and leather—strangely pleasing—that hung around him like cologne.

'Is he not behaving himself?' she enquired innocently. 'He might respond better to a gentler approach. Would you like me to try to retrieve him for you?'

Her offer was met with a long, unreadable look. Those inscrutable brown eyes fixed on her and to her unease she felt her pulse skip faster. Probably it was just her body reacting to how much she disliked him, but it was uncomfortable that he should have any effect at all and it didn't abate even when he inclined his head.

He stood aside. It couldn't have been clearer that he wanted her to summon Comet quickly so he could cut their meeting short and for the first time she found she agreed with him.

'Comet? What have you found?'

There was a good deal of rustling among the undergrowth, but no spaniel appeared. It was impossible to see through the snarled branches and leaves and only their continuous shaking implied the dog was still somewhere inside.

She could sense Lord Harnham watching her. Admitting defeat was out of the question and she leaned over a little more, balancing on her tiptoes now as she tried to see into the very middle of the thatch.

'Come on. Come out now, please.'

This time her words saw a result. The undergrowth shuddered and there came the sound of loudly snapping twigs—and then something exploded upwards into her face.

There was no time to duck out of the way. Disorientated, the terrified pheasant beat its wings against her in its desperation to escape, forcing back her bonnet, and she felt something slice across her chest. The bird thrashed and struggled, and Louisa staggered back, her hands in front of her, to ward it off as its talons flashed near her face. The accidental attack was over in seconds, but even when the pheasant disappeared into the treetops she couldn't catch her breath, too shocked and reeling to make any sense of what had happened in one frightening blink of an eye.

'Miss Burcombe! Are you hurt?'

She peered dazedly upwards. Lord Harnham was in front of her, gazing down in such concern that she almost didn't recognise him as the man who had riled her so only moments before. When he wasn't cultivating an expression of blank uninterest his face came to life, making him infinitely more attractive, but she wasn't able to admire the change for long. A raw stinging at the neckline of her gown abruptly drew her attention and she looked down, her head swimming alarmingly at what she saw.

The pheasant must have raked her with its powerful claws, she thought dimly as she lifted a hand to touch where pain was beginning to set in with a vengeance. Talons had etched a set of crimson lines from her collarbone to the top of her gown and her horror increased tenfold as she realised her flesh wasn't the only thing that had been torn. The flimsy fabric of her bodice was rent, showing her stays and a glimpse of skin as clear as day above them, and she gasped as she fumbled to cover herself, fire kindling in her cheeks as she saw Lord Harnham realise what was wrong.

He didn't leer or stare. He looked away the very moment he understood her predicament, at last behaving like the gentleman he was purported to be, but she knew he'd caught a flash of soft, secret skin and her throat contracted as a thought streaked through her mind.

*What happens now?*

Gabriel swung round so sharply he almost lost his footing.

'Here. Perhaps you have need of this.'

With his back firmly to her he shrugged off his jacket and waved it in Miss Burcombe's general direction. He heard her shuffle forward to take it, but he didn't turn, making sure to keep his eyes resolutely fixed dead ahead.

*Face front. Whatever you do, don't look round.*

She mumbled a mortified word of thanks although he barely heard it. His mind was already racing, one thought after another flinging themselves at him as he tried to stay calm enough to decide what to do.

If they were caught together like this...

The skin beneath the tatters of her gown was as smooth and pale as the finest satin, some disobedient part of him acknowledged before he could shut it out. It was a sight he should never have seen, the sort of intimacy meant only for a lover's eyes, and he tried to tamp down rising dread at what he feared could all too easily come next.

'Miss Burcombe. You must leave at once.'

She didn't answer. There was only some faint rustling behind him as she pulled the jacket into place, and he couldn't help allowing apprehension to sharpen his voice.

'Did you hear me?'

'Yes, I heard you. Can I at least have a moment to gather myself?'

'No. There are no moments to spare. If you were seen in such a state, wearing *my* jacket, I doubt you'd like the consequences. Return to the Hall immediately and be sure not to let anyone see you go.'

He knew he spoke harshly, but he also spoke the truth. The rest of the shooting party would surely come looking for him soon and he had no intention of being found in a position so compromising it would force him to do something he'd sworn never to do again.

His throat felt as though he'd drunk a tankard of sand. The reputation of a young lady discovered alone with a man, with her undergarments showing and his jacket around her shoulders, would be ruined beyond all saving. No respectable gentleman would wed such a scandalous woman, sentencing her to a lifetime of spinsterhood unless the man complicit in her shame could be prevailed upon to marry her instead.

Miss Burcombe was protected by her family who would surely insist on a wedding if word of the morning's events were to become known and, as Gabriel had no intention of there ever being another Lady Harnham, he had to act fast.

Fortunately, it seemed Miss Burcombe agreed.

'You're right. My uncle would keep this a secret, but I don't know that we can trust his guests.'

She sounded on the edge of panic, just as aware of the potential danger as he was. A union between two such unwilling parties was a truly terrible prospect, although even so it was difficult to imagine any marriage being more disastrous than his first.

Frederica's ghost lingered just out of sight, an eerie presence he felt almost as strongly as when she'd been alive. She still came to him occasionally, usually to remind him how badly he'd been wrong, and she hovered now as if to pity him for making yet another mistake.

The sand in his throat turned to splinters of glass. Seven years ago, he'd all but run to the altar, so eager to marry the woman he loved that he'd missed all the signs she didn't feel the same. Her pretence of devotion had been so convincing he hadn't dreamed it wasn't sincere, or that it was the ambitions of her self-serving parents that had forced her down the aisle rather than her own desires.

She'd been moulded into becoming the perfect bride almost since birth, he'd learned only after her death, shaped by her mother's cynical schooling and father's bullying into a pliable net to entrap a wealthy husband, and the fact their daughter had been in love with another man at the time of her marriage hadn't prevented them from seeing their plan through to the bitter end.

Frederica had become Lady Harnham, one of the richest women in Staffordshire, and for that her unhappiness had been a price they'd been willing to pay. Their daughter had been little more than a pawn to them and even after everything that had happened Gabriel couldn't blame her. His love for her had long since vanished, but he was still able to feel some sympathy for how she must have felt torn in two.

Only one good thing had come from the doomed match. Leah was a blessing he was thankful for every day—and so it was of deadly importance that Frederica's cold, grasping parents never learned the secret regarding the little girl that he and Miriam would take to their graves. His sister was the only person who knew what had truly happened on the day Frederica died and why it had made him so determined never to wed again, the rest of the world wrongly assuming it was either guilt or grief that now made him so resolved to keep himself apart.

There was a crunch of leaves. Miss Burcombe was probably dithering, debating which way to flee, and he could well imagine the terror in her eyes. The idea of being tied to him for the rest of her life probably seemed like a fate worse than death, although he acknowledged that was his own doing. He'd been deliberately rude to her since the moment they'd met, determined to make her keep a safe distance, and it was uncomfortable to realise he'd been right to feel concern.

Despite his growing unease, he couldn't quite put the thought of that little flash of skin out of his head. It had looked so soft, the pallor of it contrasting with the crimson that had bloomed in her cheeks when she'd realised the damage the pheasant had done to her gown, and that had brought problems of its own.

She was pretty when she blushed and that wasn't something he wanted to notice, just as trivial as how well her auburn hair set off the green of her eyes. She was an attractive woman and that made her dangerous, tempting a man to blind himself to what was real, and the threat she posed didn't stop there. Miss Burcombe had met his incivility with spirit, refusing to be cowed, and if there was one thing he'd come to value it was people who knew their own minds…

Comet, or 'that damned dog' as Gabriel was now privately calling him, gave an excited bark, and from behind him he heard Miss Burcombe suck in a sharp breath.

'Louisa? What on earth is going on here?'

Emanuel's booming voice sent Gabriel's heart dropping into his boots. He almost didn't dare turn around—*is she decent yet?*—but he knew he must, his host demanding an explanation it was his job in part to supply.

Miss Burcombe's face was the colour of milk as she gazed wordlessly at her uncle, and when she seemed unable to speak Emanuel turned abruptly to Gabriel.

'Harnham? What is this?'

There was angry mistrust in his tone and Gabriel didn't blame him one bit. He knew how the scene must look to the other man: his niece like a trapped rabbit, all round eyes and fear wrapped in a near-stranger's coat, and the near-stranger in question so taciturn it was impossible to know what devilry he might be thinking. It was probably lucky Emanuel had evidently left his gun with his loader, arriving blessedly unarmed; he seemed increasingly ready to leap in to defend his niece if necessary and hurriedly Gabriel held up a steadying hand.

'There was a pheasant. Comet drove it up from the undergrowth and it slashed the lady with its claws as it tried to fly away.'

Her uncle frowned. He didn't look completely convinced and it was a small relief when Miss Burcombe summoned a nod.

'That's just what happened, Uncle. It tore my dress and Lord Harnham was kind enough to lend me his coat to cover myself as I returned to the Hall.'

Emanuel's expression shifted. 'To cover yourself. I see.'

He was still frowning but now it was troubled rather than angry. Clearly, he had just come to the same realisation as his guest and niece: that she had been alone with a man while in a state of exposed disarray, and that if anyone was to know of it, she would be ruined before the day was out. Emanuel had to be aware Miss Burcombe's affections lay elsewhere, making the idea of a hasty engagement to anyone else unbearable to her, and Gabriel's hopes lifted as her uncle took control.

Emanuel moved swiftly to her side. She was holding the jacket closed with one hand, but the other grasped her uncle's and clung on, her wide eyes searching his face. She hadn't straightened her bonnet after the pheasant had disturbed it and a few stray waves of coppery hair fell around her cheekbones, making her look slightly disheveled, but in so comely a fashion that Gabriel had to turn sharply away.

He heard Emanuel's urgent mutter. 'Quickly, my dear. Before the others come. We can still salvage the situation if we all just—'

How Emanuel would have finished that sentence if he hadn't been interrupted Gabriel didn't know. All he could be sure of was the dismay in Miss Burcombe's strangled gasp as three figures emerged through the trees, his own horror segueing swiftly into numb resignation as he realised all hope was lost.

At once Emanuel stepped to the side to hide his niece from view, but the damage had already been done. The newcomers must have seen that it was a man's jacket she wore and Gabriel was the only one in his shirtsleeves, the white of his linen making him stand out with painful clarity. After that it was the work of a single moment to guess why she might have need of a gentleman's clothes, a gentleman who had been missing from his party easily long enough to have managed all manner of wickedness, and as he saw all three men reach the same conclusion, he knew there could be no escape.

Miss Burcombe huddled behind her uncle, trying to hide from his guests—one very much in particular. Sir Christopher Stanhope was among the three men now awkwardly shuffling their feet and, despite his own dread, Gabriel felt a twinge as he caught a glimpse of her face.

It was taut with shame and distress, and he recalled how different she had looked as she'd laughed with the young knight at dinner the previous evening. It was obvious to anyone who had seen them together that he was the one she wanted but would now never be able to have, all her hopes for the future torn apart with the same finality as Gabriel's own.

For one hideously long beat no one spoke. Miss Burcombe probably couldn't and Sir Christopher and his friends undoubtedly didn't know what to say, and even Emanuel seemed uncharacteristically lost for words. For Gabriel's part he could only stand silently, longing in vain to snatch back the past half-hour and wondering at how quickly everything had gone wrong.

After what could only have been a second or two, but felt like an eternity, Emanuel stepped into the breach. 'Well, gentlemen. We were all searching for Comet and here he is. What say you take him back to the guns and make him earn his keep?'

He sounded bluff as ever, but for once his cheeriness was forced, something his guests couldn't fail to have noticed.

'Of course. We'll save a few birds for you, Sir.'

Sir Christopher whistled for the dog. By some miracle Comet obeyed and the three men beat a hasty retreat, the spaniel bounding ahead to lead them away. The crunch of fallen leaves beneath their boots grew quieter and then they were gone, leaving Gabriel to wish he could have vanished along with them and left this waking nightmare behind.

He heard a tiny breath of a sound, like a cry quickly repressed. Miss Burcombe was peering out from behind her uncle, her eyes fixed on the gap between two trees through which Sir Christopher had disappeared, and the mystery twinge that had assaulted him previously lanced again through Gabriel's chest.

Her expression held the same kind of desperate despair he imagined his own had when he'd first learned the truth about Frederica's betrayal. She looked as though her last chance at happiness had slipped through her hands, like a bottle of the finest wine poured wastefully on to a cold stone floor, and it struck him somewhere far too close to the bone. She wanted Sir Christopher to come back to claim her so badly, just as Frederica must have longed for *her* real love to carry her away, although he couldn't help but notice the young knight hadn't seemed to feel that same pain.

Sir Christopher had been bewildered, yes, but not unduly disturbed, and had shown no suggestion of the jealousy or rage a man might be expected to show at his sweetheart's disgrace. Perhaps the feelings Miss Burcombe cherished for him weren't returned with quite the same fervour...but any further wonderings were cut off when Emanuel turned to him with a heavy sigh.

'Come up to the Hall, Gabriel. I'm afraid we have things to discuss.'

Emanuel patted him on the shoulder, a gesture full of sympathy and regret. He knew of Gabriel's determination never to remarry—although of course not the real reason why—and Gabriel saw unease in the older man's face.

*Maybe he's worried I won't marry her. Maybe he thinks I'll leave her to whatever fate the* ton *sees fit to mete out to young ladies whose morals are no longer above reproach.*

For one breath he was tempted to prove those fears right.

Nobody could *make* him marry her, he realised as he let the idea unfold. He was a baron and she was the daughter of a respectable but unremarkable gentleman with no power to make him act against his will. If he so chose, he could simply leave Cressex Hall and never see Miss Burcombe again, a possibility he strongly considered—but then Leah rose to the forefront of his mind.

If someone ever treated her the way he was contemplating treating Miss Burcombe, he would be heartbroken and furious in equal measure. Leah's well-being was the most important thing in the world and the idea of her facing any kind of public scorn was almost more than he could stand. If any man dared ever expose her to disgrace, he would hunt the villain down and make him answer for it, and he would be the worst kind of hypocrite if he did to someone else's daughter what he would never accept for his own.

Sometimes a man had to do the right thing even against his strongest inclinations—although as he watched Emanuel begin to walk slowly in the direction of the house, for the first time in his life Gabriel wished he had a son instead of a vulnerable little girl.

Miss Burcombe hadn't yet moved. Probably Emanuel assumed she would follow him, but she wavered, uncertain and miserable as she peered around at the trees. It seemed she was still holding on to some last scrap of hope that Sir Christopher might reappear, a faith so baseless Gabriel felt another shred of reluctant pity in the depths of his carefully flint-cold heart.

He should say something to her, he thought vaguely, but what? His own dismay was so deep he could have drowned in it, the waters fast flowing and rising above his head. He was just as horrified by the turn the morning had taken as she was, yet something in the slump of her slender shoulders wouldn't let him walk away without a word.

'Your mama will be pleased, at least,' he ventured grimly, realising far too late that he sounded as though someone had a gun to his head. 'A title generally has that effect on mothers.'

Miss Burcombe looked round. Her gaze settled on him, but she didn't seem to see what was before her, her green eyes empty but for bleak disappointment that Gabriel felt like a cool touch on his skin.

'Yes, my lord. But not necessarily on their daughters.'

## *Chapter Three*

Louisa had never seen her father so grave as he regarded her over his steepled fingers. For once she commanded his full attention and it was a pity that it had taken such unfortunate circumstances for her to experience it.

'I'm sorry. There's no other way.'

'There must be. Papa, I don't want to marry that man!'

She leaned forward desperately. Mr Burcombe had arrived at Cressex Hall within an hour of Emanuel sending for him and had summoned her to the study, where they now sat opposite each other across Emanuel's leather-topped desk. She'd changed her ruined gown and applied some yarrow ointment to her chest, but the morning's catastrophe showed no signs of going away, just as her father showed no signs of changing his mind.

Trying to suppress climbing panic, she took a deep breath. 'Please. I hardly know Lord Harnham and what I *do* know of him I do not like. I'm certain he feels the same way about me. He's consented to this marriage out of obligation, nothing more. Surely there must be something you can do?'

Mr Burcombe didn't address her hopeless plea. 'Of course he doesn't dislike you. Who could? As you said, you barely know each other. I'm certain that on better acquaintance his regard for you will grow, the same as yours for him.'

Louisa's hands, already clasped in her lap, clenched so hard she felt her nails bite into her palms. 'I don't want a husband who has to learn to tolerate me. I'd hoped for a marriage based on real feeling. My brothers married where they wished and none of them have a romantic bone in their bodies—surely I can do the same?'

It was too important a situation for her father to laugh, but as usual he didn't appear to take her input seriously.

'Louisa. Did you truly think all three of your brothers just so happened to fall in love with heiresses?' he asked, not unkindly. 'They didn't object to the matches your mother and I intended for them, it's true, but I can't pretend the sums your sisters-in-law brought with them were of no interest either. Even where there is fondness there must also be practicality. In your case, the latter is simply coming first, but I have no doubt the former will follow. How can it not when you are such a good girl?'

Pressing her lips into a tight line, Louisa looked down at her lap. She wasn't a *good girl*. She was a grown woman who knew her own mind, not a child, and if her father had ever bothered to learn anything about who she was as a person he would have known it, too.

'But, Papa...he isn't the one I want.'

She was glad she couldn't see Mr Burcombe's face as she muttered the last few words. Apparently her unhappiness touched him and she heard unexpected regret in his voice as he sighed.

'I know. Your mother told me of your liking for Sir Christopher and he seems a pleasant young man. But he saw you. I'm afraid any offer he may have been considering making will not be forthcoming now.'

Still gazing down at her skirts, Louisa nodded. Of course, she'd known that really. The moment she had seen Christopher appear through the trees she'd realised any chance of becoming his wife had vanished, along with the possibility of a friendship that might one day turn to love, but some foolish part of her had refused to abandon all hope. His attention would shift to another lady now, since she was compromised beyond salvation, and unless she wanted to spend the rest of her life either dishonoured or alone she had no choice but to accept her lot.

'So I must become Lady Harnham,' she said bitterly. 'All because of one stupid mistake.'

'Yes,' her father agreed firmly. 'But don't be downcast. Many of Warwickshire's ladies would give anything to be in your place. You'll have a handsome house, lands and more money than you know what to do with, and Eliza tells me Lord Harnham himself wasn't always as unapproachable as he seems now. Apparently, the death of his first wife affected him to a great extent, but a new one such as yourself is sure to bring him back to life.'

Surprise overcoming some small fraction of her wretchedness, Louisa looked up. 'His first wife? He was married before?'

Somehow, she couldn't quite picture it. Lord Harnham seemed too singular to have been part of a couple, the kind of man more comfortable on his own than with other people. Certainly he was only marrying her out of duty rather than the desire for a partner, although if what Eliza said was true…

If her aunt had made a point of remarking on the change in him, he must have been noticeably different before his wife had died. Perhaps it was grief that had made him so detached, an emotion so strong it could reduce even the liveliest person to a shadow of their former self? For her loss to have had such an effect on him surely meant he'd held this mystery woman in high regard and to her renewed surprise Louisa felt a dart of sympathy.

*No wonder he didn't express any interest in any of the ladies here. He must still be missing the first Lady Harnham, not looking for the second.*

Mr Burcombe tapped the desk's top briskly as if to signal the conversation was at an end. 'Yes. I don't know anything more than that. Eliza gave me the impression he prefers not to speak of her.'

Louisa watched her father push back his chair. He rose to his feet, but she remained seated, her stomach tied in a knot.

There had never been much probability Lord Harnham would turn out to be the kind of husband she'd prayed for, but now she had no doubt whatsoever that she would ever find the mutual fulfilment she craved. If he was still lamenting the loss of his first wife, there was even less chance of him opening himself to his new one even if she'd wanted him to, any last faint possibility of an affectionate match gone up in flames.

He was sure to see her as an interloper trying to step into the shoes of his real love and the tangle of her insides pulled harder as she wondered how much he must resent the imposition that would once again force her into second place. If she hadn't gone for such an ill-timed walk none of this would have happened, and although she'd never intended the morning to take such a strange turn, she still couldn't shake the feeling he would think her wholly to blame.

*I can only hope he doesn't believe I set out to trap him. If I'd known he was grieving, I would have given him an even wider berth than his unfriendliness invites already.*

There was a knock at the door. Her father looked

as though he'd been expecting it, but Louisa jumped at the sudden sound, so tense that even the smallest thing made her flinch. Mr Burcombe answered it and then she almost flinched again when she heard a deep, carefully controlled voice fill the room.

'I hope I'm not interrupting.'

'Not at all. Come in. Louisa and I had just finished our discussion.'

She stood up hurriedly. Lord Harnham was in the doorway, but he didn't have the chance to say anything more before Papa swept him inside.

'That's it. If you'll excuse me, I'll just step into the next room. Emanuel has some maps I'm keen to look at. One of the finest collections in the county, if you believe his boasting.'

To Louisa's horror her father moved smartly for another door on the opposite side of the study and disappeared through it, leaving it slightly ajar. While strictly speaking they might not have been unchaperoned it still felt very much as though she was alone with the unsmiling Baron once again and she became aware she had nowhere to hide.

*Oh, Papa. When I said I barely knew him, I didn't mean for you to leave us to rectify that the very next moment.*

Lord Harnham gave her one of his curt nods. He didn't quite meet her eye and she wondered briefly what her father had said to him in their interview before she'd been summoned for hers. Had Papa had to plead for him to take her as his wife? Had Lord Harnham been cajoled and persuaded not to turn his back, ground down until he'd finally agreed to do what must be done? It was a humiliating thought, but she couldn't think of anything else as Lord Harnham advanced, with some reluctance, further into the room.

'Miss Burcombe. Or perhaps I ought to call you Louisa now. It seems you won't be using your maiden name for much longer.'

She couldn't tell if his tone held any hidden meaning. It was measured as ever, although the gruff precision with which he formed the three syllables of her first name wasn't altogether displeasing.

'Please do. In turn, I shall call you—'

She tailed off. What was his given name? She was to marry this man and she didn't even know what he was called, that most basic and essential of requirements. If she needed further proof that the whole premise was absurd, then surely this was it, an opinion the flicker of Lord Harnham's right eyebrow implied he shared.

'Gabriel. If you want to.'

'I do.'

Now he was before her she had the chance to say what was on her mind, although that was more difficult than it should have been while fixed with those dark, searching eyes.

Up close they really were the colour of sweet cocoa—but that was of no importance.

'I want you to know that I never meant for any of this to happen,' she began awkwardly. 'I wouldn't want you to think there was any element of entrapment, with you being so eligible and me a young... ish...woman hoping to find the right match. If I'd had any idea—'

'You needn't worry.' He cut across her, his interruption no more polite than she would have expected, but at least sparing her from stumbling over any more words. 'I never thought for a moment that you might have wanted to be in this position. If anything, I understand it's the reverse.'

Louisa's spirits sank even lower. Was he referring to the fact she obviously disliked him, or that she wished Christopher was there in his stead? They'd yet to have a civil conversation and it seemed the discord between them could easily get worse before they were even wed.

If they were to spend the rest of their lives together they should at least *try* to find a way to get along, even if it was clear tolerance would never turn to the regard she'd wished for so fervently, and as Gabriel showed no indication of bending she supposed she would have to make the first move.

With some hesitation she drifted towards one of the windows overlooking the gardens, unsure whether he would follow. It would have been more in keeping with his previous behaviour if he'd strode off in the other direction, so it came as a relief when he allowed himself to be led further away from the door her father had left open.

'I believe the reason Papa left us here together was so we could get to know each other a little more. Perhaps we might give it a try?'

'If you wish.'

He didn't sound very enthusiastic and Louisa steeled herself against a prickle of disappointed irritation. Was he even going to *try* to meet her halfway? It would be impossible for their connection to improve if he made no effort, although a sudden recollection of the reason for his reticence gave her pause.

*Don't forget he lost his wife. I suppose such a thing would suck the joy from any man, even if he'd been cheerful enough before.*

The idea of Gabriel ever having been cheerful was difficult to believe, but the thought of his suffering helped her regain at least some of her patience. It would be unreasonable to expect a bereaved husband to show much interest in a woman he was being forced to wed and she made sure to choose her next words with care.

'My father told me you were married before,' she said quietly, deliberately looking out of the window instead of up into his face. 'I'm very sorry for your loss. I wasn't aware.'

There was a short silence. Out of the corner of her eye she saw Gabriel was watching the gardens, too, although she could tell his full attention was on her words.

'How could you have known? It happened three years ago, long before I moved here. An admirable quality of your Aunt Eliza's is that she doesn't talk endlessly of other people's affairs. There was no reason for her to mention anything about my past until this morning made it necessary for your father to know more about me and my intention to take care of you.'

He spoke with his usual economy, not saying any more than he had to, but all the same his last clipped phrase took her by surprise.

*Take care of me?*

Her circling apprehension shifted slightly, making the smallest sliver of room for something else: not unpleasant, but certainly unexpected. She hadn't thought Gabriel would give any consideration to her well-being and to find she'd been wrong made her sneak him a quick, inquisitory glance.

He was still gazing out at the grounds, his profile a strong, stern line set against the light. She couldn't see his expression fully, but she imagined it was grim-faced determination, the look of a man who would do what needed to be done whether he wanted to or not.

The knowledge she was an unwanted burden to him made shame creep over her, but that nameless feeling still lingered, reinforced by her growing awareness of how much taller he was as he stood at her side. He was certainly physically imposing enough for her to believe he would protect her—more so than Sir Christopher, in truth—and that he was apparently willing to do so was something she hadn't anticipated.

They had strayed into delicate territory, evidenced by the tension she could sense in his frame. Even without touching him she knew he was holding his shoulders defensively, their already impressive width increased by being braced so high and tight.

He must have been uneasy she might ask further questions, as he changed the subject with breakneck speed. 'Another thing you doubtless won't be aware of: I have a daughter.'

Louisa's eyebrows rose before she could stop them. Solemn, stoic Gabriel had somehow managed to create something as fragile and full of life as a little girl? 'Have you? What's her name?'

'Leah. She's six years old.'

He turned away from the window, only slightly, but enough for Louisa to catch a glimpse of his face and what she saw there did something odd to her insides.

After the pheasant had burst out at her, leaving her dazed and bleeding beneath the trees, she'd seen something in Gabriel's eyes that had caught her off guard. For the most fleeting of moments he'd shown genuine concern, light sparking where previously there had been nothing but the darkness of indifference, and the change it had made to his appearance was like the removal of a mask.

Real, human emotion made him look alive rather than the statue he usually resembled, handsome in a far less severe way—and the same thing happened when he spoke of his daughter, a gleam of life igniting that made it suddenly difficult for Louisa to look away.

'She's currently away staying with my sister and her children, but I'll bring her home after the wedding. I'd prefer everything to be settled and calm before she comes back to Sisslehurst Manor.'

'Of course.' Startled by her unconscious reaction, Louisa nodded quickly. 'Have you an idea as to when will that be? The wedding?'

'As soon as I can get the licence.' Gabriel cut her a swift look with those inscrutable dark eyes. They were impossible to read again, the animation in them when he'd spoken of his daughter now deliberately hidden away. 'I thought a quiet wedding at home might suit you better than having the banns read. A public fuss might invite more scrutiny than you'd like, given the circumstances of our match.'

'Oh.' Louisa hesitated at his disorienting consideration. 'I would indeed very much prefer to avoid that. Thank you for taking my wishes into account.'

He dipped his chin brusquely, apparently discomfited by her gratitude. All trace of the softness he'd worn when talking about Leah had disappeared and Louisa found herself wishing it would return, a desire she neither understood nor wanted her soon-to-be husband ever to suspect.

'Yes. Well.' He frowned, turning his attention back to the sunlit grounds beyond the glass. 'Even if it wasn't by choice we're to be joined together now and that's not a responsibility I take lightly. It's my duty to shelter and provide for you the best I can and you'll find I'm not a man who shies away from what honour demands.'

Alone in his bedroom later that evening as he changed for dinner, Gabriel scowled into the mirror.

'"What honour demands"? When did you become such a pompous ass?'

He buttoned his collar with an irritable jerk. He'd dismissed his man, preferring to dress himself in peace, and he wondered if it would be possible to strangle himself with his own cravat as he tied it around his neck. It was a slightly more appealing fate than the prospect of another dinner spent beside Miss Burcombe—or Louisa, as he must call her now—although an unwelcome murmur at the back of his mind niggled that he might be protesting a little too much.

'Nonsense.'

He turned away before his reflection could betray what he was *really* thinking. In truth, deep down the beginnings of apprehension was starting to grow, and there were few things Gabriel liked less than being afraid.

The situation was so similar to what had transpired with his first marriage that it almost gave him chills. A woman who preferred another was being forced into wedding him and he was powerless to stop it, just as he feared he might not be able to stop himself from making another catastrophic mistake.

The image of Louisa as she'd been in her uncle's study that afternoon came to him again and he elbowed it aside, although not quite quickly enough. The way she'd looked at him when he'd told her about Leah had taken him by surprise and he nearly ground his teeth into dust as he clamped them together tighter still.

*So what if for half a second she regarded me with something other than aversion? And that when her eyes opened wide like that they looked as green and brilliant as jewels?*

He'd challenge any man not to enjoy being peered at with such interest and the fact that he hadn't immediately turned away from it was concerning. Noticing her charms was the first step to appreciating them and that was a slippery slope he never wanted to tumble down again. The first time he'd seen Frederica he'd been captivated by her long eyelashes and it was a dangerous development that he'd observed Louisa's were the same, a pretty sweep of black over green that made him realise how keenly he had to be on his guard.

His feelings for his first wife had made him vulnerable and he could still recall the pain when he'd learned the truth of where her heart lay. At least Louisa had made no pretence of having a regard for him as Frederica had, but that only made it more essential that he never let sentiment creep in where it didn't belong.

Straightening his cuffs, he gave a dry snort. As if there was any chance of *that*. No matter how unexpectedly tempting Louisa might turn out to be, he wouldn't lose his head. The only person in his house he was willing to love was Leah—besides, he doubted his grudging fiancée would have gazed up at him quite so pleasantly if she knew the rumours surrounding the first Lady Harnham's death.

Frederica's ghost tried to rise again, but he left it behind as he pulled open his bedroom door and strode towards the stairs. If he had to put in an appearance at dinner, he preferred to get it over with, although he knew his back was ramrod straight with distaste at what he predicated was to come.

He was right.

The moment he stepped into the crowded drawing room the hum of conversation ebbed. Every eye turned in his direction and he felt himself skewered by what seemed like a hundred hungry stares, each one made ravenous by the rumours that must have spread through Cressex Hall like a plague.

It seemed he couldn't escape being whispered about no matter where he went. The other guests might not be muttering about the same scandal that had dogged him miles away, but the effect of their hushed tones was the same and Gabriel felt his blood begin to warm. They were looking at him as though he was an animal in a zoological exhibition and he had no patience for it, the sudden appearance of Eliza coming as a welcome distraction.

'Gabe. I'm glad you're here. I was worried you might not come down.'

She spoke quietly, but even so her anxiety was plain. Caught between concern for her niece and cousin and trying to maintain the façade of an unflappable hostess, she was in an unenviable position and Gabriel felt a tweak of conscience for his part in her unease.

'You needn't have been. I wouldn't leave you or Louisa to deal with this mess without the person who caused it.'

Eliza pursed her lips. 'Don't be too hard on yourself. Neither you nor she could have imagined this would happen.'

'Perhaps not, but I should have been more careful.' He glowered over her shoulder, making no effort to acknowledge it when two ladies muttering together in a corner gave him knowing smiles. 'You're aware I didn't intend to marry again and now that very thing is coming to pass.'

His cousin sighed. 'She has a good heart, you know. I realise Frederica's loss hurt you deeply, but if you gave Louisa a chance you might find—'

It was a mixed blessing that the drawing-room door opened again just in time to cut Eliza short. On the one hand it saved him from having to dodge explaining why he had no interest in his new wife's heart, good or otherwise, but on the other it brought Louisa hesitantly into the room and he wasn't sure he liked how easily she seized his attention along with everyone else's.

Her parents walked in arm in arm with the definite air of presenting a united front, but Louisa herself faltered a few steps behind. Just as when he had entered the voices faded before starting up again in earnest and he saw her curb the instinct to withdraw, her cheeks flaring the same rosy pink as when she'd realised he had seen the ruin the pheasant had made of her gown.

She hesitated, her eyes darting around at the staring faces before fixing on the carpet. Nobody approached her and she didn't seem able to follow her parents' resolute progress across the room. She was like an island, adrift and alone in her uncertainty, and despite his good sense insisting he stay exactly where he was Gabriel realised his legs had begun to move.

'Good evening.'

She looked faintly disconcerted by his stiff bow, but she recovered well, dropping into a curtsy that wouldn't have been out of place at court.

'Good evening, my lord.'

The muttering around them reached new heights. Clearly seeing the two of them together was what the other guests had been waiting for, although the hum of rapidly exchanging opinions receded into the background as he watched Louisa's unhappy colour rise.

He'd known he couldn't avoid her all evening, but he hadn't intended to be so drawn to her, either. Something in her hunted air touched a nerve—she wasn't enjoying the whispered speculation encroaching on all sides, her shoulders slightly hunched as if to protect herself from the thoughtlessly flung words, and it was a feeling he knew only too well.

He cleared his throat. Small talk had never been one of his strong suits and he felt his discomfort grow as Louisa looked up at him, apparently waiting for him to speak. She wore a dress of emerald silk that made her eyes seem greener than ever, so pretty that he'd never been more relieved to hear the dinner bell ring.

Eliza leapt into action. Clapping her hands together, she managed to draw her guests' attention and her smile could easily have been mistaken for genuine as she flashed it around the room.

'Wonderful. Shall we go through?'

There was a polite commotion as everyone took their places. Both Mrs Burcombe and Emanuel shot him encouraging glances that he would have preferred to ignore, but he took their meaning well enough.

Feeling as though he was putting it in a snare, he held out his hand. 'May I?'

Louisa hesitated. Probably the prospect of him leading her into dinner was like something from a bad dream, but with so many people watching she was left with little choice.

'Yes. Thank you.'

Tentatively she placed her palm on the back of his hand. It was the first time she'd touched him, he realised, the pressure of her fingers as light as a feather drifting on a breeze. Her hand felt small. If he turned his over hers would surely be swallowed inside it, just as Frederica's had been, and he sternly instructed himself not to notice such a thing again as he guided her into the dining room and pulled out her chair.

She sat gracefully, although he could still sense her apprehension as she looked around. He saw her eyes flicker sideways beneath the glossy curve of her lashes and knew she must be looking for the man she would have preferred was in his place. Sir Christopher was seated at the far end of the table in a tactful move on Eliza's part, but he didn't cast her way in return. His focus was on a young lady sitting opposite him who appeared to be very much appreciating his attentions and Gabriel almost pitied Louisa when she swallowed and quickly looked away.

The young knight was the only one who displayed

a lack of interest in her, however. Secretive mumbling had accompanied them from the drawing room to the dining table and Gabriel knew he wasn't alone in disliking how inquisitive eyes followed his every move.

To his surprise he felt her lean a little closer. 'I must say again how much I appreciate your kindness in procuring a licence rather than the banns. I can't pretend to enjoy being whispered about so obviously.'

Her voice was soft and distractingly close to his ear. 'Nor I,' he muttered, definitely more gruffly than was warranted. 'But we can endeavour to ignore them.'

Her gratitude did not feel deserved. Having the banns read would advertise publicly that he was marrying again and he had no desire for word to reach Staffordshire, the fact he was taking another wife sure to stoke the rumours there about him into a frenzy.

The more people talked, the greater the risk Leah might catch wind of something untoward, the adjustment of gaining a stepmother enough of a challenge as things were. He needed to write and tell her—*and Miriam, for that matter*—but for now the words escaped him, the situation developing so fast he could barely keep up.

Briefly he wondered what Louisa thought of the new role she was set to adopt. If she and Leah didn't take to each other, it would make an already difficult situation infinitely worse. Did she even like children? It was often assumed all women were maternal by nature, but that wasn't always the case; or perhaps she longed for motherhood and would expect him to provide her with a child of her own?

It was a startling thought. In all the haste and confusion, he hadn't considered what having a new wife would mean in real terms and he found he didn't want to examine it too closely. He'd never expected to have a woman in his bed again—not permanently, at least—and to think it would be Louisa's fiery hair spread out across his pillows made him reach for his glass of wine.

On the very edge of his field of vision he saw her surreptitiously press a hand to her chest. She wore a lace *fichu* at the neck of her gown to hide the marks left behind by the pheasant's claws, but clearly they were still sore. It was on the tip of his tongue to ask how she fared, but the words melted away when his mind strayed to the flash of bare skin he'd seen peeking above her stays. Its pearlescent softness was a memory he wished he could erase, altogether too tempting when he'd resolved to put such weakness aside...

There came the sound of metal clinking against glass. 'May I have your attention, please?'

The chatter died down as Emanuel stood up at the head of the table. Mr and Mrs Burcombe sat on his left side and Eliza on his right, and all four were smiling with such determined cheer that Gabriel knew at once what was coming next.

'Before we dine, I'd like to make an announcement.'

Emanuel beamed down the table at him and Louisa, whom he sensed stiffen in her chair. 'Further to what some of you may have already heard, I'm delighted to confirm the engagement between my niece, Miss Louisa Burcombe, and my dear wife's cousin, Lord Harnham. I hope you'll all join me in wishing them every happiness.'

There was a smattering of applause. A few significant looks were swapped, but being brought out into the open made the news less salacious than when it was clandestine gossip. Facts were never as exciting as fiction, after all, and as glasses were raised in a toast, he hoped any unwanted attention would be swift to move on.

Under cover of the repeated congratulations, he glanced at Louisa. She was staring straight ahead, smiling just as her parents were, a fixed curve shaping the fullness of her lips. Someone catching sight of her from a distance might have believed she meant it—and Gabriel was certainly the only one close enough to notice that her hands shook slightly as she folded them in her lap.

## Chapter Four

Tucking her shawl more comfortably around herself, Louisa burrowed further into her father's old armchair beside the library fireplace. She must have read *The Female Quixote* at least ten times, but as her life was currently in a state of turmoil predictability was the one thing she craved.

Already that morning Mama had dragged her from milliner to modiste to milliner again and would have done so all afternoon, too, if Louisa hadn't feigned a headache just to be alone, her relief when her parents had left the house an hour earlier to meet with the Reverend knowing no bounds.

The resulting solitude, far more in keeping with what she was used to than the novel flurry of parental activity she had unwittingly inspired, *should* have been soothing. Reading was usually able to distract her from whatever was happening around her and yet this time it wasn't quite up to the task.

It didn't help that the book was one she'd discussed

with Sir Christopher, both of them agreeing how much they had enjoyed it, and that any thoughts of him led naturally to Gabriel. In the few days since she and her parents had left Cressex Hall she'd heard nothing from him aside from a sparse note informing her he was leaving for London to see about the marriage licence and his absence had given her far too much time in which to think.

She sighed, letting the book sag in her hands. What was he doing at that moment? Was he sitting in some tavern, almost insensible from the amount he'd had to drink in order to force himself to meet with the Archbishop? A man as wealthy and well connected as Gabriel would surely have had no trouble in getting what he wanted, although her cynicism was tempered by the grudging appreciation she knew he was owed.

It showed more consideration than she'd thought him capable of to go to the trouble of procuring a special licence. In avoiding having the banns read, she could also avoid three Sundays of being stared at in church while everyone speculated on the circumstances of her rapid engagement and for that at least she was grateful.

It made her question whether some of the more agreeable man he'd apparently been before the death of his first wife was still in there somewhere, although it would have to be buried deep down if it was. Without having to wait for the banns their wedding could take place within days instead of weeks and soon enough that confusing man would be her husband, a creature so contrary she felt she still didn't know him at all.

*And then of course there's his daughter to think of. I wonder if she's as perplexing as her papa?*

Her book forgotten, she tried to imagine what any child of Gabriel's could possibly be like. Surely a little girl wouldn't be anywhere near as cool and uncommunicative? If Leah was six now, it meant she'd been three when her mother had died and Louisa felt a pang of compassion that the child would probably hardly remember her mama. As a stepmother she would have to try her best to fill that space, even if she had no idea where to begin, and she could only hope that Gabriel's daughter would be inclined to accept a stranger making Sisslehurst Manor her home...

From somewhere beyond the closed library door came the clang of the front bell.

She sat upright. Had someone come calling? For the most part she'd been able to sidestep the well-wishers who had come to offer their congratulations, pleading the exhaustion of wedding planning to hide from their avid curiosity. It was difficult to feign enthusiasm for long and any hint of reluctance would feed rumours Gabriel hadn't been her first choice. That might have been the truth, but that didn't mean everyone else had to know it, the fact that both she and Gabriel were aware neither of them had ended up with whom they really wanted already quite uncomfortable enough.

Listening intently, she heard the front door open. The servant would bring the caller inside and deposit them somewhere while he went in search of her, despite her feeling less and less willing to be found. What she really wanted was to be left alone and her frustration grew as she heard approaching footsteps in the hall.

It would be some friend of her mother's, she was certain, one of the good-natured gossips Mama surrounded herself with and exactly the type Louisa currently wanted to avoid. She was in no mood to make conversation or play the gracious hostess and, when the footsteps seemed to be heading directly for the library, she hurriedly made up her mind.

She dropped her book and stood up. The windows at the back of the room were open to a gentle breeze that made the long curtains on either side ripple slightly. If she slipped in behind them, nobody would know she was there. Acutely aware she was being ridiculously childish, she did exactly that—and not a moment too soon.

Concealed behind the curtains, she heard the library door creak.

'If you'd care to wait in here, I'll go to inform Miss Burcombe.'

The servant ushered her unwanted guest into the room, just as she'd feared he would, and she held her breath as the floorboards squeaked beneath an intruding pair of shoes. She'd be able to tell which of Mama's friends it was by the caller's reply and she was careful not to make a sound as she waited.

'Very well. Thank you.'

Louisa's throat dried instantly.

It was not the voice she'd been expecting. All of Mama's friends spoke in a genteel high pitch, but the one that came from the other side of the curtain was so low it was almost subterranean. She would have recognised Gabriel's masculine tone anywhere and she froze, too horrified even to blink.

*What is he doing here?*

The servant withdrew, closing the door behind him. Unable to move, Louisa stood like a statue, listening as Gabriel paced slowly across the room. The moment she'd realised it was him her heart had leapt into a beat so hard she was terrified he'd hear it and it didn't slow as she wondered desperately what to do.

If it had been one of her mother's acquaintances, she could have simply waited it out. The servant wouldn't have been able to find her and her guest would have left, but Gabriel was different. He wouldn't have bothered to come to see her unless he had a good reason and she needed to know what it was, preferably while her parents weren't there to overhear, but she'd left it too long to pop out now without making herself look like an utter lunatic.

*Isn't he supposed to be in London? When did he return?*

They were questions she wouldn't find answers to

while huddled behind a curtain. It would serve her right for being so unsociable and she made a mental note never to try hiding from a caller again, although all the good intentions in the world wouldn't help her now. If he found her, she'd be mortified beyond belief and she felt herself flush, her palms prickling with panic-stricken sweat.

She strained to listen. What was he doing? It didn't sound as though he was walking around any more, but that was hardly comforting. If she couldn't hear him, she didn't know how close he was to her hiding place. She had to find some way to escape and there was only one viable option.

The window behind her was open *just* enough for someone to squeeze through. If she could climb out on to the patio, she could run round the side of the house and in through the kitchen door, implying to the servant looking for her that she'd been in the garden the whole time. He would take her to Gabriel and neither man would be any the wiser, her moment of idiocy going undiscovered and her dignity left intact.

Assuming, of course, that she *could* climb out.

Being caught in the act of creeping through a window was possibly more humiliating than hiding behind drapery. She'd have to check he was distracted and that meant risking a peep out through the narrow gap between the curtain and the wall.

Painfully slowly she edged towards it. The gap gave a fair view of the room and she took a deep breath as she leaned forward to peer through it, willing the boards beneath her feet not to creak.

At first, she couldn't see him. For one short moment she thought he'd left the library, but then her eye fell on a tall figure sitting in one of Papa's old armchairs and the anxiety in her chest turned abruptly into something else.

His chair was turned partially away from the window, but she could still see his face, lit clearly by the sunlight at her back. He was concentrating on a book in his hand, his eyebrows lightly furrowed, and it was the smallest suggestion of something lifting the corners of his mouth that made Louisa's ribs feel oddly tight.

She hadn't seen him smile before and she realised she was staring at the unconscious shape of his lips. The soft arc contrasted strikingly with the granite angle of his chin as he gazed down at the book, his dark eyes moving steadily across the page. Unaware he was being watched, he seemed far less tense than she'd ever known him, and when he wasn't frowning or looking as though he'd rather be miles away...

She'd already noticed Gabriel was handsome—she had eyes, after all—but darkly brooding good looks weren't usually her taste. She preferred men who smiled to those who didn't and it was an unwelcome discovery to find that a smiling Gabriel had a distinct effect on her pulse. There was a subtle difference between knowing a man was attrac*tive* and actually being attrac*ted*, and that already fine line seemed suddenly in danger of disappearing entirely.

He turned a page. Still apparently unable to look away, Louisa watched him settle back in his chair and rest one ankle on the opposite knee. Had his legs always been so long? And his hands, as he held the book up in front of him—had they always been so strong-looking and large, the kind that could easily lift a woman without breaking a sweat?

*Stop it. Stop it right this instant.*

Peering at men from behind curtains was not the behaviour of a lady and she felt another wave of embarrassment sweep over her. What would he think if he caught her? She was acting as though she'd never seen a handsome man smile before and she dragged her eyes away from his face, determined to fix them on anything other than the upward tick of his mouth.

They settled on the cover of the book in his hand. She'd been too distracted to make the connection any earlier, but now she recognised the leather binding and the jumble of her feelings grew even more confusing as surprise rose to join in.

He was reading one of her favourites, she realised. She didn't dare check if the smile was still there, but she was certain it had been prompted by the book she liked so much herself. It was the first time they'd had anything even remotely in common and although it was only the tiniest, most tenuous of connections

Louisa felt herself tempted to grab hold before it faded away.

She was probably grasping at straws, she thought as she crept silently back towards the window, but what else did she have? Anything that might draw Gabriel into a civil conversation was worth knowing about, although a traitorous murmur at the back of her mind questioned why such a thing was suddenly so important. At one time talking to him had been as appealing as pulling teeth and she didn't like that the sight of one smile was apparently enough to make her reconsider.

*Of course it wasn't that. I'm not so shallow that a handsome face is enough to sway me.*

It was difficult to muster much conviction, however. The impression of Gabriel's smile followed her as she lowered herself on to the sill and noiselessly swung her legs over to dangle outside, her heart hammering hard enough to feel it in her ears. Just as when he'd spoken about his daughter, she had the sense she'd just caught a glimpse of the real person behind the determined indifference, and even as she dropped lightly down on to the sunlit patio and began to scurry towards the kitchen, she couldn't deny she'd liked what she'd seen.

His eyes had crinkled slightly at the corners…and when they weren't glaring, she could have sworn they'd looked almost kind…

\*\*\*

Gabriel's eyes narrowed. 'Have you been running?'

'Running? Of course not. What a question.'

Louisa patted the slightly dishevelled knot of curls at the back of her head. She certainly *looked* as though she'd been hurrying somewhere, but as he supposed she'd have no reason to lie he let the subject drop.

'Apologies for calling unannounced. I wasn't aware your parents wouldn't be at home.'

Her mouth twisted. 'I think we're past the point of needing to be chaperoned, don't you? That ship has most definitely sailed.'

He grunted in sardonic agreement. It would indeed be a little redundant now if her parents insisted on supervising his visits, although the realisation he and Louisa were very much alone together made him pause. There would be no one to frown if he reached for her hand, for example, except of course the lady herself, and he was quick to remind himself that he'd never entertain doing any such thing.

She gestured for him to sit in one of the multitude of chairs dotted around the room. Evidently her father liked his library to be comfortable and out of the varied selection available Gabriel chose the same armchair he'd risen from at Louisa's entrance. She settled into another close by, smoothing her skirts down neatly over her lap, and when she looked up again it was with barely hidden curiosity.

'I wouldn't have expected you here today. I thought you were to be in London this week?'

'I was. I've only just returned.'

Reaching into his waistcoat pocket, he drew out a folded piece of paper. Attached to the bottom of it was an impressive seal and he saw Louisa's eyes widen as she spied it. 'I was able to arrange the licence. It occurred to me I should probably let you know sooner rather than later.'

He leaned forward to pass it to her, noting the slight unsteadiness in her hand as she took it. She read it quickly once and then again more slowly, running a finger over the Archbishop's crest before giving it back.

'Good. Yes. What a relief.'

In truth he thought she sounded more apprehensive than relieved as he tucked the licence safely back into his pocket. 'I thought you and your mother would want to decide on the date.'

'Thank you. I'm sure she'd like that.'

She gave him what might have been intended as a smile. She never looked completely at ease in his company, for which he didn't blame her, but it struck him that today she seemed even more skittish than usual. Rather than looking straight at him, she kept directing her eyes just above his shoulder or took a sudden interest in one of his ears, and he was just beginning to wonder what the matter was when she gave a small, self-conscious cough.

'I'm sorry for keeping you waiting in here, by the way. Did you find something to amuse yourself while I was being fetched?'

There had only been a few minutes between the servant leaving and returning with Louisa in tow and he wouldn't have thought the delay worth commenting on. She was waiting for an answer, however, and with minor bemusement he indicated to a book resting on the arm of his chair.

'I suppose so. I started flicking through this.'

'An interesting choice. Have you read it before?'

He shrugged. 'A few years ago, when I was at university. Why do you ask?'

Louisa's gaze switched from his left ear to his right. 'I was just wondering if you'd enjoyed it. It's one of my favourites.'

'Is it?'

'Yes. I read it for the first time when I was twelve and then perhaps once a year ever since.'

'Hmm.' It was an unusual book for a child to have read and Gabriel couldn't deny he was mildly impressed. It had been one of his set texts at Oxford and carried memories much happier than those he'd made over the past few years, some of which he'd revisited as he'd skimmed through the pages while waiting for Louisa to appear. He might even have smiled to himself once or twice, a rare occurrence these days, and to his alarm he realised he'd very nearly done so again.

'You've read the following volume?'

Her enquiry helped him wrest back control of his wayward mouth. Frederica had always told him he looked so much more approachable when he smiled. As the idea of Louisa approaching him was not one to encourage, he made sure instead to keep his face carefully blank.

'I haven't had that pleasure.'

She slid him a quick glance, the first direct eye contact she'd made since entering the room. 'My father has it here in his collection. I could fetch it for you, if you were interested.'

His immediate instinct should have been to refuse... yet for some reason he found himself hesitating.

He'd meant to call in, tell her about the licence and then leave right away, he thought uncomfortably. There'd been no intention to stop and chat and certainly not to start swapping book recommendations, and every particle of his good sense told him it was time to go. The fact he was still sitting there was worrying, therefore, and made even more so if he were to admit it was that fleeting flash of green that had made him reluctant to move.

Somehow, when she looked at him with such deft directness, for a second or two it felt as though he was pinned to the spot. Doubtless she had no such objective but that was unarguably the result, and he cursed himself for his momentary weakness as she interpreted his silence as a 'yes'.

Rising from her chair, she crossed to one of the

bookcases built into the far wall. It stretched from floor to ceiling and he watched with grudging interest as she pulled a rickety-looking ladder towards her. Clearly, she was preparing to climb to one of the shelves far above her head and Gabriel hastily stood up.

'Don't go to such trouble. My being well read is a poor exchange for you falling.'

'It's no trouble at all. I spent the greater portion of my childhood in this library. I've been up and down this ladder like a chimney sweep since I was a girl.'

'Even so. Either forget the book or let me go up in your place.'

Her only reply was to set her foot on the first rung and begin to climb. The ladder creaked alarmingly as it took her weight and Gabriel found himself moving closer, drawn nearer almost against his will.

If it were to break…

Louisa climbed higher. Her little, slippered feet were now level with his head and he stepped back half a pace to peer up at her. Her eyes were set on some distant shelf and her lips in a determined line, but it wasn't her expression that seized his attention in a sudden and powerful grasp.

The ladder was propped up very close to the window and in the sunlight pouring through it he could very nearly see straight through her gown.

He looked away again so hurriedly he jarred his neck, but it still wasn't fast enough. The image had seared itself into his brain and the desire to take another peek was so strong he almost obeyed it, only just able to stop himself in time.

The lines of her body beneath the thin fabric were like a landscape barely covered by wisps of cloud. Her figure was displayed against the light in the most tantalising silhouette Gabriel had ever seen, from the slender length of her legs to the subtle arch of her waist as she stretched up in search of her prey, and he was helpless to halt the involuntary spiral of his thoughts.

Would those secret curves feel as good beneath his fingertips as they looked?

It was a mystery he suddenly longed to solve—and that made his chest tighten as though it was caught in a vice.

*I ought to leave. Quickly.*

He took another step back. Louisa was too intent on the bookcase to notice his unease but that didn't make it any less intense. For one worrying moment he'd felt the same desire Frederica had managed to provoke in him when they'd first met and all at once the parallels between her and the woman now triumphantly waving a book above his head felt far too clear.

'Here. I knew this was where I'd find it.'

Louisa's insistent gesturing wouldn't let him retreat any further. Every time she moved the ladder gave another threatening creak and taking care not to look up at her too closely he reluctantly approached to take the book from her hand.

'Thank you. You really needn't have bothered.'

'I didn't mind. It only took a second—'

The ladder interrupted her with a sharp, splintering *crack*.

He heard her gasp as the rung gave way beneath her foot, but by that time he had already moved.

Instinct had told him what was going to happen a split second before the ladder broke. Something in the way it shook as Louisa cautiously descended it had set alarm bells ringing, so he was perfectly placed to catch her as she tumbled backwards into his arms.

She fell against him, her back pressing squarely to his chest, and his natural reflex was to drop the book and wrap her in a steadying hold. One hand braced around her waist while the other flattened across her midriff and he felt his heart turn over as the answer to his earlier question was revealed.

The shape of her beneath his palms was every bit as enticing as her shadow against the window had suggested.

Her figure was different from Frederica's, he realised at once. Her curves were more pronounced, her body rounder and softer than Frederica's had ever been, although that was by no means a failing. She was shorter, too, the back of her head coming just to his chin, and he was overwhelmed by the scent of lilac that floated from her hair.

For one mad moment he feared he might bury his face in it, to inhale the sweet smell of flowers that was more intoxicating than he ever could have imagined, and it was only by summoning the last shreds of his self-control that he managed to resist.

He wasn't sure whether to be relieved or disappointed when she regained her footing and snatched herself away. She stumbled out of his grasp so hurriedly he wondered if she might fall again and his hands twitched with the desire to touch her once more, a longing so unexpected and unwelcome he felt dread skitter down his spine.

*I cannot allow that to happen again.*

He looked down at her, wishing her lips weren't slightly parted in surprise. She was close enough that he could have bent down and kissed them if he'd had a mind to and the knowledge that he was tempted to do exactly that helped him to take a smart step back.

It would be folly to indulge even the faintest of feelings for his soon-to-be wife. The old adage of once burned twice shy had never been more apt than in the case of his marriages and he was damned if he wouldn't take some kind of lesson from the carnage of his first. Louisa wanted Sir Christopher just as Frederica had wanted that gutless wretch Sir Cecil Allenby and no amount of perfumed curls or pretty-looking lips would make him forget it.

The thought left a sour taste that he attempted to rinse out with words. 'Are you hurt?'

'No.' Louisa shook her head, apparently unwilling now to meet his eye. 'It's a good thing you were there to catch me. Thank you.'

'Think nothing of it.'

He dismissed her thanks with the lift of a shoulder, glad that he managed to sound more offhand than he felt. A growing awareness of something was stealing over him and he had absolutely no intention of Louisa guessing he was not as unmoved as he might appear.

It wouldn't have been the first time a woman he was responsible for had suffered a fall, he recognised dourly—although at least on this occasion nobody had died.

It was a reminder he neither wanted nor needed. The circumstances of Frederica's premature death haunted him unceasingly and even after three years the mess of guilt and regret was impossible to unpick. For Leah's sake he had allowed the falsehoods his former parents-in-law now told about that day to go unchallenged, the truth he'd have to reveal otherwise far worse than the lies, and he wasn't looking forward to the day when Louisa began asking questions of her own.

*She'll want to know about Frederica eventually. The question is—how much will I tell her when she does?*

Unwilling to confront that prospect while Louisa was still within touching distance, he bent to pick up the book that had caused so much trouble before sweeping a stiff bow. 'If you're sure you're unhurt, I must ask you to excuse me. I've stayed longer than I should have.'

'Of course.' Louisa bobbed him a curtsy almost as substandard as his bow. She still didn't seem disposed to look at him, instead busy fiddling with the lace edge of one cuff. 'I'll tell my parents about the licence. I imagine Mama will want the wedding to be quite soon.'

'Very good. Whatever you decide.'

He turned away. A few short paces took him to the door and when he glanced back he didn't expect her to be watching him. She was, however. The instant their gazes met hers flew to some point on the opposite wall, but he knew what he'd seen and the expression in her eyes wasn't one he'd ever thought to catch there. She'd been looking after him in the way only a woman who was interested in a man could look and sudden confusion almost made him forget what he'd paused to tell her.

'Oh. And I'll be sure to read the book.'

## Chapter Five

Despite having seen it almost every day of her life, Louisa barely recognised the best parlour as her father practically carried her inside.

Her legs might have been shaking uncontrollably, but still she marvelled at how Mama had transformed an ordinary room into a wedding venue almost fit for Queen Charlotte herself. Whatever her failings as a mother, Mrs Burcombe's hosting skills couldn't be faulted: the walls had been repapered in a pale blue to match the new velvet curtains at every window while great lengths of white muslin swagged across the ceiling made it feel as though the space was enveloped in a cloud.

Flowers spilled from every available surface, their scent filling the air, and even the chair legs had received a fresh application of gilt. Quite how her mother had managed such a feat in just three days—or why she'd gone to such measures when the private ceremony meant nobody of note would see them—

Louisa didn't know, but as she took her place at the top of the makeshift aisle the sight of Gabriel waiting for her eclipsed all other thoughts.

Heads turned as Papa guided her forward, a blur of faces she was too nervous to tell apart. Her brothers would be there among them, along with their wives and perhaps a couple of their older and more well-behaved children, as well, of course, as Uncle Emanuel. As far as she was aware the only member of Gabriel's family in attendance was Eliza, although she had no attention to spare to look for her aunt.

Papa gave her arm an uncharacteristically encouraging squeeze. Her head felt light, but the dark intensity of Gabriel's eyes drew her onwards, pulling her to him as if she had no say in the matter. He looked freshly shaved, with his hair artfully pushed back and the close-fitting navy coat he wore emphasising the firm shape of his shoulders—things she wasn't sure she would have noted quite as keenly before the afternoon in her father's library that had made her think twice.

Ever since she'd felt Gabriel's hands on her she hadn't been able to get the sensation out of her head. His grip had been strong as he'd steadied her and the warmth of his palms had spread through the thin muslin of her gown to reach the skin beneath, sending a cascade of *something* flooding through her. It had lasted but a moment, but in that brief splinter of time she'd felt safe, somehow completely convinced that he wouldn't let her fall, and it was hard to reconcile that with the gruff man she was getting to know.

He was still distant and brusque, yet that single act had shown her there was something in him a woman might be able to rely on if she could just tease it out—nothing close to affection, but perhaps at least a support when life became too difficult to navigate alone. A wife ought to be able to depend on her husband after all, she thought distantly as she reached the front of the room, and that his touch had made her feel dazed as well as secure was neither here nor there.

The string quartet arranged in the corner fell silent. She'd been so distracted she'd hardly noticed they were playing, but in the ensuing quiet she was aware of every tiny sound, from the rustling of Mama's new dress to the insistent hammering of her own heart. Standing directly in front of Gabriel, she could have sworn she could hear him breathing, the subtle movement of his chest far more measured than she could manage herself. He seemed calm as ever, which to her was something of a miracle—but then, of course, he had done all of this before.

*It's my first time getting married, not his. He's already an old hand.*

Dwelling on his first wife while about to become his second wasn't something she wanted and she made an effort to gently banish the previous Lady Harnham from her mind. She could only hope Gabriel was doing the same, at least temporarily, although she knew the chances were slim.

For all her determination to wed only where there was true feeling, she had still fallen into a trap and the knowledge she was yet again to be second best was a bitter thing to swallow. In her husband she'd always wanted to find someone who valued her in a way she'd never known before, but for Gabriel someone already occupied the space she'd dreamed of filling. His thoughts were tied up in the past, not the future, and just as her brothers had unwittingly pushed her out, she suspected the first Lady Harnham would do the same, no longer alive but her presence lingering before Louisa's married life had even begun.

With one last press of her arm Papa stepped back to take his seat beside her mother. She didn't need to look to know Mama would be beaming from ear to ear, the prospect of her daughter becoming a baroness a prize she never would have dreamed to aim for. The Baron himself wasn't smiling, however, his face as always damnably difficult to read, and so it came as a surprise when he bent his head to murmur something only Louisa could hear.

'You look very well.'

From anyone else such an underwhelming compliment would hardly have felt like a compliment at all, although from Gabriel's lips it seemed like high praise indeed.

'Thank you.'

Her mouth was so dry she feared the words would escape as a croak. It was ridiculous that even such meagre approval should please her and yet she couldn't deny that it did. She and Mama had gone to great trouble in selecting her gown and the best way to put up her hair and for him to make any comment at all suggested he didn't altogether dislike what he saw. As much as their union had been born of necessity it was still finally her long-awaited chance to be a bride and she'd intended to make the most of the one day she was supposed to feel like the most beautiful woman in the room.

It was unlikely Gabriel thought of her as such, but all the same his eyes didn't leave her face as the Reverend cleared his throat. Evidently he was waiting for his cue to begin and the fine hairs on the back of Louisa's neck stirred when Gabriel muttered to her once more. 'Are you ready?'

'As much as I think I ever will be.'

One dark eyebrow flickered slightly. Perhaps he was thinking much the same thing, although his nod to the clergyman was as self-assured as ever.

'Dearly beloved...'

The Reverend's voice rang out clearly in the silent parlour. It was something she'd waited years for and yet now it was happening she couldn't seem to concentrate on the words, the Reverend hardly any distance away but all her focus directed elsewhere. It was the other man standing close to her that had captured it and she found herself unable to break away, his presence so all-encompassing there might as well have been no one else in the room.

She swallowed. When had *that* happened? She'd been under the impression she disliked him, so why now could she barely tear her eyes from his face? Perhaps it had been the secret glimpse of his smile that had done it, or the strength of his hands when he'd prevented her from falling to the ground? Either way it had to be a purely physical attraction and nothing deeper than that, but surely even that much had the potential to lead to trouble when there was no hope of it being returned…

The Reverend went on talking. At the furthest reaches of her vision she caught a movement that might have been Mama dabbing her dry lashes with a lace handkerchief purchased especially for the occasion, but it was Gabriel's eyes that commanded her attention. They were trained on hers, coffee-brown meeting green in a look that to her immense surprise was almost reassuring. It was as if he knew her legs felt weak and was encouraging her to stand on them anyway, and her confusion didn't abate when he reached out for her hand.

Her already tight throat clenched shut as he began to roll down her glove. He did so with astounding gentleness, his fingers tracing across the back of her hand, and the sensation of his fingertips grazing her skin almost made her knees buckle. It felt altogether too intimate, the kind of thing that ought to be done in private rather than in front of an audience, and she thought she caught a faint reflection of her own shock mirrored in Gabriel's face. It was gone again the next moment, disappearing so quickly she wondered if she'd imagined it, although the rapid tattoo of her heart against her ribs wouldn't let her forget.

She spoke her vows through lips that barely moved. She had no choice: every muscle in her body was on high alert, held tense and ready for what she knew would come soon after the ring was slipped on to her finger. Once that was done the only thing left would be for them to share their first kiss and the knowledge it was fast approaching veered dangerously close to anticipation.

It wouldn't just be her first kiss with Gabriel. It would be her first real kiss with *anyone* and that was what she tried to tell herself was the reason a swarm of butterflies erupted as he slid her wedding ring into place.

She would have been excited and anxious no matter who was about to press their lips to hers and that it was Lord Harnham who'd have that honour didn't mean a thing. Sir Christopher had kissed her hand once or twice—*don't think about him now!*—but of course that hadn't been the same. She'd wondered endlessly what it would be like, but all her daydreams vanished as reality abruptly pushed to the fore.

The brush of Gabriel's mouth on hers was over before she could blink.

Stunned, Louisa stared up at him. He had bent his head and then pulled back again so quickly she'd barely felt anything…aside from a rush of something worryingly close to disappointment.

*Was that it?*

Gabriel wasn't looking at her. The small congregation had broken out into applause she knew she had to acknowledge, although it was a struggle to find a smile as she peered around at the delighted faces. Dismay and embarrassment flowed over her like cold rain and she almost recoiled when he placed her hand into the crook of his arm and prepared to lead her back down the aisle, all her expectations dashed and the butterflies faltering in their flight.

*He could barely even bring himself to kiss me. What kind of start is that for a marriage, even one built on duty?*

It was a dismal thought, but one that shouldn't have surprised her, she chided herself as she let her new husband guide her towards the door. His arm beneath her fingers was firm and the musculature inviting, but they weren't things she was supposed to notice. He'd married her against his inclinations and she should remind herself she felt the same about him, too, never forgetting that to Gabriel she would always be second best.

It wasn't anything like how she'd always wanted

to feel on her wedding day. For years she'd hoped for happiness and mutual affection that might even lead to real love—but that wasn't to be her destiny and, as Gabriel's shadow fell over her as they walked out into the sunlight, it was a stark reminder to be careful what one wished for.

It was growing dark by the time Gabriel handed Louisa down from the carriage. Sisslehurst Manor's windows glowed with candlelight, casting a yellow haze over her face as she looked up with some uncertainty at her new home.

He followed her gaze as it travelled the vast distance from the gravelled drive all the way up to the chimneys. It still didn't feel quite like home yet for him, either, and he wondered whether her being there would make him feel more or less as though he belonged.

A surreptitious glance showed she was examining the uppermost windows. With her head tilted back, more of her face was visible beneath her veiled bonnet and he couldn't help but appreciate the way the candlelight emphasised the soft line of her profile. In her bridal gown of shimmering ivory she looked positively angelic, the fabric flattering the creamy blush of her skin, and he couldn't deny his first glimpse of her at the end of the aisle had almost made him choke on his own breath.

He bit the inside of his cheek in a warning not to

let himself go any further. Was it really relevant that it wasn't just her features he'd admired, but the determination with which she'd carried herself as her papa had walked her closer? Any woman could look fetching in an expensive dress, but it was the proud lift of her chin that had caught him.

She didn't want this marriage any more than he did and he'd been able to tell she was nervous, but she'd stood up in front of everyone none the less and only someone watching her very closely would have seen the anxious tightness around her mouth. It showed a strength of character previous events had made him value far more than a comely face, although nobody looking at Louisa that day could have argued she didn't possess both.

'Allow me to escort you inside.'

She took his outstretched arm with a breath of hesitation. All afternoon she'd been surrounded by her family and friends, but now they were alone and he thought he sensed tension in the way her hand rested on his sleeve.

Together they climbed the marble steps. On the evening of his first wedding, he'd carried his bride across the threshold, but somehow he didn't think Louisa would take kindly to the same treatment—not that he'd intended to try. She'd barely spoken to him since the ceremony and she hardly looked at him now as he pushed open the door and let her go in ahead of him, aware of a strange apprehension as he waited to see her reaction to her first glimpse of her new domain.

He needn't have worried.

She stopped on the threshold, her eyes widening as she took in the tasteful grandeur of the hall.

'Gabriel...!'

There was something uncommonly pleasing about hearing her gasp his name and he struggled to keep his expression impassive. It was a sound suggestive of the bedroom rather than an entrance hall and his pulse ticked up at what *that* implied. Had her mother explained what usually happened on a wedding night?

The idea of lying with Louisa was far more appealing than it should have been and that was reason for concern—even their first kiss as man and wife was kept deliberately chaste to stop himself from desiring more. She was hardly likely to be looking forward to what must eventually happen to make their marriage legally watertight and he determined there and then that unless she raised the subject he certainly would not.

'Will it do?'

At his question she graced him with a short laugh. 'Will it do? I think this entrance hall alone is bigger than Mama's entire dining room. And that chandelier...'

She gazed up at it, the multitude of candles illuminating her rapt face. The crystal droplets gleamed, but her eyes sparkled brighter, or at least it seemed to Gabriel as she slowly shook her head.

'I knew you were a baron, of course, but somehow I never quite made the connection with what that *meant*. I suppose I should have expected such a magnificent house.'

Gabriel frowned, although he was by no means dissatisfied by her response. 'It's unusual for people to forget the material privileges of a title. Perhaps that makes you more deserving of your own.'

He glanced away from her, her enthusiasm encouraging him to look around as though he was seeing the manor for the first time again himself. It was more impressive even than the ancestral seat he still owned in Staffordshire, but would be reluctant to return to, both for the whispers it would prompt as well as the memories that haunted its walls.

*Frederica never forgot my title and its advantages for so much as a moment—or perhaps I should say, her parents didn't.*

They had enjoyed those advantages at every opportunity, he recalled unwillingly, using his devotion to their daughter to ask for money and favours he'd at first been ready to grant. His wealth and status had let them into the upper echelons of society and after Frederica's death they had tried to cling on to him through Leah, feigning interest in her to keep him and his pocketbook at their disposal.

By then, of course, he'd begun to see through them:

they cared for their granddaughter only as a means to a lucrative end and not for herself at all, and to protect her from their scheming he had cut off all contact—as well as financial assistance—soon after Frederica's coffin had been lowered into the ground.

It couldn't have been clearer that they desired to use his daughter in the same way they had weaponised their own and he wouldn't allow them to sink their claws into his child, a decision their subsequent act of vengeful spite had confirmed beyond any doubt had been the right one.

Again, shadows of the past had tried to break out into the light and again he forced them back. Aside from Frederica herself, her parents were the very last individuals he wanted to think about and he was glad when Louisa interrupted his train of thought with a tentative gesture towards one of the doors leading from the hall.

'Can I…?'

'Please do. Go wherever you like. This is your home now as much as it is mine.'

It was a bizarre notion, but he thought he caught a trace of something like relief. She must have been worried about his reaction to her being there, he realised belatedly, and he thought her step seemed marginally lighter as she handed her bonnet to a waiting maid and crossed to the nearest door.

He followed. She'd chosen what he'd imagined would be her parlour and her delight at the pretty room was clearly sincere. The floor-to-ceiling windows afforded a good view over the landscaped gardens and she lingered in front of the darkened glass, her reflected expression one he abruptly thought would look well captured in paint.

'Is there a library?'

'Of course. This way.'

He led her from the parlour back into the hall. The library stood on the opposite side with the door slightly ajar and, just as he had on their entrance to the manor, he drew aside to let her go first.

Another uncomfortably agreeable gasp was his reward. The best way to describe her as she stared around at the flame-lit shelves was looking as if all her birthdays had come at once and to his amazement—and concern—he found he had to fight back a smile.

'It meets with your approval?'

In place of words she darted to the nearest bookshelf and ran a hand across the leather spines. Many of the books were from his late father's private collection, built up over the years of Gabriel's childhood, and he was glad now he'd gone to the trouble of having them all brought down-country when he'd abandoned his previous house. It was gratifying she seemed to appreciate their worth, the corners of his mouth still threatening to turn upwards as he watched her edge closer to his desk.

'Oh?' She picked up the book lying next to his quill rest. 'You read it, then?'

'Of course. I said I would.'

He detected a hint of surprise in the way she turned over the book she'd lent him. Perhaps she'd expected him to set it aside without touching it and to find instead he'd done as promised was…pleasing?

'I should have known you were a man of your word. And? What was your verdict?'

'I enjoyed it. Very nearly as much as the first.'

It was the truth. He'd read it from cover to cover within two days, but he wouldn't be admitting what had been on his mind almost the entire time. The memory of her silhouetted against the window as she strained up to fetch the book in question had left its mark, alongside how she had felt in his grasp, and he doubted he would ever be able to read it again without the same associations pressing forward with every page.

Fortunately, she didn't seem to guess his thoughts. She returned the book to his desk and looked again around the room.

'Does your daughter like to read?'

'She does. It's a habit I was pleased to instil in her as early as I could.'

'You must have missed her today. It's a shame neither she nor your sister were there. I would have liked to have met them sooner.'

Gabriel curbed a frown. Was that really how she

felt, or was she just being polite? For his daughter and new wife to form a good relationship was of the upmost importance and it would be disastrous if they disliked each other on sight, neither of them having much choice in suddenly being saddled with the other.

'It was for the best. Until all the dust has settled and you feel more at home I'd prefer to keep Leah away.' He straightened a book sitting haphazardly on a shelf, hoping he sounded suitably offhand. 'She enjoys spending time at my sister's house—besides, Miriam is a terrible traveller. As she only has to look at a carriage to start feeling bilious I thought I'd save her the trouble of coming here for the wedding. You'll meet her when we go to fetch Leah.'

'Of course. I shall look forward to it.'

Louisa nodded reassuringly with no sign of any hidden meaning. Her jaw was clenched and by the sudden tightness of her cheeks he could tell she was holding back a yawn.

'Are you tired?'

'Aren't you? It's been a long day.'

'It has. I'll have someone show you to your room.' She paused. '*My* room? Surely you mean *our*?'

The instant the words left her mouth he knew she regretted their clumsiness. If he'd ever seen someone more mortified he couldn't recall it, his own discomfort surging upwards sharply in turn.

'I didn't want to assume.'

'I wouldn't have thought you had. I know what's

expected.' Looking as though she wanted the ground to swallow her, Louisa mumbled in the direction of the carpet. 'There are certain things a newly married couple must do, Mama has informed me, unless you don't want…?'

It seemed she couldn't bring herself to finish her sentence. It hung abandoned in the air and Gabriel felt a thread of tension stretch out between them he had no idea how best to break.

What she was referring to was so outrageously tempting it took all his self-control not to immediately correct her. To have the chance to explore her body, this time without layers of linen in the way, was an opportunity he wanted to grab before she changed her mind—and yet he couldn't immediately bring himself to accept. She'd only raised the subject out of obligation and he refused to impose where he wasn't wanted, the very idea going against everything he believed.

However…

Louisa was studying the carpet as if her life depended on it. Her face was aflame and her hands tying themselves in knots, and he knew he couldn't win no matter what answer he made.

If he accepted, she might feel uncomfortable, but if he refused, she would doubtless feel rejected and even more embarrassed than she was already. It was difficult to think clearly while ungentlemanly thoughts clouded his mind and he tried to shut them out, attempting to banish the memory of how good she'd felt in his arms.

The rational part of him knew it would be better to go along with what her mother had prepared her to expect, as well as it being all but required to formalise the marriage, although he had to sternly remind himself that desire should play no part in his decision.

'No. If you've no objection, then of course we should do what is proper.'

Straddling a line between sounding too enthusiastic and not enthusiastic enough was like balancing on a tightrope. Both sides made very persuasive arguments and he could only hope he'd said the right thing, Louisa's glowing face giving very little away.

Of his own feelings he was certain. Anticipation had begun to build somewhere deep down inside him and, try as he might, he couldn't ignore it as his new wife bobbed her head, the candlelight making her hair shine like burnished copper.

'Very well. Don't bother sending for a servant. I'm sure I can find my own way.'

Gabriel nodded in return. His heart had picked up speed and he felt it thudding beneath his shirt. 'I don't doubt it. It's the first set of rooms on the left as you go up the stairs.'

Louisa lay very still beneath the coverlet.

The bed she now found herself in was enormous. From what Mama had hinted she'd gathered *some* proximity to one's husband was required, but she couldn't bring herself to move more towards the centre of the mattress. She had no idea which side of the bed Gabriel usually slept on and until he came upstairs, she'd just have to guess, along with answers to all the other mysteries about which she had barely any information at all.

*It's all very well for Mama to say Gabriel will know what he's doing, but what about me?*

She clasped her hands tighter over her stomach. Every breath was shallow and she could feel the soft flutter of her pulse at her wrists, aware of every tiny movement as she lay in the darkness and waited for him to walk into the bedroom they were now expected to share.

A creak from the landing directly outside made her heart shoot up into her mouth.

Through a gap in the bedhangings she watched as the bedroom door opened and Gabriel stepped inside, his face lit by the feeble light of a single candle. The lone flame cast shadows under his cheekbones and the sharp edge of his jaw, making him appear more severe than ever, and Louisa hardly dared look at him as he set the candle down beside the bed and began to unbutton his shirt.

An invisible hand wrapped around her and squeezed as tight as it could. Was he really going to undress there? Right in front of her, with no preamble at all? She tried to tear her eyes away, but found she couldn't, instead following the steady progress of his hands until the shirt's collar hung open across his chest. In the gloom it was impossible to see clearly, but what little she *could* see was enough to make her mouth run dry.

He looked up. For the briefest of moments their eyes met through the curtains' narrow gap and her heartrate spiked at the dark glitter in his. He must have known she was watching helplessly, but he didn't seem offended, his face barely changing as he took hold of the hem of his shirt and pulled it over his head.

If she'd been finding it difficult to breathe before, Louisa feared she might now suffocate.

The dim light made his bare skin glow golden, the moving flame both revealing and coyly concealing the broad set of his shoulders and sculpted shape of his chest. There was a scattering of hair on it, she saw with fascination, black, curling hair that wound a meandering path down his toned abdomen and into the waistband of his breeches, drawing her gaze there with effortless ease.

It was the first half-naked male form she'd ever seen and her embarrassment couldn't eclipse her appreciation for the firm swell of his biceps, his arms as strong looking as they had felt that day in the library when she'd found herself locked in their accidental embrace. *Then* of course they had been covered by his sleeves, but now there would be no barrier at all if she touched his skin with her fingertips, perhaps tracing a line from his wrist all the way up to his neck...

His hands had dropped to the fastening of his breeches, but now he hesitated. Another glance at her seemed to help him make up his mind and, to what Louisa acknowledged was an undignified degree of disappointment, he leaned down and blew out the candle.

The room was plunged into darkness. The sudden absence of light was momentarily disorientating, but she regained her senses with a jolt when she felt the bedcovers move and something heavy settle beside her—something that smelled of fresh woodsmoke and leather, a scent she'd already discovered was more pleasing than any cologne.

She lay as stiff and silent as a plank of wood. There was some rustling and shifting as Gabriel made himself comfortable, but she didn't move, staring directly upwards and barely able to snatch a single worthwhile breath.

*Is...is he... The breeches...?*

She'd never been gladder of complete darkness. At least Gabriel couldn't see how her face was aflame as she wondered whether he was wearing anything while lying less than a hand's span away. She could sense how close he was without even needing to see—her nerves were alive, her skin tingling at his nearness—and the overwhelming temptation to reach out a tentative finger was so strong she feared she had little hope of holding it back.

As it turned out, Gabriel beat her to it.

Any last panicked thoughts stuttered to a halt as she felt a light touch on her arm.

'You're sure about this?'

His voice came out of the darkness, so close and deep it sent a nameless thrill the full length of her spine. It was unspeakably intimate, the first low murmur of her husband in what was now their bed, and it brought an answer instinctively to Louisa's tongue.

'Yes.'

She heard a scarcely audible noise that might have been a swallow. The idea that Gabriel might be apprehensive about whatever was about to happen was ridiculous, so it must have been for some other reason that he paused before closing the space between them. His hand still lay on her arm and she felt herself tense as it travelled—very gently—inwards towards her waist, his fingers brushing her nightgown in a barely-there caress.

She gave an involuntary gasp. Her nightgown might as well have not been there at all, the fabric acting as no barrier whatsoever against the warmth of his body. His breath was soft against her ear, his face obviously now mere inches from hers, and the deliberate slowness with which he slid his hand across to rest just below her ribs made it almost impossible not to writhe against the sheets.

His breathing stirred the curls at her ear. It didn't sound completely steady and the thrill that had streaked down her spine came again to realise *she* was affecting *him*. His fingers were drifting backwards and forward, circling her navel, and although she wasn't sure exactly what it was she wanted Louisa knew she wanted more.

Gabriel's voice was hoarse. 'The first time isn't usually the best for a woman. Try not to be too tense—and don't be afraid. If at any time you want me to stop, I'll stop.'

Louisa shuddered. Feelings she didn't fully understand were coursing through her and they made it very difficult to concentrate on anything other than the movement of Gabriel's fingers. They were wandering lower, heading towards the place where a novel sensation was beginning to grow, and she couldn't help a sound of protest when he abruptly took his hand away.

'Louisa. I'd like to hear you say it. You'll tell me if you want me stop?'

'Yes,' she barely managed to choke out. 'I'll tell you.'

'Good.'

The hand reappeared. It slipped around her waist, effortlessly turning her on to her side, and then her heart stopped as she felt Gabriel's lips settle over hers.

It wasn't a kiss like the one he'd given her at the end of their vows. That had been a chaste anticlimax, nothing like she'd always imagined her first real kiss, but then this one didn't match her daydreams either. Nowhere in the books she'd read had there been any mention of a soft start that grew more and more firm, or of how unconscious desire would lead to a gradual dance of tongues that sent fire flooding through her veins. Even with no experience she seemed to know what to do and she found herself moving to his rhythm, her mind blank as she let her body take control.

Gabriel's hand was at the small of her back, pressing her closer against the unyielding lines of his body, and she realised her own hand had settled somewhere on his side. A flat plane of muscle lay beneath her palm and she couldn't stop herself from following it, sliding higher until she found the broad expanse of his back. His skin was hot to the touch, all but blistering her fingers, but she had no time to register it before Gabriel broke the kiss and dipped beneath her jaw.

Her nails dug lightly into his back as he kissed from her throat to her ear, her bones liquefying when he traced the very tip of his tongue over the lobe. He'd risen up on one elbow and Louisa felt him above her, his chest pressing slightly against hers as he rolled her on to her back. Her nightgown was tangled around her legs and the ribbons at her neck hanging free, and she'd never felt such a longing to pull the damn thing off altogether as when he began carefully inching its hem up towards her thighs.

Her heart beat so hard she thought it might burst

through her ribs. Gabriel's light touch along the sensitive skin of her inner thighs should have tickled, but instead it felt wonderful, unfamiliar and yet awakening something within her that had been waiting to break free. She hadn't known such feelings existed and for it to have been the solemn, serious Lord Harnham that prompted them was almost laughable, the unhappy start to their match making such a thing hard to believe.

*I thought I disliked him? And I thought he disliked me in return?*

Her mind was too busily engaged elsewhere to give her questions much thought. Gabriel's mouth had found hers again and between the movement of his lips and his fingers she was suspended in a mute, pleasure-drenched stupor. The hem of her nightgown had almost reached the point of no return and she just about managed to wonder vaguely if he now regretted extinguishing the light, unable to see exactly what he was uncovering with such teasing slowness—

Her eyes flew open.

The bedroom was completely dark. Without even the smallest spark from a candle it would be impossible for her new husband to tell who he was caressing, and her stomach gave a sudden lurch as she realised what that meant.

'Stop.'

Gabriel's hand stilled immediately.

'Louisa? Is something wrong?'

He sounded like a man teetering on the edge of something uncontrollable and she shivered, her body reacting to the gravel in his tone. What she wanted more than anything was to pull his face down to hers again and let him do what he would, but a growing fear spiked through her and refused to fall back.

At the end of the wedding ceremony he'd given her the briefest kiss he could get away with, and yet in the darkness he seemed much more enthused. Had he deliberately blown out the candle so he couldn't see her—perhaps to help him pretend she was someone else?

Her hands had been pressed flat to his shoulders, but now they dropped away from him, landing beside her on the mattress with a soft thud.

She had absolutely no proof her worries were true, but they were strong enough to overcome all rationality. Now the thought had occurred to her she couldn't stop it from bedding in, burrowing down inside her like a worm turning a good apple's core bad, and the embers that had been setting fire to her blood now cooled to frigid ash.

He hadn't married her for love. She knew that, but the idea of her new husband thinking of his first wife on their wedding night was too much to bear. When she'd dreamed of marrying it had always been to someone who cared for her and her alone, not a man who would always long for another, and to her horror she felt a sudden prickling behind her eyes.

'I don't... I can't... Forgive me.'

Gabriel shifted away. It wasn't the abrupt withdrawal of an angry man, however, it was the tactful giving of space and Louisa was grateful for it, although she still felt a strange sense of loss when he gently lifted away his hands.

'I understand. There's nothing to forgive.'

In the darkness she heard him roll on to his back. He might have been staring up at the canopy, wondering what had gone wrong, but Louisa didn't stay to find out. The insistent pulse inside her that had driven her on had been silenced by doubt and unhappiness and she hoped Gabriel wouldn't realise it as she moved on to her side, squeezing her eyes shut as she turned her face to the wall.

'It's been such a dizzying day. If you don't mind, I think I'd like to sleep.'

A soft sound from the direction of his pillow might have been him nodding. He didn't speak and she was relieved his silence meant she needn't say anything more, embarrassment and dismay making the stinging behind her lashes more intense.

A lump of wretchedness rose in her throat. He probably thought she was a prissy thing now, unwilling to undertake the duties expected of a wife. Her failure would only make the first Lady Harnham seem even more saintly by comparison and she was about to bite her lip against a hot rush of tears when a careful touch on her back interrupted the flow before it could begin.

Gabriel's hand found her hunched shoulder. It landed softly and Louisa's breath caught as it rested there, only for a moment and taking her almost as long to understand.

There was no sense that he was making any kind of demand of her. He touched her with the same gentleness one might use to offer comfort and to her amazement she realised that was his intention. He withdrew again before she could react and she made no attempt to stop him, too shocked to move even if she'd wanted to. It was kindness of a sort she'd never have expected from him and she didn't know what to make of it, only that no part of her had felt the urge to pull away.

She lay there for a while, frozen in place by the jumble of feelings she was too confused to unravel. Gabriel still didn't speak and eventually she heard his breathing slow, becoming deeper and more measured until she knew he was asleep.

Rest didn't come to claim her, however. She remained awake long after a clock somewhere struck the hour, its distant chimes echoing through the unfamiliar house she was somehow supposed to think of as home.

## Chapter Six

For the next few days Louisa spent as little time in Gabriel's company as possible.

At one stage that would simply have been because she disliked him, she thought as she crept down the staircase and into the hall on the fourth morning after their wedding, but now her reasons were less clear cut. After their disaster of a wedding night, he hadn't tried to touch her again and it was how much she wanted him to that now made it necessary for her to keep away.

Her eyes were gritty with tiredness as she peered round the dining room door, half-hoping and half-fearing Gabriel was already seated inside. She'd barely slept again—it was almost impossible to drift off while every inch of her was alert for any movement on his side of the bed, waiting for an exploratory hand that never came.

Part of her was glad he had evidently decided to keep a respectful distance, but another worryingly vocal part wanted him to try again, uncertain which of the two opposing factions inside her would triumph if he did. On the one hand she was afraid it was his first wife he'd be imagining if she let him impose upon her, while on the other...

Louisa gave an involuntary shudder. His expert mapping of her body had awakened her in ways she hadn't known she was capable of, the memory of his fingertips ghosting over her bare skin another reason she found it so difficult to sleep.

She almost wished she'd ignored the insistent doubt that had pushed itself to the front of her mind, instead blocking it out to concentrate on the unfamiliar delights her husband was intent on introducing her to, but of course now it was far too late. She'd let her misgivings get the better of her and now the atmosphere between them was uncomfortable in a way different from any that had gone before, with embarrassment on her side and the bite of rejection probably very much on his.

Leaning against the wall, she took a deep breath. Loitering in the hall all morning wasn't going to help matters. Any awkwardness would only dissipate if she made an effort to confront it, although that was far easier said than done when she recalled the hand that had settled on her shoulder at the moment she'd needed comfort the most. Such a sweet, simple gesture coming from a man she'd thought was anything but was still something she didn't fully understand,

and it didn't help quell the uncertain feelings for her new husband that had begun to develop despite her attempts to stamp them out.

Gabriel was indeed already at his breakfast when she pushed open the dining-room door. He looked up at her entrance, his face impassive as he gave one of his signature nods.

'Good morning.'

'Good morning.'

It was hardly a riveting conversational opening, but it was the best Louisa could do as she took her seat on the other side of the table. It was the first time she'd seen him that morning, Gabriel having slipped from their bed before she'd woken from her latest fitful snatch of sleep, and she found it much safer to study the sugar bowl than the man in front of her.

From the glimpse she'd caught as she sat down he looked almost as tired as she did, but somehow the shadows beneath his eyes enhanced the darkness of his gaze rather than the reverse, giving a brooding edge to his handsomeness that was almost as appealing as the rare smile he still didn't know she'd seen.

*Has he not been sleeping well either?*

It was a question she wouldn't dream of asking. If he had been lying awake night after night, it was doubtful it was for the same reason sleep had been evading her. He was surely more likely to be reflecting on the disappointments of his new marriage than waiting breathlessly for her to slide towards him on the mattress and she quickly turned her attention to the toast rack to distract herself from any such thoughts.

Gabriel was flipping through the morning news-sheets as he ate, his eyes mercifully downturned, but when the quiet between them went on long enough for even him to notice it, he looked up.

'Will you have some coffee?'

'No, thank you. I prefer tea.'

He returned to his paper. No further attempts at conversing seemed to be forthcoming, although he didn't need to speak to command Louisa's attention.

Every time he turned a page, she was aware of it. He held the newssheet loosely at the edges and it gave her an uninterrupted view of his large, strong hands as they rested on the table. She'd never really given much thought to those parts of a man before, but apparently Gabriel's had taken on a fascination all their own and she tried to concentrate on the teapot instead as she poured herself a cup. It was hard to ignore them when she knew how warm they were, however, and how they could be so much gentler than they looked, even strangely comforting when the need for such a thing arose...

'I thought I might ride out on the estate today,' she blurted out more loudly than she'd intended. 'If you have no objection? I'd like to see a little more of the grounds.'

Gabriel set his paper aside. 'Of course. I'll have one of the horses readied for you.'

He frowned as if an afterthought had occurred to him. 'I'm afraid I can't accompany you. I have some business in town I need to attend to, but I'll arrange for a groom to go with you.'

'There's no need. I'd enjoy going out by myself.'

He studied her for a moment. 'How competent a rider are you?'

'Not very. I don't think I could manage an opinionated horse.'

'In that case I'll ask for Nutmeg to be saddled. She's steady and ideal for a lady.' Gabriel's gaze sharpened suddenly. 'I must, however, insist that you take a groom.'

Both his tone and expression suggested any disagreement was unwelcome and Louisa tried to hide her surprise. Why did he sound so determined she didn't go alone? In truth, that was the very thing she wanted—she needed the time and space to make sense of what was going on inside her head, her opinion of Gabriel slowly beginning to change into something she didn't fully recognise.

If she took a man with her, she wouldn't be able to retreat into herself without interruption, the thread of her thoughts too tangled to unravel while pretending there was nothing on her mind, but another peep at her husband's serious face made her think the better of arguing.

Surely he was just being polite? She'd said she wasn't much of a horsewoman, which was certainly accurate—her parents had never arranged riding lessons for her and in the absence of proper tuition she had taught herself the best she could, trotting about on her middle brother's long-outgrown pony while his expensive hunter had left her in the dust. Probably Gabriel sensed she wasn't very confident on horseback and thought having a groom nearby would be helpful to her and she couldn't think how to correct him without revealing too much.

*What would I say? I want to be alone so I can think about you without interruption?*

Taking the servant with her was clearly out of the question. She wasn't in the habit of lying, however, or making promises she had no intention of keeping, so instead of replying she merely picked up her cup.

She took a sip of tea. She'd put far too much milk in it and the taste wasn't especially pleasant, but drinking it gave her an excuse to do something other than look at her husband as she deftly changed the subject.

'Will your business take you away for long?'

Thankfully Gabriel didn't seem to notice the diversion. 'Until late afternoon, I would imagine,' he replied with little enthusiasm. 'I find once lawyers start talking, they're often reluctant to stop.'

He pushed back his chair. 'Would you excuse me? My appointment is in less than an hour and I need to see about your horse before I leave.'

She couldn't tell whether he was annoyed by the added delay and she sat forward swiftly, ready to stop him as he stood up. 'I'm sorry, I didn't realise. If it's too much trouble—'

'It isn't.' He silenced her with a decisive shrug that again invited no dispute. 'My being punctual is nowhere near as important as your safety.'

Louisa blinked as he strode to the door, surprised and—yes, she'd admit it—pleased by his response. In truth, it was the kind of considerate thing she'd always hoped any husband of hers would say and she wondered whether Gabriel was aware he'd flustered her as he reached the door and turned back.

Unless she was very much mistaken, she thought she caught the smallest suggestion of a smile and it stoked the fluttering beneath her bodice without mercy.

'Enjoy your ride. I hope the grounds meet with your approval.'

As soon as Gabriel rode back through Sisslehurst's front gates he knew something was wrong.

His lawyers had indeed talked for far longer than patience could endure and so it was against a backdrop of gathering dusk that he saw his servants, many of them clutching torches and lanterns, assembled on the front steps. Every face turned towards him at his approach and a sense of dread overcame him as he pulled to a halt and slid down from the saddle.

'What's the matter? What's happened?'

At first nobody answered. None of the footmen or even his butler seemed to want to be the bearer of bad news, but then the youngest of his housemaids spoke up.

'It's Lady Harnham, my lord. She hasn't returned from her ride.'

'What? The one she took this morning?'

He looked around at the servants spread out on the doorstep, hoping one of them might correct him. 'But that was *hours* ago. She and Conway haven't been seen since?'

There was an exchange of nervous glances. A hesitant movement came from the back of the crowd and then a man stepped forward.

'I'm here, my lord. The mistress went out alone.'

'Conway?' Gabriel stared at the visibly uncomfortable groom. 'Why aren't you with Lady Harnham? I was clear she was to be accompanied when she went for her ride.'

'I know you were, my lord. I'm very sorry.' The man shuffled his feet, looking as though he would rather be anywhere but in his present position. 'She was just so firm that she didn't want an escort and I didn't know how to insist without giving offence. It didn't seem right to argue.'

Gabriel's heart sank like a stone. He'd told Louisa to take a servant with her for a very good reason, but she'd ignored his request, and now no one had set eyes on her for almost eight hours…?

Instinctive fear seized him, but he tried to shake it off. There might be any number of reasons she hadn't returned aside from the one that immediately sprang to mind. She could have got lost or been waylaid by poachers, or perhaps…perhaps she might have left of her own accord?

He hesitated, uncertainty circling like a pack of wolves. Surely Louisa wouldn't have run away? It was true their marriage hadn't got off to the best of starts, but even so…

Ever since their abortive wedding night he'd tried to maintain a polite distance, taking his lead from her example. She spent much of each day hidden away in his library and he had no intention of intruding where he wasn't welcome, especially given her reaction when he'd approached her in the privacy of their bed.

At first, she'd seemed to *want* him to touch her, blossoming under his hands like an unfurling flower, but then she'd abruptly changed her mind, and it had come as a worryingly intense disappointment to have to make himself stop. He'd tried his best not to frighten her, but obviously he'd failed and his stomach dropped to wonder if he had chased her away.

*No. She wouldn't just leave without a word.*

He dismissed the thought although it brought no relief. His fear grew quick and keen and another attempt to contain it was no more successful than the first, the possibility that frightened him the most pushing to the forefront of his mind.

Surely lightning couldn't strike in the same way twice?

Gabriel swore under his breath. Dusk was rapidly changing into night, any daylight already faded away. The Sisslehurst estate was huge and finding her would be even harder in the dark. 'Why didn't anyone think of looking for her earlier?'

He asked the group at large, but it was the groom that answered. 'We thought she must have just been caught up with exploring the grounds, my lord. She certainly seemed keen to get out and see them this morning. It wasn't until Merlin came back without her—'

'Merlin?' The fear in Gabriel's gut splintered into stark horror. 'Lady Harnham wasn't on Nutmeg?'

Conway shook his head apprehensively. 'She'd thrown a shoe, Sir. I would have told you, but you'd already left.'

Gabriel passed a hand over his face, struggling against a sweeping current of panic. This was getting worse and worse. The horse the groom had readied for Louisa was the tallest in the stable, good-natured but jumpy and with absolutely no common sense. The smallest thing was enough to frighten him into a blind charge and only the most confident of riders had any hope of controlling him, something that by her own admission Louisa was not. It was a recipe for disaster and her absence was surely proof something hideous had occurred, perhaps bad enough even to match the events of three years before.

'I'm sorry, my lord. I didn't know Merlin was a poor choice. He's large, but I thought as he's so gentle he might do for the mistress.'

'You're not to blame.' Briefly Gabriel patted the other man's shoulder, although his attention was elsewhere. The memory of the first occasion on which a wife and a horse had proved a devastating combination drowned out everything else, echoes of that terrible night reaching icy tendrils into the present. It seemed almost impossible that the same tragedy could happen again, but he knew better than to trust probability, already half-convinced that any woman forced to marry him must be cursed.

'I should have been more explicit, but that's for another time. Now I just want her found.'

His butler came to the fore. Resuming control of the other servants, he began to divide them into smaller groups, but Gabriel didn't stay to listen to the search parties' instructions. He was back in the saddle before anyone could say a word more, turning his horse's head in the direction of the trees standing in a great gloomy mass on the other side of the park.

It seemed the obvious place to start: far from the house, with the trees so dense that it would be easy to lose one's way unless familiar with the land, and of course the sound of creaking branches eerie enough to scare an unwise horse. If Louisa was anywhere on the estate, he'd place money on her being in the thickest part of the woods and his fear as he tapped his horse into a gallop was less whether he'd find her and more what state she'd be in when he did.

There was a chill in the air that buffeted against his face as he rode. Autumn was well underway and a glimpse upwards showed a clear sky strewn with countless stars. It would soon be cold and he doubted Louisa was dressed for a night out in the open, his jaw hardening as he tried to claw back some of his usual determined calm.

*How badly is she likely to be hurt? It's a long way to fall if Merlin threw her and if she's caught a chill in addition to anything else...*

He tried desperately to skirt around the true crux of his worry, but it came anyway, caring nothing for his state of mind.

*Or she might be dead already. You might be too late to save her—just as you were for Frederica.*

He shied away from the idea instantly, nausea rising in his gullet.

*Stop*, he instructed himself savagely, immediately beating back the inevitable barrage of memories that tried to flash before his eyes. *You can't think like that. Until you know otherwise, you mustn't assume the worst.*

Grim-faced, he spurred his horse on even faster.

The trees loomed up out of the darkness, holding out their branches like grasping skeletal arms, and he hardly slowed at all as he reached them and plunged into the maze of groaning wood.

'Louisa? Can you hear me?'

His horse's ears twitched at his shout, but Juniper was far steadier than Merlin would ever be. The mare could be trusted to carry him without direction and Gabriel all but abandoned the reins as he peered this way and that, trying to make out any shapes among the shadows. There was nothing but the army of tree trunks, however, standing as straight and silent as a regiment on parade, and he called again as his horse took him deeper into the murk.

'Louisa? Are you there?'

Listening hard, all he could catch was the hiss of stirring leaves and occasional rustle of some small creature fleeing through the undergrowth. Aside from that and the rhythmic thud of Juniper's hooves there was nothing and in spite of all his efforts to control it he felt the flames of his dread flicker hotter.

'Louisa?'

He called again, hearing his voice crack. There was still no sign of her and it occurred to him he might have been wrong. He could be wasting valuable time looking for her in the woods rather than elsewhere, each minute he squandered doubtless increasing her distress. She was cold and alone and the thought of her lying injured somewhere gnawed at him—if indeed she was still alive...

'Gabriel? Is that you?'

He pulled Juniper to an abrupt halt.

The faintest thread of sound had carried towards him on the night air. It was so quiet he almost missed it and he sat like a statue, straining to hear whether it came again.

'Please, is someone there?'

His chest lurched painfully. 'Louisa?'

He sprang from the saddle, following the direction from which he thought the feeble little voice had come. 'Where are you?'

'Down here...a gully, I think...'

Leaving Juniper behind, Gabriel crashed through the tangle of shrubs and undergrowth, pushing aside low branches with an impatient hand. There was only one place Louisa could be and he rebuked himself for not thinking of it sooner.

'Don't worry. I'm coming.'

Lowering his head, he shoved his way through, not slowing even as roots tried to trip him as he passed. All of his energy was centred on getting to her and he didn't stop until he suddenly found himself teetering on the edge of a steep-sided drop, a great yawning trench almost completely camouflaged by a line of trees.

He peered down into the shadows, his heart beating hard. There was nothing to see, only darkness and piles of fallen leaves, and for one horrible instant he thought he'd been mistaken before an uncertain movement caught his eye.

'Gabriel?'

A heap of what he'd taken to be loose earth transformed into a human figure as Louisa stood up, her face an ivory smudge in the gloom. 'Oh, Gabriel. Thank heaven. I've been down here for hours. A bird startled Merlin and he threw me off into this ditch.'

She sounded exhausted, but the sight of her set a flood of relief crashing through him. He could *just* make out she was bareheaded, her hair loose around her shoulders with a smattering of blotches across her cheeks that might have been dried mud. She was standing, however, clearly not badly hurt, and he didn't even try to hide how glad he was of it as he crouched down on the edge of the pit.

'Are you injured?'

'No. I was winded when I fell, but fortunately nothing worse than that. I tried to climb out, but the walls are too high and too steep.'

She staggered closer, peering up at him with her hands pressed to the gully's crumbling side. At this distance he could see she looked every bit as exhausted as she sounded and he hurriedly dropped to lie flat on the floor, sparing no thought for how the dirt would ruin his coat as he stretched to reach down as far as he could.

'Let me pull you out.'

Louisa seized his hand without hesitation. Her grasp was weak, but Gabriel's was not and with ease he hauled her upwards, pulling until she found a foothold and managed to scramble the rest of the way herself.

She folded down beside the chasm's edge, trying to catch her breath. Repeated attempts to climb out by herself must have wearied her and Gabriel gave her a few moments to collect herself before once again extending a helping hand. She needed far more time to recover, but everything in him wanted to take her home that very instant, some illogical fear insisting that until she was safe within the Manor's walls some danger could still strike.

'Do you need assistance to walk to the horse?'

'I think that might be best. I'm so tired and hungry I'm afraid I might fall again.'

Carefully she pushed herself up from the ground. She faltered and immediately Gabriel reached for her, not sure he ought to take quite so much pleasure from the feeling of her sinking into his arms. She leaned against him and there seemed little choice but for him to slip a hand around her waist and mould her to his side, although the coolness of her forehead as it brushed his chin made him frown.

'You're cold. We need to get you back to the Manor at once.'

'I'd be very glad to go. I only hope the horse you brought to take us there isn't Merlin.'

He couldn't help a dry laugh despite his lingering unease. Even when famished and dirty she still kept her sense of humour? 'I'm afraid not. Try not to be too disappointed.'

He couldn't see her face as they began to walk, he almost carrying her, but he imagined she wore the wry smile he'd seen there a few times before. It gave her lips a pleasing curve and he was just wondering whether she'd ever show it to him again when he heard her speak.

'I wasn't sure you'd come looking for me.'

'What? Did you think I'd leave you out here all night?'

'I don't know. I suppose I wasn't sure you'd notice I wasn't at home and even if you did…'

He waited for her to finish, but she didn't seem inclined to say anything more. The head just beneath his chin was turned away, any expression hidden behind a curtain of loose hair. There was something on her mind and, although she was reluctant to voice it, he thought he could hazard a guess.

'You were thinking that perhaps I wouldn't care even if I *had* noticed?'

There came the smallest of almost imperceptible nods. 'I confess the thought did occur to me.'

He felt something uncomfortable hitch beneath the front of his waistcoat. It was more proof she didn't have a very high opinion of him, but wasn't that what he'd wanted? From the very first he'd tried to keep her at arm's length, relying on bluntness and silence to make himself seem like an unpleasant prospect for any young woman on the hunt for a husband, and Louisa couldn't be blamed for assuming the worst.

He hadn't wanted her to get too close, the events of his first marriage making such a thing intolerable, although somehow his plan hadn't quite worked. All he'd managed was to make her believe he didn't care about her while his *real* feelings paid no attention to his attempts at caution. It wasn't her fault Frederica had made the prospect of opening himself to anyone again feel so ill advised—but still the betrayal of the first Lady Harnham cast a shadow over the second, no matter how unfair that might be, and it would take far longer than such a brief marriage for him to entirely separate the two.

'I won't insult you by pretending I don't understand why you'd think that,' he said quietly, aware his lips were very close to the delicate curve of her ear. 'But you're my wife. On our wedding day I vowed to take care of you and that's a promise I intend always to keep.'

He felt her make a tiny involuntary movement similar to a shiver. Was she cold? Carefully he tightened his grip on her waist, drawing her nearer to tuck her more warmly under his arm. The closer contact made his baser instincts sit up and take notice, but he made himself ignore them, his attention caught by something Louisa was saying behind the muffling curtain of her hair.

'I meant my vows, too. I may not have been your choice, but I'll try my hardest to be a good wife to you and a loving stepmother to your daughter. That's a promise *I* mean to keep.'

Gabriel's chest tightened. For her to entertain any kind of regard for him was a tempting possibility, but the reference to Leah fled straight to his weakest point.

Somehow it felt as though some line had been reached and then stepped over, leading them into territory unknown. When he'd left that morning he hadn't imagined he'd return to such a frank exchange of views but he couldn't say he regretted it, even if such truthfulness left him vulnerable to more following in its wake.

It appeared Louisa had also realised the change in the air between them. She still leaned against him as he beat a path through the knotted scrub towards where he'd left Juniper, but he thought he sensed a slight reticence in the way she pushed back her hair, at last revealing her face beneath the moon's uncertain light.

'As we seem to have strayed into being honest with each other…'

She paused, then continued in a rush. 'May I ask—what happened to her? To Leah's mother, I mean. Your first wife.'

His throat had been tight already, but now her question made it feel as though a beartrap had closed around his jugular.

He didn't stumble. There was no subject he would rather have discussed less, at this moment or any other, but he'd known it had to come and he was faintly relieved that he managed to keep his voice level when he replied.

'There was an accident,' he said shortly. 'Frederica went riding in a storm and she fell from her horse.'

He caught Louisa's sharp intake of breath. She was looking up at him, but he didn't return her gaze, his eyes fixed instead on the indistinct shape of Juniper waiting beneath a nearby tree.

'I found her the next day,' he heard himself go on. 'She must have been knocked from the saddle by a low-hanging branch. The doctor said she'd broken her neck; death would have been instant.'

Some ungovernable impulse made him glance down. Louisa's face was pale even by moonlit standards and so quietly horrified he wondered if he ought to have done more to soften the blow. He hadn't meant to upset her, only to give her an explanation without veering too close to his secrets, but she looked dismayed all the same and it prompted a pinprick of guilt.

'I'm so very, very sorry. I shouldn't have asked. Please forgive me if I've caused you more pain.'

Her sorrow sounded so genuine he *almost* corrected her. Her concern for his feelings was touching, yet wildly misguided. Nobody could have caused him more pain than Frederica herself, but as they drew closer to the horse Gabriel reminded himself Louisa didn't need to know it. She might ask what his first wife had done to wound him so deeply and whatever answer he gave would come far too close to touching Leah for him to allow.

'There's no cause to apologise. It's natural you should want to know.'

His assurances didn't seem to lift her remorse. 'That's why you asked me to take a groom. I thought you were just trying to be civil. If I'd known…'

'Don't reproach yourself.'

He guessed how she would have ended her sentence. It would do nobody any good to point fingers and although he wished she *had* done as he'd asked, he could also understand why she had *not*. She was a grown woman and she couldn't be expected to obey his commands as though she was a child, especially when he hadn't explained the reasoning why. He'd grown too used to keeping his own counsel and that wasn't something he'd imagined would need to change, although it seemed Louisa might force him to think twice.

'I had my own motives for wanting you to take extra care, but perhaps if I'd been more open about them you might have been more inclined to agree to my request.'

He had never been more relieved to see Juniper,

standing placidly where he had left her. She gave him the perfect excuse for a rapid change of subject and he imagined Louisa was glad of the same as he lifted her into the saddle as easily as he might have carried a sleeping Leah to bed.

'No cause to worry. Juniper's very sensible. She'll take us home safely, which is more than could be said for Merlin.'

She didn't speak as he climbed up behind her. For a moment she sat stiffly, leaning slightly away from him, but as he tapped the horse into moving he felt her sway. She was too tired to maintain her rigid posture, or perhaps the tentative new understanding between them meant she felt safer in his arms; either way by degrees she began to relax, allowing her back to settle on his chest and, despite the swirl of mixed emotions revisiting Frederica's last day always inspired, he found himself enjoying his wife's soft, warm weight against him as Juniper carried them home.

## Chapter Seven

'You're certain the journey isn't tiring you? Doctor Gibson *did* tell you to rest.'

'I'm fine. It's been days since the fall and all I have to do is sit here. Besides, didn't you say we're nearly there?'

Louisa watched Gabriel's nod from the other side of the gently rocking carriage. 'Yes. Less than an hour, I should say.'

'Well, then. I doubt I'll faint between now and reaching your sister's house.'

She peered out of the window, watching the countryside slip by. That was what she was pretending, at any rate, and she hoped Gabriel hadn't noticed she could see his reflection in the glass. She'd discovered that useful little trick of the light soon after they'd left Sisslehurst Manor and she'd studied him on and off ever since, what could have been a tedious journey made far more interesting by snatched glimpses of her husband's face.

Settling more comfortably in her seat, she peeked again at the ghostly outline of Gabriel's profile. He was reading his paper, just as he had for much of the time they'd spent rattling down country roads, and she found herself lingering over the slight unconscious frown he maintained as his eye moved down the page. He looked as stern as ever, but in the most handsome of ways—and now of course she knew more about why his smile was so rare.

He'd told her not to blame herself for refusing to take the groom when she'd ridden out, but that was far easier said than done. Her stupidity had forced him to relive something indescribably dreadful and she'd admonished herself for it ever since, certain she had unwittingly wrenched open old wounds. If he'd been angry with her, she would have thought him justified, but to his credit he'd shown great forbearance, treating her with far more grace than she applied to herself as she struggled to overcome the worst of her guilt.

Finding the body of his first wife must have been the most terrible moment of Gabriel's life and she couldn't begin to imagine how he must have felt. To know he'd seen the woman he loved stretched lifeless beneath the trees made her want to reach out for his hand and squeeze it until the bones creaked, but something held her in check.

He'd lived with his nightmares and grief for three years, sharing them with no one, and she didn't want him to regret the insight he'd given her as to what lived inside his head. He didn't want a romantic partner, but if she was careful, he might accept a friend, although she'd be lying if she pretended friendship was the extent of the feelings that had begun to unfurl deep within.

The carriage rounded a corner and she braced herself against the back of her seat, wincing as it caused her shoulder to throb. She'd twisted it when she'd rolled down into the dry ditch, or so the doctor had said, and the intermittent pain made her inclined to believe him. Aside from a few small cuts and bruises, however, she'd managed to escape otherwise unharmed and she knew she'd been lucky not to have done more damage, although her pretty hat was lost and her new riding habit torn almost beyond repair.

Gabriel had been generous in offering to replace them, but she hadn't accepted, unsure as to whether she ought. Allowing him to buy her clothes was what a *real* wife would do and, although she'd assured him she intended to be a good one, she wasn't yet sure where the boundary lay.

It would be all too easy to get caught up in her budding desires if she let Gabriel behave like the affectionate husband he would never truly be, she reminded herself. He only meant to be kind to her following her accident and yet the undeserved consideration he'd shown her since that day made some foolish part of her hope for more.

When she'd fallen into the gully, she'd feared he

wouldn't care enough to come to find her and to realise how wrong she'd been sat heavily over her heart, glad she'd misjudged him yet increasingly regretful that her new-found regard for him would surely not be returned.

*It's Frederica he wants. If she hadn't died, they would still be together and I'd be even less to him than I am now.*

That thought bordered on being selfish and she dismissed it as quickly as she could. Her one-sided attraction to Gabriel paled into insignificance when set against his very real grief and she determined not to think about it any more, casting about for something else to take its place.

'I'm looking forward to meeting your sister and Leah.'

Gabriel looked up from his paper. 'Are you nervous?'

'Perhaps a little,' she admitted. 'A man's sister is often harder to impress than his mama, after all. I should know—I have three brothers.'

'Do you dislike your sisters-in-law?'

'Not at all. They're very pleasant and made an effort to befriend me, just as I shall with Miriam.'

He glanced back down at the newssheet in his hand, although he didn't resume reading. 'Don't be upset if she doesn't take to you straight away,' he said after a pause. 'It won't be a personal slight. I don't believe

Miriam was expecting me to marry again and it took her by surprise.'

Louisa nodded, unable to completely subdue a flicker of unease. Probably her new sister-in-law had been almost as fond of Frederica as Gabriel and felt the introduction of a new wife was an affront to her memory. It would be difficult to win Miriam over if she'd been close to the first Lady Harnham, but she would attempt it anyway, even if it was another instance in which she would always be outshone.

'Then I shall just have to try twice as hard.' She dredged up a smile, her heart giving a flutter when Gabriel gave her a small one in return. 'And what of Leah? Is there anything I should know that might help me make a good impression?'

The subtle upward tick of Gabriel's lips increased, drawing Louisa's gaze like an arrow to a target. 'You might try talking to her about horses. She loves them, even if they're currently an unknown quantity. She can't wait until she's old enough to ride.'

'You haven't allowed her yet? Not even on a pony?'

'No. I suppose, given what happened to her mother, there's a chance I may be slightly over-cautious about accidents.' A shadow crossed his face. 'I can't keep her locked up for ever, though, no matter how much I might want to. The next time she mentions lessons I think I might have to give in.'

His hard-won smile had faded and Louisa realised how much she wanted it to return.

She sat forward a little. 'You know, if the idea troubles you, I'd be happy to take lessons with her. Recent events have taught me the necessity of improving my riding and there would be an extra pair of hands to make sure nothing happened to Leah if I was there, too.'

Gabriel's eyebrows rose. 'You'd do that? Get on a horse again after Merlin could have killed you?'

'If it would help put your mind at rest, yes.'

He looked at her for a long moment and she felt her cheeks grow warm. As ever it was hard to tell what he was thinking, but he didn't seem displeased—perhaps, in fact, the very opposite.

'Thank you. I very much appreciate you making such a kind offer, although I'm not sure I could let you back in the saddle so soon. Remember the doctor said you needed rest.'

'*Let me* back in?' It was Louisa's turn to lift her brows towards her hairline. 'Surely that would be my decision?'

Gabriel shrugged. 'Not necessarily. If I had to lift you down from a horse and carry you back to the house myself, then that's what I'd do.'

Her mouth opened, ready to defend herself, but it snapped shut again when she caught his eye. For the first time she thought she saw humour in their brooding depths and it set the warmth in her face scuttling down to settle in her stomach.

Once she never would have thought he was capable of teasing, but the faint quirk at one corner of his mouth said otherwise. 'Very funny. Is that the thanks I get for trying to help your daughter?'

'Not at all. My gratitude was sincere, but so is my very real regard for your safety.'

The carriage turned another corner, bringing them under cover of an avenue of spreading trees, and she was glad when the sudden shade made him look away from her towards the window.

'Look. That's Miriam's house just up ahead.'

A smart town had begun to fan out around them and as they emerged from the trees, she saw a large house perched proudly on the crest of a hill. It was handsome and well proportioned, just as one might expect the home of a baron's sister to be, and as they drew nearer Louisa felt her apprehension rise.

'Will her husband be at home, too? Sir…?'

'Duncan, and no. In my sister's letter she said his father has been ill and he's gone to visit him. It'll just be Miriam and my nieces this time.'

She nodded, although in truth whether the man of the house would be in residence was neither here nor there. It was her new sister-in-law she was really anxious about meeting and Leah even more so. What if the child didn't like her? What if one look was enough to convince the girl that having a stepmother was the worst thing in the world? Leah hadn't asked for her father to remarry and she'd be within her rights to despise any woman trying to take her mama's place, and Louisa's innards felt as though they'd been put through a mangle as the carriage turned on to a curving, hedge-lined drive.

The house was getting closer. She could see smaller details now, like the door knocker in the shape of a lion's head, and her fingers tightened in the folds of her skirts.

'Don't look so frightened. Nobody is going to eat you.'

'I know that. I just don't want them to dislike me on sight.'

She heard Gabriel exhale through his nose. 'They won't. Nobody looking at you could find anything wanting.'

A couple of the nervous butterflies winging their way through her insides stopped mid-flap. Probably he was just trying to put her at ease, but all the same the compliment made her flush, her heart skipping with more than just anxiety as the carriage slowed and then rocked to a final halt.

Gabriel stood up. 'Ready?'

At her tentative nod he stepped out through the door opened by a waiting servant, then turned back. 'Here. Let me help you down.'

She rose and shook out her skirts, buying a second to collect herself before reaching for his outstretched hand. Her fingers weren't completely steady and she couldn't tell whether it was apprehension or the proximity to her husband that was responsible for the slight tremor as she slipped them into Gabriel's palm.

He drew her forward, carefully guiding her down the carriage's steps. Since her fall from Merlin, he seemed to think she risked capsizing at any moment and she might have smiled at his caution if his hand hadn't felt so strong on hers, his grip so firm she almost forgot she was afraid of what was to come.

'It'll be fine. Trust me.'

His voice was low and it made a curious rippling sensation snake down the back of her neck. At one time if he'd asked her to trust him, she would have laughed at his presumption, but now somehow the idea didn't seem quite so farfetched and she wished she had more time to get used to it before a figure emerged from the front porch.

'Gabe! I was beginning to think I'd have to send out a search party.'

A woman stood at the top of the steps and Louisa followed as Gabriel began to climb towards her. Somehow, she hadn't let go of his hand after alighting from the carriage and he didn't seem in any hurry to surrender hers either, his grip still reassuringly firm as they reached the top step.

'Were you? Since when were you so easily alarmed by a half-hour's delay?'

His sister—for there was no one else a lady so like Gabriel could possibly be, Louisa reasoned—sniffed. 'It wouldn't have been on my account. Leah has been asking when you're to arrive since daybreak. Much longer and I think she would have gone to look for you herself.'

'That sounds about right.' Gabriel's mouth quirked briefly, but then his usual seriousness returned. 'I'm here now, however, and I'd like to introduce you to my wife.'

Louisa had been following the exchange from slightly behind the shield of his broad shoulder, but now he brought her forward, his fingers pressing gently down on hers as he nudged her on to centre stage.

'Miriam, this is Louisa. Louisa, meet my sister.'

She dropped into a curtsy, hoping the brim of her bonnet would hide her uncertainty. Miriam's first look at her hadn't been particularly warm and the unease from the carriage circled round again as she thought she must have been right. Perhaps Miriam was indeed displeased her brother had married again and might not be inclined to hide it. Gabriel had said his sister was surprised at his marriage, but *surprised* wasn't how Louisa would have described the expression on her new sister-in-law's face.

'Louisa.' Miriam dipped a curtsy of her own, coming up with a tight smile. 'A pleasure to meet you. May I call you by your first name? Or perhaps you prefer Lady Harnham instead?'

It struck Louisa that something was being implied by the pointed remark, a reference she didn't understand, but she was given no chance to voice her confusion.

'First names will do very well,' Gabriel cut in, giving his sister a look that only added to Louisa's puzzlement. 'Louisa isn't in the habit of flaunting her title.'

Miriam's lips thinned a little. 'It's as well to ask. Some people enjoy preserving the distinction of rank, after all—as well you know.'

Brother and sister seemed to be trading coded glances and Louisa's discomfort increased. Something unspoken hung in the atmosphere and she feared she'd inadvertently caused it, an impression that didn't lift even when Gabriel changed the subject.

'Where's Leah?'

'In the garden. I tasked her cousins with keeping her occupied, so she didn't drive herself mad watching for you out of the window.'

Turning, Miriam gestured for them to follow her into the house. Gabriel complied at once, his enthusiasm—and grasp of her hand—encouraging Louisa to copy him, although the heaviness inside her didn't lighten as she allowed herself to be led through the entrance hall.

Miriam glided ahead, the hem of her expensive gown brushing her exquisitely polished floor, and she didn't turn around as Louisa reached up on tiptoe to mutter into Gabriel's ear. 'You weren't joking when you said she might not take to me immediately.'

She saw him hesitate. 'As I said, it's nothing personal. As an older sister she's always been protective, and ever since—'

Gabriel stopped talking. Whatever he'd been about to say was swallowed again, his mouth shutting so tightly it immediately piqued her curiosity.

'Ever since? Ever since what?'

He shook his head. 'Nothing. It's of no consequence.'

Louisa wrinkled her nose. It was on the tip of her tongue to argue—the new furrow of his brow made her suspect that whatever was on his mind was *not* of no consequence at all, but as they emerged into the sun again a high-pitched cry from the other side of the garden interrupted any further investigation.

'Papa!'

A cannonball blew past Louisa and crashed square into Gabriel's midriff. It was testament to his strength that he wasn't knocked to the ground, but all the same he had to catch his breath before he could seize hold of the little girl wrapping her arms around his waist and fling her into the air, catching her again as she squealed a laugh.

'Who's this, calling me Papa? The only person allowed to call me that is Leah and you're far too tall to be her.'

The girl laughed again, clinging to Gabriel's arm as he lowered her to the ground. 'It *is* me, Papa. Aunt Miriam says I grow like a weed.'

Louisa took a discreet step away. She'd wanted to

get this daunting first meeting over with as soon as possible, but now had no desire to intrude. Leah was clearly delighted to see her father and Gabriel no less pleased to have his daughter in his arms again, his smile the warmest Louisa had ever seen him wear as he looked back at her.

'Louisa. There's someone I'd like you to meet.'

Slightly reluctantly she came forward, not wanting to interrupt their reunion, but unable to resist the pull of that smile. It knocked years from his face and made him look almost like another person, one who wasn't weighed down by tragedy and grief. Perhaps when Leah came back to Sisslehurst Manor Gabriel would be happier more often, the prospect of seeing him so causing butterflies to take wing again, but then the little girl peered up at her and Louisa made herself concentrate on the matter at hand.

'This is my daughter, Leah. Leah, this is Louisa—my wife.'

The child stared at her with wide, uncertain eyes. They were blue, about as unlike the cocoa richness of Gabriel's and Miriam's as they could get, while the curls streaming over her shoulders gleamed gold in the autumn sun.

There was no resemblance to her father at all, Louisa realised; certainly not in the colour of her hair or even the slant of her nose, no trace of Harnham present in any of her features. The girl must have taken after her mother in every respect and Louisa felt her nerves rise again to know she was stepping into the other woman's shoes, the spectre of Gabriel's first wife hovering over her as she bent down.

Aware the eyes of her husband and his coolly observing sister were on her, she made sure to keep her voice as gentle as her smile. 'I'm very pleased to meet you, Leah. I've been looking forward to it.'

Leah peeped up at her father. Taking some reassurance from his nod, she shuffled a little closer, although she spoke so shyly Louisa had to lean down further to catch her reply.

'Am I to call you Mama?'

Louisa's innards scrunched. She'd thought the little voice would have been too quiet for Gabriel to have heard, but she realised she'd been wrong when she sensed him stiffen. It was a question she had no idea how to answer and she had to guess as to the right response.

'Only if you want to. Perhaps you might like to start with Louisa and see how you feel as time goes on?'

To her immense relief the girl nodded. Most of the wariness left her rounded face and Louisa sensed Gabriel relax likewise. Her insides unknotted slightly, but she was careful not to look at Miriam as she straightened up from her crouch. Her new sister-in-law still didn't radiate much of a welcome and apparently Leah's approval didn't make a difference, although Louisa herself was touched when the child held out her hand.

'Will you come and meet my cousins? They're guarding the orchard against poachers and I need to go back to help.'

'Of course.'

She took the warm little hand without hesitation. It slotted into hers as though it had been made to fit there and she didn't have to pretend to be willing as Leah began to lead her away. It came naturally, she was surprised to find, as easily as her fondness for the nieces and nephews she was always glad to play with whenever her brothers came to visit, and she barely had time for more than a single swift glance back at Gabriel before Leah broke into a run, dragging her along towards what must be the orchard gate.

It was only the briefest moment of eye contact, a second at the most, but even so she knew what she saw in that dark gaze. There was gratitude and amusement and even a touch of relief—but also something startlingly close to affection, and Louisa couldn't tell if it was for Leah alone or whether, against all odds, some tiny fragment of it might have been meant for her.

Looking down from a window of the upstairs gallery, Gabriel watched as Louisa motioned for the three little girls milling around her to sit beside her on the grass. His daughter and nieces had followed her around the gardens all afternoon, shy at first, but quickly growing bolder, and now they made a very pretty picture as they gathered round to be taught how to make daisy chains. Leah had taken to her almost immediately, but he felt no jealousy that he'd been temporarily forgotten, his feelings instead verging on something he didn't dare say out loud.

Watching them together, seeing his new wife take such pains to make friends with his daughter…it made the hollow place Frederica had flayed open feel warm and filled with possibilities, and that was as worrying as it was a delight.

Leah had picked a fistful of flowers and was trying to copy Louisa's method of pushing each stem through the next to form a link. He couldn't see their faces as all four bent over their work, but he imagined they were smiling, the sunlight glancing off their downturned heads. Louisa seemed to have mislaid her bonnet and her hair glowed copper beside his nieces' brunette curls, neither of the two girls in any way similar to the blonde child they called their cousin. As far as they knew, that was right; and Gabriel would never correct them.

He only realised he'd been smiling when he felt it slide from his face. Had Louisa noticed Leah bore no likeness to him? He'd been so preoccupied with hoping they got along that he hadn't spared a thought for whether she might suspect anything, but now he saw the two of them sitting side by side fresh worry began to stir.

'There you are. I was wondering where you'd disappeared to.'

Miriam's voice broke into his uncomfortable musings. A backwards look showed her coming towards him and he moved so she could join him in looking out through the glass.

'It's going well, wouldn't you say? As good an introduction as one could wish for.'

'Yes. Louisa certainly seems pleasant enough.'

'I note the emphasis on *seems*.' Gabriel sighed. 'Go on, then. Speak your mind. If you've something to say, I'd like to hear it.'

His sister shrugged. 'You know what I think. After the wreckage Frederica made of your life, I never expected you to wed again, and given you were fooled once I don't want you to repeat the same mistake.'

'You worry I might fall in love with Louisa, only to find she never cared for me at all?'

'In part. You know more than most how a title attracts fortune hunters like rotting fruit attracts flies.'

Gabriel let out a flat laugh. He'd known that was what Miriam had meant by her remark to Louisa when they'd first arrived, but on that score at least she'd been wrong. Frederica—or rather, her parents—had indeed loved to show off her rank at any opportunity, but Louisa seemed to forget she was a baroness more often than she remembered, her amazement at seeing Sisslehurst Manor for the first time still fresh in his mind.

'I take your point, but remember: Louisa didn't want to marry me, title or no title. She's never made any pretence of being in love as Frederica did. From the very start she's been open as to her opinion of me and I don't expect that to change.'

'Even so.' Miriam's dark eyes flashed. 'I saw how much the whole business hurt you. If your second wife turns out to be anything like your first—'

'She isn't.'

His words came more abruptly than he'd intended, taking him by surprise. He hadn't meant to jump to Louisa's defence quite so sharply and he tried to back-track as he went on. 'Or at least, that's what I'm coming to believe.'

His sister pursed her lips. 'I'm yet to be convinced. Recall that Frederica tricked us all in the beginning. We didn't suspect a thing. If I hadn't seen her and Allenby with my own eyes, I'd never have believed she'd be unfaithful to you.'

Gabriel tensed at the unwanted reminder. 'Neither would I.'

It wasn't a fact he needed any help to recall. He'd remember the day Miriam had told him what she'd discovered for the rest of his life, her face white as he'd stood in mute disbelief. He hadn't wanted to believe her, but Frederica had admitted the truth and from there everything had gone wrong, the world he'd built crashing down around him like a wall formed on sand.

'Don't worry. I've no intention of offering Louisa my devotion. Our marriage was one of duty and

I know that as much as she does. I won't be getting too close.'

He spoke with conviction, although he couldn't completely dismiss a nagging doubt. For all he was determined to keep his distance, he couldn't seem to stop himself from wanting to be near her, a desire that another glimpse out of the window didn't help to quell.

Leah was half-sitting on Louisa's lap now, he saw, their heads close together as they spun their chain of flowers, and the sight came warm as sunshine on the frost he'd tried to pack around his heart. If she made his daughter happy, then his icy defences might melt away altogether and he didn't like how vulnerable that would make him, the sorrows of his past casting long shadows over the present.

'So you won't be telling her? About Leah?'

With some effort he turned away from the window. 'I have no current plans. If I'm right about Louisa's character, then she wouldn't think any less of Leah for knowing the truth, so what would be the point in revealing it? But if I'm wrong—' He broke off, something unpleasant twisting deep inside him. 'If I've misread her, then it would be dangerous for her to know. She might tell someone who might tell someone else, then all the world would find out that Leah is not my child.'

He rested a hand on the window ledge, hardly aware his fingers had balled into a fist. Usually he avoided voicing the fiercely held secret aloud and doing so made his unconscious frown deepen. Speaking the words made them worse somehow, forcing him to admit the situation was real, and he knew Miriam felt the same by her grim-faced nod.

'And by all the world you mean, of course, Frederica's parents.'

Gabriel's lip lifted in disgust. 'You know what they'd do if they found out I wasn't her natural father. They would try to take her from me and make her into another puppet for their use, just as they did their own daughter. Her happiness would count for nothing and they would argue that it was none of my business since they are her blood and I am not, even though I have more love for her in my little finger than they do in both their bodies combined.'

'They will never take her.' His sister raised her chin with the determination people soon learned not to underestimate. 'I won't ever tell anyone Frederica had a lover and neither will you. Plenty of children favour one parent more for looks than the other. As long as we keep quiet, nobody will have any reason to suspect Leah is Allenby's child and not yours.'

Gabriel pressed his knuckles harder against the window ledge, feeling wood chafe over bone. 'Yes. Only silence will keep Leah safe, even if half of Staffordshire believes that silence means the rumours about me must be true.'

'That couldn't be avoided,' Miriam insisted. 'You

couldn't tell anyone why Frederica was *really* out in that storm the night she died. If you ever admitted she was leaving you for Allenby, people would have begun to question Leah's paternity at once and of course there was no way you could have that.'

'No. I couldn't.'

Gabriel felt his shoulders slump in bitter regret. 'It meant I had to keep my mouth shut while her parents slandered me to anyone who would listen, however. They were determined to punish me for cutting them off and what better way to do that than to destroy my reputation? That storm was far too dangerous for Frederica to risk going out in it without good reason and no reason could be more pressing than fleeing from a husband who supposedly beat her black and blue.'

The old ache, the one that had sat inside him for three years, unleashed a flurry of pain like the throb of a fresh bruise. For what might have been the hundredth time he wondered what he could have done differently, the events of that terrible evening coming once again as if called forth by his words.

Should he have tried harder to stop Frederica from getting on to her horse that night and riding off into the rain? She'd been so determined to leave there and then, apparently relieved she didn't have to hide her affair any longer, and she hadn't wanted to tarry for even a moment to let the weather pass.

Once the truth had come out, she'd had no reason

to stay, after all—not even for the daughter she was prepared to abandon in her pursuit of her new life with the one person she truly loved. Her selfishness had sickened Gabriel even more than her infidelity. If he'd prevented her from leaving, she would still be alive... but part of him had *wanted* her to go, appalled by what he'd learned, and now he had to live with the guilt of knowing he'd missed the chance to save her life.

The rumours had begun a short time later. In their malice and spite at having their greed denied Frederica's parents had accused him of driving their daughter away with his cruelty and, as he couldn't correct them, he'd had no choice but to wear the shame they had heaped on him ever since.

His lungs felt as though they were being crushed. All the horror and hurt he'd managed to lock away threatened to break through and it was only by gritting his teeth he managed to withstand it—that, and turning back to the window to take solace in the view below.

'I've loved Leah from the moment she was born,' he said quietly, watching as Louisa threaded daisies through his daughter's blonde curls. 'Even when Frederica admitted she wasn't mine my feelings didn't change. I'd rather an entire county thought I was a brute than have just one person call her a bastard or try to use her for their own selfish gains.'

Out of the corner of his eye he saw Miriam about to speak, but he hadn't yet finished. 'That wretch Allenby wouldn't want to know. He has children all over the country and he doesn't claim a single one of them. I don't know how many women he's ruined, but Leah will not be one of them by association.'

Miriam laid a hand on his arm. 'Of course she won't. Between us we'll keep her safe. You don't ever need to worry about that.'

If his usually prickly sister felt the need to try to soothe him, he must have looked unhappy indeed and he tried to muster a smile at her concern. 'I know. Who would dare try anything when she's under your protection?'

The hand on his arm gave a robust squeeze. 'Yours, too…and perhaps even Louisa's, one day, if she turns out to be worthy of the knowledge.'

'Perhaps.'

He looked down again at the four figures spread out on the grass below. Although he couldn't hear what they were saying he could see his nieces were chattering away and Louisa was nodding patiently, Leah now sprawled fully across her lap. It seemed it hadn't taken long for his daughter to decide her new stepmother was acceptable and he found himself hoping her judgement was sound.

'I ought to go down. Just because Louisa looks as though she's enjoying herself doesn't mean she might not need rescuing.'

Miriam gave him a long, knowing look. 'I'm sure you're right. Just…be careful. Make sure I won't have to rescue *you*.'

\*\*\*

Sitting on the lawn amid a heap of small girls, Louisa looked up as a shadow fell over her.

The maker of said shadow possessed a fine pair of boots attached to an even finer pair of legs, which drew her gaze up higher, over a broad chest, until she reached a face shaded by the palm of an upheld hand.

'Good afternoon, ladies. I hope I'm not interrupting?'

There was a touch of the Greek god about Gabriel as he stood in a halo of sunshine. Certainly the smile he wore made him handsomer than ever and it was fortunate Leah's reply made it unnecessary for Louisa to attempt one herself.

'Look, Papa. We've been making crowns.'

'So I see. Very beautiful they are, too.'

Suddenly supremely conscious of the circlet of flowers on her own head Louisa almost reached up to remove it before changing her mind. It might look childish, but Leah had been the one to bestow it on her and she'd rather risk looking slightly foolish than hurt the feelings of the little girl she was already starting to like.

The worries she'd had as to their first meeting had vanished as if they'd never been and she wondered if Gabriel could tell how deeply she was relieved that his daughter had taken to her so quickly—as well as being relieved himself.

'Louisa taught us,' Leah confided to her father. 'She

said we can make crowns now and then at Christmas she's going to show us how to make kissing balls.'

Gabriel's mouth curved upwards a little more. 'Is that so?'

Louisa felt herself flush. It was dangerous to mention kissing while his lips looked so inviting and she hoped he wouldn't notice the colour that had rushed into her cheeks.

'If you've no objection.'

'None at all. I'll look forward to seeing the results.'

He turned to his nieces. 'Your mother wants you inside, girls—you, too, Leah. Apparently the cook has done something new and exotic with marzipan and you're needed to test it.'

All three young ladies were on their feet at once. With a flurry of skirts and high-pitched voices they were gone, disappearing into the house and leaving Louisa alone to squint up at her husband outlined against the sun.

'Can I help you up?'

'Thank you. I think my leg has gone to sleep, sitting like this.'

Taking the proffered hand, she allowed Gabriel to pull her to her feet. She was right—one of her legs had taken the opportunity to lose all feeling and she stumbled slightly, almost glad of her weakness when it prompted him to pass his free hand around her waist in a steadying grip.

'Are you unwell? Perhaps you've had too much sun. You should sit down in the shade for a moment.'

She very nearly argued that she'd done nothing of the sort. It was indeed a sunny day, although not particularly warm, and she was about to say as much when something intervened. Somehow the gentle pressure of Gabriel's palm at the base of her spine made her willing to overlook his mistake and she found herself, quite by accident, letting him escort her across the lawn to a pretty folly set against one wall.

He deposited her on a stone bench well sheltered from the sun. There was a short pause, but then he sat down beside her, his knee brushing hers as he took his seat.

She straightened her skirts, trying not to notice how close they were to his breeches. 'I'm not sure this was warranted. My leg was numb from sitting on the ground, that's all.'

'Even so. After your fall Dr Gibson gave strict instructions that you were to rest and wrangling Leah and my nieces is hardly relaxing.'

'It wasn't *that* arduous a task. They're all sweet girls.'

'I agree. I'm glad you think so, too.'

Gabriel stretched, apparently rolling some stiffness from his shoulders. A few seconds passed, during which birdsong in the trees on either side of the folly was all Louisa could hear, but then he turned to her.

'She isn't as frightening as you feared, then. Leah, I mean.'

'No. I think perhaps I was envisioning you, but smaller.'

'Thank heavens that isn't the case—for her as well as you.'

Some of the feeling was returning to her leg. It gave the unpleasant sensation of pins being driven into her skin, distracting enough that she didn't guard her tongue as well as she should have done. 'That may not have been completely fair. You aren't *quite* as horrible as I once imagined. In truth, I'd expected to be unhappy, but now...'

Immediately she stopped herself, but the damage was already done.

Gabriel had stilled. 'Now?'

Her heart lurched. Why had she opened her mouth? She had no intention of telling him what she was really coming to think: that a decent man still existed just below the unapproachable surface he pretended was his true nature. The loss of his first wife and the traumatic events surrounding it had wounded him so deeply he'd retreated where he couldn't be hurt again, but watching him with Leah only confirmed what Louisa already thought, gaps in his armour hinting at what goodness lay beneath.

He was studying her closely. There was no way of escaping that direct gaze other than to get up and run, so she was left with no choice but to answer.

'I see how you are with Leah,' she began unwillingly. 'She brings out another side of you I didn't realise you had at first. I know you'll always wish you had Frederica here instead of me, but I wonder…perhaps, if we tried, we might find some kind of contentment in what we have?'

His eyes didn't leave hers. He held her captive for some unmeasurable span of time, probably only a second, but feeling far longer. Worse than that, however, he didn't answer her question and she felt regret claw at her, horribly aware she'd said far too much.

His gaze flickered to the top of her head. 'Your crown's crooked.'

Louisa blinked. Was that all he could say? She'd just made herself vulnerable with her honesty and he was going to dismiss it with some paltry remark?

'Oh.' She could barely speak, embarrassment beginning to spread through her. 'I'd forgotten I was wearing it.'

She lifted her hand to slide the circlet of flowers from her head, but to her surprise Gabriel gently pushed it back down.

'Don't. The daisies look pretty in your hair—' He broke off, a note of something edging into his voice that stirred the hairs on the back of her neck. 'If you'll permit me?'

Louisa managed an unsteady nod. Her heart had picked up speed and she could feel her pulse flitting faster as Gabriel carefully straightened her crown, his touch so light, yet igniting every nerve. His face was very close to hers and she struggled to take a proper breath when she saw his eyes drop down to her mouth, lingering there with such sudden intent that she knew exactly what he was about to do.

She leaned forward at the same moment he did and all rational thought melted away as his lips met hers.

He'd kissed her twice before: once at the end of their wedding vows and then again later in the privacy of their bed, but this time was nothing like either of the others. In front of the congregation the brush of his mouth had been disappointingly chaste while in their bedroom she'd feared the darkness meant he was thinking of someone else, but in broad daylight there could be no mistake. He knew exactly who he was kissing and his passionate striving told her he *wanted* to, neither duty nor obligation entering into the way his fingers tunnelled into her hair.

Her eyes were closed, touch the only sense worth paying any attention to as Gabriel's mouth moved over hers. Her hands had tangled in his shirt and she could feel the thundering of his heart beneath thin linen, its haphazard tempo matching the galloping of her own. Heat had begun to build low inside her, sparks stoked by every skilful stroke of his tongue, and if he hadn't dropped back she didn't know what her rising desire would have made her do next.

His breathing sounded uneven as he leaned away, his eyes still on her mouth. There was a kind of hunger in them and it made her tremble, although she could tell he was trying hard to control it as he ran a hand through his hair.

'I think you might be right. Contentment could be something to strive for.'

She swallowed. He looked and sounded on the brink of reaching for her again and she would have allowed it if a voice from the direction of the house hadn't cut through the aching tension like a knife.

'Papa? Are you coming inside? There's some marzipan here for you, too.'

Both she and Gabriel started. Fortunately, the trees surrounding the folly shielded it from the house, but he still got quickly to his feet.

'That's good,' he called back, hurriedly straightening his lopsided cravat. 'I was hoping you'd save me a piece.'

Louisa laid the back of her hand against her hot cheek. Desire still coursed through her, but confusion was beginning to join it, a heady mix she had scant hope of untangling.

What did it mean that he'd kissed her? Had something changed between them, or was all as it had been before?

Gabriel looked down at her. 'Will you join us? I'm sure there's enough to go around.'

'I'd be glad to.' She tried to smile, although her mouth, much like the rest of her body, didn't want to do as it was told. 'I'll just sit here for a little while first.'

'Of course. Take all the time you need.'

He watched her for a moment. His eyes roved from the flowers in her hair down to her mouth and she saw a muscle twitch as he tightened his jaw. He didn't seem displeased, though, or appear to regret what had just occurred, but it was impossible to tell what a man as determined to distance himself as Gabriel was truly thinking and she was left with more questions than answers as he turned and walked away.

## *Chapter Eight*

Despite feeling as though she was about to jump off a cliff, Louisa gave Leah a bright smile as Conway helped her on to Nutmeg's back.

'See? There's nothing to be afraid of. You'll be absolutely fine.'

The girl peered up at her doubtfully. For almost the entire week since she had returned to Sisslehurst Manor Leah had chattered excitedly about the riding lessons her papa had promised she could finally begin, but now the time had come to get into the saddle she didn't seem quite so sure. In truth, Louisa wasn't either, the memory of her fall from Merlin still fresh, but she had no intention of letting Leah know.

'You can do it. Look—Bracken's waiting for you.'

She nodded—rather than waved, which would have required her to loosen her tight grip on the reins—towards the stout, reliable-looking pony standing on the other side of the mounting block. Privately she thought she'd much rather ride him than Nutmeg, who although reassuringly calm was still taller than she would have liked, although of course that was an opinion she couldn't possibly voice.

'What if I fall off?'

'You won't. Conway assures me Bracken is perfectly safe and so does your papa.'

She deliberately avoided glancing towards where Gabriel was watching proceedings from a few steps away. Ever since their encounter in Miriam's garden, she hadn't been able to meet his eye without blushing and she was still none the wiser as to what his kiss could have meant, the two of them now apparently trapped in some kind of strange standoff where each waited for the other to make the first move.

*Were* they going to try to make the most of the situation they'd been forced into, just as she'd suggested moments before Gabriel's mouth had found hers? They'd been interrupted before anything more could be said and they hadn't revisited the subject since.

Now that Leah was at Sisslehurst there were limited chances for Louisa to speak to Gabriel privately. Even if she had snatched an opportunity, she didn't know what she would have said. How skilled his lips were was the only thing that was clear to her, how they could start so softly and then kiss her into a stupor, and she only realised she was on the verge of drifting off into yet another daydream when Leah had to tap on her foot to get her attention.

'I said, will you be with me the whole time?'

'Yes. Conway will lead you and I'll follow behind on Nutmeg.'

'But you said you'll be learning, too. Who will be leading *you*?'

The answer came from an unexpected source.

'I will.'

Louisa spun round as best she could while seated on a horse. 'What? I thought...'

She tailed off as Gabriel came to stand by Nutmeg's head. He was looking at Leah, smiling so encouragingly Louisa's heart missed a beat, but it was she he addressed as he patted the horse's neck.

'The groom who was supposed to come up to help you has been taken ill. I wouldn't know where to begin in teaching a child to ride so I'm of no use to Leah, but I could give you some direction as to where you might improve if you'd like.'

He glanced up at her in a brief dark flash. He didn't seem entirely sure of her reaction and Louisa wasn't certain what it should be either, both delight and apprehension coming at her from opposite sides.

In order for him to instruct her, wouldn't he have to walk very closely to her horse, his shoulder practically touching her leg?

It would be the most intimacy they'd shared since Miriam's house, she thought as she twisted a phantom curl back into place to hide the reddening of her cheeks. Leah's sleep had been disturbed since her return, the little girl struggling to settle alone at night after weeks spent sharing a room with her cousins, and Gabriel had taken to dozing in a chair beside her bed instead of in his own. When Leah woke from a nightmare it was her father she wanted and Louisa was glad he was so ready to comfort her, although it meant they'd barely had a moment alone to explore what, if anything, their kiss might have set in motion.

'If you'd prefer to wait for a groom, however, I won't be offended. It's entirely up to you.'

It was as though he knew what was going on in her mind, the dance between wanting to be close to him and not trusting herself enough to do so, and she wasn't sure what decision she would have made if it had been left in her hands.

Instead, Leah's voice held a wobble that shattered any illusion of choice. 'You won't wait, will you, Louisa? I don't want to go on my own.'

The little girl looked aghast. She'd progressed to stroking Bracken's velvety nose and Louisa could tell she was at last warming to the idea of getting on to his back.

There was nothing else to be done.

'No. No, of course not. If your papa is kind enough to help me, then I'm sure I'm happy to accept.'

Her eyes were on Leah so she missed whatever might have passed over Gabriel's face. Whether he was pleased she'd taken him up on his offer or not it was impossible to tell, although Conway certainly seemed glad a decision had been made.

'Up you get then, Miss.'

The groom lifted Leah and deposited her carefully into the pony's saddle. She froze, gripping the pommel so hard Louisa could see her knuckles standing out beneath her little gloves, but Gabriel shook his head admiringly.

'Brave girl. You have a natural seat.'

There came a suggestion of a smile. Clearly her father's approval made all the difference and Leah unclenched slightly, her hands moving to the reins rather than holding on to the saddle as if her life depended on it.

'I'm ready, Conway. Louisa, will you still follow?'

'Yes. I'll be right behind you.'

The groom took hold of the pony's lead rein and gently urged him forward. Bracken stepped out obligingly, causing Leah to redouble her grip, but there was a determined tilt to her chin and Louisa was about to express her own admiration of the girl's nerve when she felt Nutmeg move.

Gabriel had come closer and was steering the horse away from the mounting block, but even his presence almost touching her skirts couldn't stave off the sudden dizziness that overcame Louisa as she shifted in the saddle. While Nutmeg had been standing still things hadn't been so worrying, but now they were in motion she felt a flicker of panic, her mind sprinting back to the moment she'd known she was about to fall from Merlin's towering height.

She recalled every detail in one snatched second: how he had reared, so tall he'd almost seemed to touch the leaves above them, and then the horrible weightlessness of her body as she'd flown through the air, landing with a thud that had knocked all the breath from her. Rolling into the ditch had been painful, stones and sharp sticks digging into her as she passed, and then the final bruising thump as she'd come to a halt against the base of a tree, confused and aching with no idea where she was or how she was supposed to get back up again—

'Louisa? Are you unwell?'

Gabriel's question seemed to come from miles away. 'You've gone white. Do you want to get down?'

Hurriedly she shook her head, stopping abruptly when it made her dizziness worse. 'No. I'm fine.'

'You don't look it.'

She glanced towards him. It was odd to be able to look down on him and she swayed alarmingly at the fresh reminder of how high up she was perched. She would have loved to slide from the horse and into his arms, but instead she clamped the reins in her nerveless hands.

'I can't give up so quickly. I don't want Leah to think riding is something to be afraid of. What kind of an example would I set if I let my fear win?'

The brim of Gabriel's hat hid his face while she saw him from above. Unless he tilted his head back to peer up at her she couldn't see his expression, and it was difficult to read anything in his voice while her anxiety ran riot.

'But you *are* afraid?'

'Perhaps a little.'

'I see.' His hat moved as if he was debating whether to look up at her, but his face remained concealed. 'Wait a moment.'

To Louisa's horror he let go of the lead rein—although he didn't abandon her for long.

'What are you—?'

Her heart screeched to a standstill while she was mid-word. A warm thigh had appeared on either side of her, pressing against her skirts, and only the firm grasp of her knee on the top pommel stopped her from sliding in the saddle when two strong arms snaked round her to reach for the reins.

'If you're so determined to stay up here, it's only fair I come up, too,' Gabriel's deep voice issued from somewhere very close by. 'But you're in control. I'm just here for support while you find your feet.'

Stunned, Louisa jerked a nod. How had he managed to climb up behind her without a mounting block? She found herself surrounded—his chest was flush against her back and his legs touching hers in the most delightful way imaginable—and she felt an overwhelming urge to settle herself even more snugly into the tight space between his thighs. Even the scent of him enveloped her without mercy, making her want to breathe him in, but instead she made herself twitch the reins and spur Nutmeg into a stroll to match Leah's amble across the stable yard.

The horses trotted through an open gate and into a small paddock set on one side of the yard. Every few steps Leah would look over her shoulder to make sure she was being watched and every time Louisa made sure to smile encouragingly, although it was almost impossible for her focus on anything other than the sensation of Gabriel's arms brushing her waist.

Conway began to lead Bracken in laps around the outside of the paddock, Nutmeg following suit. Louisa could hear him giving Leah instructions and she seemed to be doing well, gradually beginning to sit up straighter and look less as though she feared she might tumble off at any moment.

Louisa's experience, however, was slightly different.

Any anxiety she might have felt at the prospect of getting back in the saddle had vanished. Her fall from Merlin couldn't have been further from her mind as she directed Nutmeg's steady stride, any nerves she felt now bound up entirely in the presence of the man sitting behind.

'May I make a suggestion?'

Another bass murmur caressed her ear. Her neat little riding hat covered less of her head than a bonnet would have so there was hardly any barrier between his mouth and her hair. His lips were scant inches from her cheek and if she turned her face to the side she might even have been able to kiss him, a thought that was too tempting to allow.

'Please do.'

'I realise it wouldn't be easy, but you might consider trying to relax a little,' he said, stating the impossible. 'Your posture feels stiff and the horse will sense your unease.'

Louisa stared straight ahead, refusing to look down at his hands so close to hers on the reins.

*Relax? How am I supposed to do that?*

It was one of the most ridiculous things she'd ever heard. How could any woman feel at ease when cradled in a strong pair of arms that subtly tightened around her with every movement of the saddle, the two of them swaying together as though engaged in the most intimate of dances? For some reason it reminded her of how her body had fitted against his on their wedding night and, if he caught a glimpse of her cheek peeping from behind her hair, she hoped he would blame the sun for how the memory made it glow a fierce pink.

'Thank you,' she muttered. 'I'll try to bear that in mind.'

She tried to release some of the tension holding her prisoner, but to no avail. If she let herself rest against him any further he was certain to sense how much she enjoyed being encircled by his warmth and she wasn't sure that was wise, the waters between them currently so muddied she'd do better to lean *away* from him rather than *towards*.

Nutmeg was still executing her repeated laps of the paddock, following behind Bracken so placidly there was very little active riding for Louisa to do. Her hands lay idle on the reins, and she almost jumped out of her skin when Gabriel's fingers grazed hers unintentionally, so attuned to his presence that even that trivial contact made her start.

She needed a distraction before she lost her wits, she thought hastily. Gabriel's knee was repeatedly rubbing against her thigh in a manner that made it difficult to think of anything else and in desperation she grabbed the first thing that came to mind.

'Leah is doing well.'

'She is.' Gabriel's voice held a distinct note of pride. 'She's always been a quick study.'

'It's a good thing you're letting her have lessons early,' Louisa went on, wishing she couldn't feel how each of his words vibrated through his chest as he spoke. 'In hindsight, I believe riding is the kind of thing best learned young.'

'Did you not receive instruction as a child?'

'Not really. My parents were never unkind to me, but with three older brothers my needs were often overlooked. I don't think it occurred to them that horse riding was something I might have enjoyed.'

She stopped to give an exaggerated smile. Leah had twisted to peer over her shoulder, the worry in her face turned to excitement, and her joy would have warmed Louisa even if it had been the middle of winter. The little girl's growing confidence was a pleasure to see and again Louisa marvelled at how quickly her new stepdaughter was stealing into her heart. Her worries as to if the child would resent her trying to take her mother's place were thankfully turning out to be unfounded, although how much Gabriel still compared his second wife to his first Louisa could only guess.

'I'm sorry to hear you say that.'

'Say what?'

'That you were overlooked.'

She lifted a shoulder, regretting it when she felt it slide against Gabriel's well-muscled arm. 'It's no great matter. That's just how things were.'

'Even so. I hope you know that now you're here no need of yours will ever be neglected again.'

Louisa didn't reply. What could she have said? In one short sentence he had shown he understood how she'd felt as a lonely child and to be *seen* so clearly touched her in a way she could never have expressed.

It was another example of the disarmingly sweet things he would say or do that made her wonder whether the man he'd been before Frederica died might be closer to the surface than he'd have her believe, and as ever she had no idea how to respond. It was tempting to think that such instances might mean he was beginning to open up again after having been adrift for so long, but of course she might be wrong.

She'd asked if he'd entertain the idea of trying to make the most of their situation and he hadn't given a real answer, a kiss the only thing coming from his mouth. If anything it had made her standing with him less clear, not more, and she still didn't know whether what she was starting to hope for might ever be realised: that he might come to have room for two women in his broken heart.

*Almost there. Only a little further.*

Gabriel closed his eyes, willing his dwindling composure to last just a few more minutes. They were circling back to the stable yard now, the end of their ride in sight, and if he could resist temptation long enough, he might just avoid embarrassing himself by giving in to his desires and trying to kiss Louisa once more.

He flexed his hands on the reins, dangerously close to her dainty fingers. Did she have any idea what she was doing to him with no effort whatsoever? For the entire duration of their ride she'd been in his arms, leaning against him as closely as if they'd been in the bedroom he'd hardly set foot in for over a week, and the way she moved so unknowingly seductively was driving him to the brink. His chin was almost resting on her shoulder and every time she looked to the side he caught a glimpse of her mouth, her lips so near yet for him utterly out of reach.

Or were they?

*'Perhaps we might find some kind of contentment in what we have.' That's what she said. And she didn't pull away when I kissed her, did she?*

The scene from Miriam's garden wasn't one to rehash while he could feel the length of Louisa's left leg pressing into his, but he couldn't seem to stop it. It had circled through his mind so many times he'd lost count and he was no nearer to knowing where it left him, aside from wishing he'd met her honesty with some of his own.

She'd been open about wanting them to form more of a partnership and, like a coward, he'd skirted around her candour. It had taken him by surprise and he hadn't known what to say, although his fragile hopes had leapt at her admitting he wasn't quite the brute she'd initially feared. If she no longer disliked him as she once had, then perhaps the hold Sir Christopher had on her heart might be weakening, maybe clearing the way for someone else to take his place...

*Is that what I want?*

Once everything had been so clear, but now... After the pain Frederica had inflicted, he'd never wanted to let another woman get under his skin, yet Louisa seemed to be doing exactly that. Physically she excited him and emotionally she drew him in with her kindness, her careful attentions to Leah raising her even higher in his estimation.

She'd been willing to set her own discomfort aside

to reassure the little girl and such selflessness only underscored what he'd already seen: a bond was growing between his daughter and wife with a speed that far exceeded his expectations, his chest swelling every time he saw them walking hand in hand or reading together in companaible silence. Another man might have rushed into believing he was on track for a happy ever after, but previous experience stayed Gabriel's hand.

If—and that was a huge *if*—he was contemplating trying to develop his relationship with Louisa into something more, he'd have to tell her about Frederica and what had happened to make him leave Staffordshire and that made him grimace. What would she think of him if she knew others suspected him of abusing his first wife, accusations he couldn't deny without bringing Leah into a mess he'd sworn she would never be exposed to?

A flash of blonde caught his attention. As if sensing he was thinking about her, Leah had turned round to wave at him from her pony's saddle and he lifted a hand in reply, hastily summoning a smile. In the autumn sunshine she looked more like her mother than ever, her flaxen curls bouncing in time with Bracken's plodding stride, although when viewed from this angle there was no denying she had her real father's chin.

Sir Cecil Allenby was a handsome man and had passed his comeliness to the daughter he never would have claimed even if he'd been told of her existence,

Leah sure to grow into a beauty to rival even Frederica in her prime. She was sweet and innocent and deserved more than the complicated existence she had been born into, and as the horses drew closer to the yard's mounting block he knew he had to put his daughter's needs before his own desires.

*I can't tell Louisa yet. For Leah's sake, I need to be sure before I confess.*

Nutmeg came to a gentle halt, obeying Louisa's twitch of the reins, and he slid down from the saddle, looking up at her as he straightened his jacket. 'You're making good progress. It won't be long until you'll feel confident enough to sit up on your own.'

'Thank you. I'm not sure I agree, but it's polite of you to say so.'

Louisa made as if to unhook her knee from the pommel. She seemed slightly hesitant, glancing from the saddle to the ground, and Gabriel seized his chance.

'Can I offer you some assistance?'

A little voice at the back of his mind chided him for wanting to touch her again so soon, but it was easily crowded out by the much louder clamour of pleasure when she nodded.

'If you wouldn't mind. Nutmeg might not be as tall as Merlin, but I still have no desire to fall while attempting to dismount.'

He needed no further encouragement to step closer to the horse. Reaching up, he held Louisa's free hand as she released the pommel and untangled her skirts, then his heart flew up into his throat as she permitted him to take hold of her waist and carefully slide her to the ground.

Her hands darted to his shoulders, gripping them to steady herself as her boots hit the cobbled yard. For a moment they were pressed together along the entire length of their bodies, chest to chest and face to face, his hands straying to her hips and her arms all but wrapped around his neck, and he realised in a streak of fire that he had no desire to let her go.

She looked up at him, her lips slightly parted. Her eyes were just as wide as they'd been in Miriam's garden when he'd kissed a fairy queen wearing a crown of flowers and his breathing stuttered as he watched her gaze drop to rest on his mouth.

'Did you see, Papa? Were you watching?'

His daughter possessed the uncanny knack of piping up at the worst possible moment. The tension broke and Louisa stepped smartly back, his hands dropping away from her as Leah skipped towards them.

'I was,' he assured her, only slightly bending the truth. 'You did extremely well. Soon you'll be a better rider than me.'

She beamed. 'Yes. I think I will.'

Conway's mouth twitched into what Gabriel thought might have been a quickly hidden smile. 'Did you want to lead Bracken back to his stall, Miss? I think he's taken a liking to you. There might even be an apple around here somewhere you could give to him.'

'I could feed him? May I, Papa?'

Gabriel dipped his chin, trying to ignore his awareness of how close Louisa still stood. 'Of course, if you want to. Shall I come with you?'

With great dignity Leah shook her head. 'No, thank you, Papa. Conway will show me how.'

Clearly any anxiety she'd felt around the pony was long gone and Gabriel had to hold back a smile of his own as she took the rein from Conway's hand.

'There's no need to come back for Nutmeg,' he told the groom. 'I can take her in myself. It's been a while since I untacked a horse and I'd like to see if I can remember how.'

'Very good, my lord. If you'd like to follow me, Miss?'

Conway guided Leah away, the pony trailing along behind them. His stall was in another part of the yard and their progress wasn't especially fast, time seeming to stretch out before they rounded a corner and disappeared from sight, leaving Gabriel very much alone with his wife.

He didn't turn back to her straight away. The frisson he'd felt at having her pressed to his chest hadn't abated and he had to take a beat to collect himself before he looked her way.

'Are you returning to the house now?'

'I'm not sure.' Louisa stroked Nutmeg's nose, not

quite meeting his eye. 'I didn't know if you might need some help with the horse. Another pair of hands, as it were.'

Gabriel paused. Untacking a horse was a simple enough task and one he'd done repeatedly as a younger man too impatient to wait for a groom. He could manage very well by himself, but somehow the answer that made its way out of his mouth wasn't the one he knew to be true.

'That would be useful. Thank you.'

Louisa followed him to Nutmeg's stable in a quiet corner of the yard. None of the stable lads were anywhere to be seen so there was no one to watch as Gabriel unbolted the door and stood aside to let Louisa enter before him, her hair turning from sunlit copper to darker red as she retreated into the shade.

The rest of the stalls were empty, Nutmeg's the only one that would be occupied, and he saw Louisa note the open doors.

'Won't she be lonely in here by herself?'

'No. She prefers it to being shut in with the others. We used to keep her stabled with the rest of the horses, but she didn't seem to enjoy it.'

He led the horse into her stall and began to remove her bridle. He was aware Louisa was studying his movements and felt his hands grow clumsy, actions he'd performed a hundred times before suddenly causing him to fumble under her gaze.

Trying to concentrate on lifting the saddle off correctly, he didn't turn when she spoke again.

'I suppose some people are like that, too. Preferring their own space.'

'Are you talking about yourself?'

'I meant you, actually.'

He peered over his shoulder. She was leaning against the stable wall, watching him from beyond the stall's open door, and she looked away when his eyes sought hers. The toe of one little boot drew a line through the straw that covered the floor, a slightly apprehensive gesture that suggested she'd said more than she'd intended.

He stopped, still holding the saddle in both hands. Was that how she saw him? Possibly lonely and definitely reluctant to get close to anyone else?

Slowly he placed the saddle back on its rack. Nutmeg shifted slightly and he patted her before leaving the stall, closing the door behind him without a thought. At his approach Louisa stood up straight, pushing herself off the wall, and she didn't move away as he came to stand in front of her.

In Miriam's garden, she'd said she knew he'd rather have Frederica than her, but she'd been wrong. She thought he still missed the woman who had broken his heart, that he lived in constant loneliness after losing her, but she couldn't have been further from the truth.

He had no notion of how to deny Louisa's beliefs about his attachment to Leah's mother without sounding callous or inviting questions he didn't want to answer, yet it felt suddenly important that he correct the assumption that might be holding them apart.

He looked down at her. A stable wasn't the most romantic of places, he'd admit, but even amid the smell of hay and faint snuffling of the horse shut in behind them Louisa still struck him as lovely in a way all her own. Her eyes were so green and the lashes veiling them so long and dark she reminded him of a deer, appearing fragile, but more than capable of running if he pushed too far.

Perhaps he didn't have to say it out loud, he thought as a rushing sound began to build in his ears. Perhaps his actions could speak louder than words and he could *show* her how he felt rather than *tell*. Words could come out wrong, after all, and once spoken couldn't be taken back; but if he took her in his arms again surely there was no way she could misunderstand.

The sigh that escaped her as he brought his mouth down on hers sounded very much like one of relief.

Her arms twined around his neck with such unthinking swiftness it was as if she'd been waiting for the moment to arrive. She pulled him to her and he went willingly, his tongue meeting hers in a jolt of static electricity he felt all the way down to his boots. He almost stumbled, overwhelmed by the readiness with which she responded to his touch, and when he backed her against the wall it was as much to steady himself as her.

His hands were on her, moving from the curve of her waist that had driven him to distraction in the saddle to the intoxicatingly feminine swell of her hips. He wanted to explore every inch of her, from the head bare now that her riding hat had been knocked to the floor to the slender insteps of her feet, a desire he knew she shared when her fingers delved into the hair at his nape and refused to let go.

Mouths moving in an instinctive, longing-filled dance, he pressed her harder against the wall, trapping her between stone and the firm length of his body. To his dazed delight he felt her shift to allow his thigh to slot between hers, a ragged gasp choking from her when he moved to apply gentle pressure to the place he knew she'd want it the most. Probably she was too inexperienced to know what she was yearning for, but he'd be glad to show her, finally given the chance to finish what they'd begun on their wedding night if she'd permit him to go that far.

Restraint hanging by a thread, he buried his face in the crook of her neck, breathing in the warm scent of her skin as he kissed along her collarbone and down towards the edge of her gown. He was too tall to reach anywhere more interesting without folding himself in two and without stopping to think he lifted her higher against the wall, supporting her weight with a strong grasp at the backs of her thighs. She gasped again to find herself off her feet, but she didn't protest, instead tilting her head back to give him more room to explore the neckline of her dress.

'Gabriel...'

His name falling from her lips in a sigh was the sweetest thing he'd ever heard. His mouth was busy, but she didn't seem to require a reply. Glancing up, he saw her eyes were closed, her head thrown back and her bottom lip held between her teeth, a picture of such abandon that he almost crumpled to the ground.

His blood was heating past the point of all endurance. Inside the cage of his ribs his heart thrashed violently, the rushing sound in his ears blotting out everything but Louisa's ragged breaths. Her fingers had crept down into the collar of his shirt and even that slight touch made him fear he might explode, his grip on her thighs tightening as he struggled to keep his desire under control.

Her skirts had hitched up to her knees, giving him a tantalising glimpse of silk stocking that did nothing to help slow the frenzied leap of his pulse. If he edged her hem up just a little further, he would find the bare skin of her legs and, with his mouth still pressed to her bodice, he began to gather her skirts in one hand, swallowing a groan when he slid his palm upwards and found a band of ribbon-tied lace.

She bucked against him when he brushed over the top of her stocking, his fingers grazing the sensitive flesh as they continued their climb. An ache was building inside him and it throbbed so hard it was almost painful, but he would have to take his time with the remedy. For all his want was raging like a wildfire he knew better than to rush, Louisa's pleasure at the forefront of his mind as he ghosted over the final stretch of skin and brushed a fingertip over the very crux of her desire—

Her thighs clenched shut around his fingers.

'Wait. Not here.'

Gabriel stilled at once. Her voice was shaky, but he heard the command in it loud and clear, and despite the hot clamour of his own longing he immediately retracted his hand.

He lifted his head from the neckline of her gown and looked down at her. Her chest was heaving and her eyes were glazed, and with her hair half-pulled down around her shoulders she would have tempted a man made of stone.

She took a deep breath. She seemed to be finding it as difficult to restrain herself as he was and she must have sensed his bewilderment as to why she'd stopped him when she gave a husky laugh.

'I'm not completely sure what happens next, but I do know it shouldn't happen in a stable. Or at least, not the first time.'

Louisa peeped up at him through the dark sweep of her lashes, a look such a heady mixture of coquettish and coy that his knees almost buckled. 'So…shall we go?'

'Go where?'

'Upstairs.'

Gabriel swallowed, nearly unmanned by a single murmured word. 'Only if you want to.'

'I do.'

His leg was still nestled between hers, helping to brace her against the wall, although it felt suddenly weak at her shy but strident need. She'd declared out loud that she wanted him as much as he wanted her and, bolting the door on any unwanted thoughts as to what that might mean, he carefully placed her back on her feet.

'Then I'd be happy to go with you. Lead the way.'

## Chapter Nine

Days at Sisslehurst Manor turned into weeks, and those weeks were happier than Louisa ever would have believed they could be.

Despite her initial fears her new role as Leah's stepmother was a constant source of joy. Nobody could take Frederica's place as Leah's real mama and Louisa would never try, although as Leah had only the haziest memories of her natural mother there was little to stand in the way of their deepening bond. That blossoming connection seemed to please Gabriel as much as it did Louisa herself, something that now made her smile to think of as she lay among the tangled sheets of their bed, his empty side still warm from having left it not long before.

She stretched, luxuriating in the softness of the mattress. Almost every night now—and, scandalously, sometimes during the day, too—her husband showed her exactly how delightful being truly married could be and the mild aches that resulted from so much activity were more than worth it. It had taken a while for them to reach such a level of intimacy and it seemed they were making up for lost time, whatever had been slow to start growing between them now racing in full flight.

Sitting up, she cast about for her nightgown. It was lying in a heap beside the bed and she leaned over to retrieve it, glad as she moved to find she didn't feel as nauseous that morning as she had for the past week. Generally, the faint biliousness disappeared by the afternoon and was surely only a sign she wasn't getting enough sleep, but she made a note to consult Gabriel's physician if it persisted as she pulled the flimsy linen over her head, pushed back the twisted sheets and got up.

She assumed it was her maid when she heard someone outside the bedroom door and her heart gave a flip when instead it was Gabriel's tall figure that entered the room. He'd already taken his leave of her that morning, treating her to a fine view of him dressing before he'd gone, and to see him again so soon was an unexpected pleasure.

'I thought you were going into Warwick today. Did you forget something?'

Thinking he would flash the smile he showed far more often these days she was puzzled when his dark eyebrows drew into a frown.

'Is something the matter?'

She had the impression he hadn't meant for his expression to give so much away. 'No. Nothing's wrong. I just came to tell you my plans for the day have changed.'

He extracted a piece of paper from his waistcoat pocket, holding it up so she could see. 'An express has just come. It seems I'm needed in Staffordshire. Some legal business to do with my estate there, all very tedious. I'm hoping to be there and back in a day.'

'Staffordshire. I see.'

Louisa shrugged on her dressing gown, pretending to tie the belt around her waist, although really she was buying herself a moment to think. Even a child wouldn't have been fooled by Gabriel's attempt at nonchalance and keen sympathy lanced through her.

*He obviously doesn't want to go back there and I can understand why.*

His other estate held memories it was probably too painful to revisit. He'd lived there with Frederica and Leah as a perfect family and being forced to remember such lost happiness would hurt. There had to be good reasons he had left his Staffordshire home and although he'd never spoken of them she knew well enough what they must be, her compassion mingling with a desire to help him whether he asked for it or not.

'Shall I come with you?'

His reply was immediate. 'No. There's no need for that, but I thank you for the offer. I was only telling you so you weren't concerned by my absence at dinner later tonight. I doubt I shall be back in time to eat with you.'

Gabriel smiled, but it was too stiff to be genuine. Clearly his discomfort ran deeper than he was willing to admit and Louisa had to stop herself from reaching up to cup a hand around his cheek.

She held herself in check, however. He was obviously intent on displaying a brave façade and she would never shame him by letting him know she saw through it. He had thawed almost past all recognition from the cold man she'd first met, but that damaged man was still there somewhere and she had no desire for him to return to the fore if she tried to dig too deep.

He crossed to the still-drawn curtains and she watched him push the heavy drapes aside. Autumnal sunlight filled the room and it lent his wary eyes much-needed illumination as he looked back at her.

'It's a beautiful day. You shouldn't spend it cooped up inside.'

Louisa nodded. The fact his gaze hadn't strayed down to her barely covered decolletage was damning evidence that he was not himself and she reflected how different the nature of their connection had become that she could now use such a thing as a benchmark for his state of mind.

Ever since she had been so bold as to invite him upstairs, everything had changed. The change had begun before that, of course, set in motion by many other things, but it had been the igniting of their physical flame that had given them the final push into something more. She could have no doubt now that Gabriel's attraction to her burned bright; but that wasn't the only way in which she was beginning to hope he might care for her.

Once it would have been impossible. Once the idea of cool, detached Lord Harnham looking at her with anything close to fondness would have been too stupid to entertain, but now, with the passing of each day, didn't he seem to be letting her in more and more?

She looked at him standing by the window, bathed in early morning light. Despite his best efforts, he still seemed distracted and her insides clenched with compassion she knew better than to show. His heart had been broken by his first wife's death and she would never dream of wanting him to forget it, but she *did* want to help him heal if she could and it felt as though he was starting to give her the chance.

*But he's still so proud. He won't accept any assistance he thinks makes him look weak, yet how can I stand by while he faces today alone?*

Affecting to tighten the knot on her belt more securely, she made up her mind. There was no choice but to take matters into her own hands. If he wouldn't willingly let her help then she'd have to force the issue, but in a way so gentle he wouldn't realise her concern.

'You're right.' She smiled, quietly glad her husband

couldn't read minds. 'I won't stay at home today. I think getting out is exactly what I'll do.'

*That was close,* Gabriel thought as his carriage pulled away from the Manor. *For a moment I thought she was going to insist on coming with me.*

It had been typically kind of Louisa to offer to go with him to Staffordshire, but of course there had been no question of him accepting. There was too great a chance of her hearing things he'd rather she didn't, although if he was honest with himself her company was just what he wanted as the carriage began to pick up speed.

He sighed, raking a hand through his hair. His hat lay on the seat beside him, but as a fellow passenger it was nowhere near as agreeable as his wife would have been. The idea of returning to a place so hostile was not one he relished and Louisa would have been a friendly face, not something he would have imagined when they first wed, but now a fact he'd make no attempt to deny. In fact, if he was determined to be absolutely truthful, *friendly* might not be the word he'd use to describe the face that swam before him as he closed his eyes and leaned his head back to rest against his seat.

He'd never been one for flowery language and, his eyes still closed, he shook his head at his own folly. Was there truly a need to put a label on how he was becoming to feel about his wife—feelings that he was also starting to suspect might be returned?

Despite the apprehension currently wringing out his innards he felt a low warmth thread through them. It was dangerous to hope for such things, he knew, given how Frederica had torn his life apart when he'd been fool enough to trust her, but his ability to hold himself back was waning fast. Surely the shade he'd thought Sir Christopher had cast over his marriage had lifted, the other man no longer keeping a monopolising grip on Louisa's heart?

Every night now she allowed Gabriel to touch her, delighting in his caresses in a way he was certain couldn't be faked, but her willingness to be close to him didn't stop when the sun rose. She sought him out now for casual conversation rather than hiding in the library all day and was always touchingly insistent on him taking his meals with her and Leah at the grand dining table her sunny presence had robbed of its austerity.

To his daughter she was kindness personified, endlessly patient and genuinely interested in all the child's likes and dislikes, and he couldn't have wished for a better stepmother for the little girl he'd allowed himself to be irreversibly tainted to protect.

His eyes opened, fixing on the carriage's swaying ceiling.

Those former neighbours that now thought so badly of him. Would they have flaming torches and pitchforks out ready for his return? If he was lucky, his estate manager had been discreet about needing the master to visit to look over the books, but one couldn't say for sure. Word had a way of getting around, especially when it was so salacious as to concern a suspected monster coming back to town, and he pinched the bridge of his nose as he wondered how quickly he could conclude his business and leave.

'Woah. Woah, there.'

The coachman's voice broke into Gabriel's dark musings. The carriage was slowing down and he frowned as he half-rose from his seat, wondering at the cause.

The answer came soon enough.

There was a low exchange of words from outside and then the carriage's door opened.

'Good morning. Again.'

Caught entirely off guard, he blinked as Louisa climbed aboard and closed the door behind her. Pausing only to rap on the ceiling with one gloved hand, she dropped into the seat opposite him, demurely straightening her bonnet as the carriage lurched into motion again as though she was an expected guest and not more on par with a highwayman.

She beamed at him, either not noticing or not fazed by his stunned silence. 'I was hoping to throw myself on your mercy. I know you said your business would be tedious, but as Leah is going out with her governess all day I'd be bored if I stayed at the Manor. Would you really mind if I came with you?'

'I—' He stared at her, still not entirely sure what was happening. 'Were you waiting for me to pass by?'

'Oh, no. I was out walking, as you know, and happened to see the carriage coming out of the drive. It occurred to me I could flag your man down so that's what I did.'

Gabriel's stomach plummeted. Louisa was settling herself into a corner as though getting comfortable for a long journey and he felt dismay wash over him as he watched her fold her hands firmly in her lap.

By what nightmare had this occurred? As glad as he was to see her, she *could not* be there. The very last thing he wanted was for her to go with him, to hear the whispers that painted him in such a terrible light. The carriage was bowling along merrily once again, however, and the prospect of setting her down from it made him flinch.

'I'd thought to go alone,' he managed tightly, praying his tone would not betray his horror. 'You would be less entertained by coming with me than if you stayed at home.'

Louisa regarded him closely. She seemed to be trying to read something in his face and hurriedly he smoothed away any trace of unease. If he made too big a fuss of wanting his visit to be a solitary one, she would begin to question why and he had no wish to offer her either an excuse or the truth.

'Even so.' She studied her lap, a trace of colour tinging her cheeks. 'Entertaining or not, I would still prefer to be with you.'

The clamour inside him quietened a fraction. Such a sweet confession made his spirits soar—but they were shot down again just as quickly by a sharp arrow of guilt.

He was trying to hide things from her, things she had the right to know, yet he couldn't bear the thought of her hearing such ugly lies. Her good opinion of him mattered more than ever and the rumours might make her think twice about bestowing it, perhaps wondering if indeed the adage of no smoke without fire might carry some weight. Warning her beforehand would take the power away from those who spread the slander, but when he tried to imagine how he might begin to explain he found that all words had fled.

When they'd first wed, he had kept silent out of concern for Leah, but any fears he had of Louisa revealing his daughter's true parentage had gone. There was no danger of her spilling the secret if she knew it: Louisa was far too fond of the little girl to risk her being branded a bastard or snatched away by Frederica's parents to be raised as their new pawn.

He could confess why Frederica had been trying to leave when she'd fallen from her horse and how he'd taken the blame for it to divert suspicion, secure in the knowledge Louisa wouldn't treat Leah any differently to how she did now...yet somehow he still couldn't make himself speak.

He glanced across at her. She was looking out of the window, her face turned towards the glass to display the clear line of her profile. The sunshine had scattered golden highlights among the deep green of her eyes, eyes it would kill something inside him to see filled with fear.

Dismay began to curdle into something stronger. Half of Staffordshire was convinced he had beaten Frederica so savagely she was willing to risk her life to escape him. He'd seen it in the way mamas steered their daughters away from him in the street, careful to avoid his gaze as they hurried by. Some of his accusers he'd known since he was a child and their judgement had hurt, such condemnation making him withdraw from society and eventually driving him from his home. If people who had patted him on the head as a boy thought him capable of harming his wife, then surely there was a chance Louisa might also, the thought of her being afraid of him turning his blood to ice.

If she hadn't been sitting opposite him, he would have dropped his face into his hands. What was he supposed to do? He could have stopped the carriage to set her down or ordered his driver to turn back to the Manor, but another study of his wife told him neither option was likely to be well received. She looked settled and comfortable in her corner. Besides, when she'd voiced she would rather spend the day with him, words that had sparked within him like a lit match, how could he refuse her anything she desired?

She must have felt him watching her. Turning towards him, she gave him another one of the smiles that made him feel as though he was standing in front of a fire, a pleasant warmth attempting to run through him that was abruptly beaten back by apprehension's chill.

'It's a shame Leah isn't with us. She might have wanted to visit her old home.'

'Perhaps, but I doubt it. There's nothing there for her to miss.'

Louisa frowned. 'But don't Frederica's parents still live locally? Wouldn't Leah have wanted to see them, at least?'

It was a reasonable enough suggestion and under other circumstances he would have been able to turn it aside with more tact. In his present state of mind, however, he had none to spare, his reply coming more plainly than he knew was wise.

'They'll never be in the same room as her again if I can help it. Some people aren't fit to be around a child.'

He shouldn't have said it and yet it came as a strange kind of relief to speak some of the truth. The secrets simmering just below the surface weighed on him and to release even part of one felt like snatching a breath. Frederica's parents deserved none of his discretion in any case—their selfish schemes had ruined lives and it would serve them right if the world knew what cruelty hid behind their genteel smiles. Knowing what effect it might have on Leah was the only thing that stayed his hand.

'Oh.' Louisa shifted somewhat awkwardly in her seat. 'I didn't realise you felt that way. I just thought that as they're the only relations she has apart from Miriam's family you might want to encourage the connection.'

'I do not.'

To his dismay he saw her face fall. He had spoken too harshly. The last thing he wanted was for her to feel she had done something wrong and manfully he summoned some lightness, forcing it from somewhere *very* deep down.

'But Miriam and company aren't all the relations Leah has. Are you not her family now also?'

It was a relief to see her smile return. 'That is my dearest wish. I hope she'll come to see me as such.'

'She will. How can she not, when the care you pour into your connection with her is plain to anyone who bothers to look?'

Louisa flushed. 'You know, you say some very agreeable things at times. It never ceases to surprise me that you possess such a silver tongue, given your reticence when we started out.'

'Yes. Well. Marriage changes a man.'

Switching his attention to the view outside, Gabriel

watched the fields spin past, determined to keep his eyes on the grass and skittering fallen leaves. Talk of tongues was risky, putting him in mind of the sweet one that lived in Louisa's mouth, and he had already noticed the subtly transfixing way she swayed with every move the carriage made. Even with what felt like the weight of the world on his shoulders he was still painfully aware he could reach out for her at any time, perhaps drawing the curtains before showing her what he could do in such an enclosed space...

He gave himself an internal pinch.

Now wasn't the time. He and Louisa would reach Staffordshire within a couple of hours and that held the potential to tear the hopes he was building into shreds. If she heard of the scandal and believed it, that would be like a knife through his heart, her inevitable fear of him and the destruction of her trust coming as a merciless double blow.

Gazing particularly hard at a dormant mill on the side of road, he tried to marshal his thoughts. They kept wanting to creep back towards Louisa's undulating waist, but with great effort he managed to herd them in a more productive direction.

*Think. Think hard.*

The Staffordshire house had a library housing all the books he couldn't fit into Sisslehurst. If he showed it to Louisa, surely there was a good chance she would spend the day ensconced inside where no whispers could reach her. It was a fragile scheme, but the only one he had at his disposal, and he tried to stir up confidence he didn't feel.

*There's nothing else I can do. If she goes out there's a possibility of someone telling her before I can find the best way to do it myself—and I'll have to eventually. Of that there can be no doubt.*

Louisa tried again to concentrate on the book in her lap, but like all her previous attempts it was in vain.

She sat back in her chair. The unfamiliar library she was sitting in boasted fine decorative coving and she let her eyes follow it the length of the opposite wall, attempting to distract herself from the roiling in her stomach. When she'd woken it hadn't been so bad, but the long carriage ride had jolted her into feeling more bilious than ever and she took deep, slow breaths to steady her shaking hands.

She pressed the back of one against her clammy forehead. Was she ill? She'd assumed it was lack of sleep that had made her feel so delicate of late, but perhaps she was wrong. Neither Gabriel nor Leah had been unwell, however, and to her knowledge she hadn't spent time with anyone who was, and she gritted her teeth as yet another wave of nausea rose and receded like the tide.

*I'll ask the doctor for a tonic. A little boost is all I need.*

What she would not be doing was telling Gabriel,

she resolved firmly. He had enough to think about already without adding her health to the list of concerns no doubt currently occupying his mind. For the duration of the journey to Staffordshire he'd seemed distracted and she didn't blame him one straw, her sympathy and desire to be of use to him growing with every mile that passed.

It must have been almost unbearable for him to return to the house that held so many memories of both happiness and horror and she almost admired his pretence of indifference. It was entirely unnecessary, but quite convincing, and it might have fooled her if she hadn't already known the truth. There was no way he could set foot in the place and remain so coolly unmoved as he appeared and she wished he didn't feel the need to keep up the charade, his pride making him reject the comforting hand she knew would do him good.

She couldn't force him to accept her compassion, however. If the most she could do was simply provide a discreetly reassuring presence when he emerged from his meeting with the estate manager, then that was what she would do—provided, of course, that she managed to keep her rising nausea at bay.

Taking another deep breath, she laid her book aside. Sitting in one place didn't seem to be helping and, gripping the padded arm of her chair so hard her fingers left indents behind, she levered herself up.

A walk was the thing to take her mind off this blasted queasiness. 'I'm sure when he invited me to view the library, he didn't mean I couldn't explore the rest of the house,' she muttered as she waited for the room around her to stop spinning. 'A stroll in the gallery, just to stretch my legs after travelling, will soon set me to rights.'

With wobbly determination she moved for the door and stepped out. Unlike Sisslehurst Manor the library here was on the uppermost floor and it seemed reasonable to assume one of the other doors leading from the landing must open on to the gallery she hoped would provide some respite from whatever was assailing her insides.

The first door she tried showed what must have been a music room, although now of course any instruments it had once contained had made their way south when Gabriel moved. Her second attempt was met with success, however, and on weak legs she tottered into a gallery that stretched what looked like almost the full length of the house.

Slowly she wandered over creaking floorboards. Tall windows to one side of the room let sunlight stream in, giving a good view of the grounds below. It was a large, handsome house with pretty gardens, but to her mind Sisslehurst still triumphed and it was strange to imagine Gabriel and Leah had once called it home.

She shivered. Ghosts were only real in Gothic novels, but she couldn't help wondering whether Frederica's might still roam the corridors of the place she'd once lived. The memory of her haunted every corner even if her spirit did not, doubtless kept alive by the husband they now shared, and Louisa suddenly felt as though she had strayed somewhere she didn't belong.

*Don't be absurd.*

She tutted to herself, ashamed of her own foolishness. *The poor woman is dead. Don't disturb her rest just to frighten yourself with shadows.*

Steadily she progressed towards the other end of the gallery. The gentle exercise had begun to have the desired effect: she was feeling less as though she might need to use a chamber pot at any moment and the cold sweat at her nape was starting to dry. A few more turns of the long room and she'd be right as rain and as she walked she looked about properly for the first time.

Paintings hung on the wall opposite the windows, she noticed now. Some were countryside scenes or pictures of horses, but others were portraits, and she slowed her pace to examine the flat faces peering back at her. Each belonged to some relation of Gabriel's, she guessed from the brass plaques attached to their frames, and she smiled slightly to trace his dark features through the generations until she came across the man himself.

Her smile segued into an expression of vivid interest as she examined the final portrait. 'That's Gabriel, albeit a few years younger, which means that must be...'

Her eyes fixed on the right side of the painting. Gabriel stood on the left and beside him, holding his arm, was a woman so like an older version of Leah that Louisa almost gasped aloud.

She stared up at the stranger held captive in the frame. Frederica—for who else could it possibly be?—returned her gaze, the painted lips curving as if genteelly amused. With her golden hair and large blue eyes she was an undeniable beauty, fair where Gabriel was dark but the two of them together making such a striking pair Louisa couldn't tear herself away.

Her stomach, blessedly calm again moments before, now dropped like a stone. She'd assumed the first Lady Harnham must have been a rare jewel for her loss to affect Gabriel so deeply, but seeing the evidence for herself struck an unexpected blow. The painted woman was elegant and refined and even when rendered in oils Gabriel's face seemed to glow as he looked at her, his adoration caught for ever on canvas and unable to be denied.

Louisa swallowed down a bitter taste in the back of her throat. She was being ridiculous. Why *would* he deny it? She'd always suspected he'd loved his first wife deeply and this was merely the proof. Jealousy was an ugly emotion and not one she'd entertain, although immediately and completely dismissing it was easier said than done.

With her attention so focused on the painting she didn't hear the approach of footsteps until they stopped directly behind.

'Did you need something, my lady?'

Louisa turned, almost glad of the interruption. A maid of middling age was standing close to her, looking mildly ill at ease, and she quickly shook her head.

'No, thank you. I've just been admiring the paintings while Lord Harnham is engaged. There are some very fine ones.'

'Yes, my lady. Some are real works of art.'

She followed the servant's gaze. The older woman was looking up at her former mistress in a manner it was difficult to place, half-wistful, half-troubled, and it intrigued Louisa enough to want to know more.

'Were you here at the same time as the first Lady Harnham?'

'Yes, ma'am. There's only a few of us left now, kept on to keep the place tidy since his lordship has moved away, but I was one who served the former mistress. All the staff at Sisslehurst Manor are new and never met her.'

'I see. And is this picture very like her?'

'Oh, yes, ma'am.' The maid seemed as though she'd been about to smile, but then a darkness passed over her face instead. 'She was a very comely young lady.

Never any bother to tend to, either. We were all very sad when…when…'

She stopped herself, appearing suddenly more unhappy than before, and Louisa laid a hand on her arm. 'Please don't upset yourself by explaining. I know what happened.'

To her surprise the maid turned to her sharply. 'Do you, my lady?'

'Why, yes. Lord Harnham told me.' Louisa couldn't help but frown at the rapid change in the servant's manner. 'There was a terrible accident. Lady Harnham went out riding in a storm and she fell from her horse.'

Her uncertainty didn't diminish at the widening of the servant's eyes. 'What? What's the matter?'

The maid took a step backwards. 'Nothing, my lady. Forgive me. It isn't my place.'

'It isn't your place to what?' Confused, Louisa watched as the servant retreated another pace. 'I don't understand. What did I say?'

'Forgive me, my lady,' the maid repeated. 'It's not for me to say.'

Increasingly baffled, Louisa looked again at the portrait. Neither Gabriel nor Frederica gave her any clues as to what had made the maid so apparently frightened, however, and with growing discomfort she turned back.

'I really would like to know what you're referring

to. If something is worrying you, I feel I ought to know.'

The maid opened her mouth as if to argue, but hating herself for stooping to such measures Louisa resorted to her winning card. 'I am the mistress of this house now and I'm afraid I must insist that you explain.'

The other woman sagged. Clearly she couldn't bring herself to disobey a direct order and Louisa felt a hot pang of guilt at the dismayed downturn of the servant's lips.

'Are you quite certain of that, my lady? I would never wish to speak out of turn.'

Louisa nodded. A strange, tight feeling had developed in her chest. For some reason the maid's abrupt and obvious fear was infectious and she felt her heart beating hard beneath her stays, the nausea that had hounded her earlier returning with a vengeance. 'I understand that. I'm grateful for your discretion.'

The maid sucked in a long breath. She glanced up at the portrait, resting briefly on Frederica's lovely painted face, and when she turned back to Louisa it was with mingled pity and dread.

'What Lord Harnham told you may not be the whole truth. Nobody can prove it, but there's talk Lady Harnham wasn't merely out for a ride when she fell.'

Suddenly abandoning the deeply ingrained deference of an experienced servant, the older woman stepped forward and grabbed hold of Louisa's hand, her eyes wide and pleading.

'Heaven save you, my lady. I would never wish to speak ill of the master, but some people say she only went out in that storm because she had to—he'd hurt her for the last time and she was finally running away.'

## Chapter Ten

Louisa barely spoke for the duration of the carriage journey back to Sisslehurst Manor. With her eyes shut and head bowed, she knew Gabriel must have assumed she was asleep and to her shame she didn't correct him. If he realised she was awake, he'd talk to her and she had no idea how to hold a conversation when she was shaken right through to her core.

What the maid had told her couldn't be true. It was slander plain and simple and she'd be doing her husband a grave injustice to allow it any space in her mind. There was no possibility Gabriel had harmed Frederica, none at all, yet what she'd heard played again and again on a relentless loop that made her want to put her hands over her ears, a constant disloyal murmur trying to make her question everything she thought she knew.

She opened her eyes the tiniest of invisible cracks. Through her eyelashes she watched Gabriel staring steadily out of the carriage window at the night beyond, his eyes unfocused as though he hardly saw what was before him. He looked deep in thought, but not as if he was wrestling with his conscience and her sickening confusion churned once again.

*He's never done anything to make me think I can't trust him. Why should I believe the gossip of strangers over my own experience?*

Still from beneath her lashes she studied Gabriel's moonlit face. A black heart could hide behind a handsome visage, but she couldn't imagine his countenance was the mask of a monster. Only a real villain would set out to hurt his wife and he had never given the impression of being one of those, not even at the very beginning when she'd disliked him above anyone else. It had been his terseness that had nettled her rather than any suggestion of violence, and now even that initial coolness had been replaced by consideration she didn't believe was feigned.

She closed her eyes again, relieved to feel some of the tension leave her stiff shoulders.

*No. There must have been some kind of mistake.*

The maid had misunderstood. The rumours had been about some other man, or perhaps twisted around until they bore little resemblance to any original fact. It was kind for the servant to worry about her new mistress's safety, but her concern had been misguided, well intentioned but still doing more harm than good.

The carriage rattled down another uneven road, the movement making her insides turn again, although this time not with unease. Horror had been responsible for making her feel so sick previously, but now the first rush of dread had subsided a different kind of nausea came in to replace it, the same sort that had chased her from the library earlier in the day. What she wanted more than anything was to lie down somewhere dark and quiet and above all still, the rocking of the carriage about as far from pleasant as it was possible to get.

'Louisa.' Gabriel's murmur was soft. 'Louisa, you may want to begin waking up now. We're almost home.'

Evidently her charade of sleep had been convincing and, fluttering her eyelids a few times, she pretended to rouse herself.

'Oh. Already?'

'Yes. You slept almost the whole way.'

'Did I? I must have been extremely fatigued.'

Covering her mouth, she affected to hold back a yawn. Gabriel looked tired himself, she saw as she peered through the gloom, the moonlight emphasising the dark shadows beneath his equally dark eyes. It seemed he hadn't taken the same opportunity to sleep that he thought she had and she felt a sudden burst of compassion for his set, careworn face.

How could anyone believe he'd harm another person? It had been grief that had awaited him in Staffordshire, not guilt for past wrongs, and her chest ached with sympathy for what the day must have made him feel. He was unlikely to admit his heart was sore, but she couldn't see how it could be otherwise, aware now that a far more sensitive man hid behind what she'd once thought was a wall of ice.

The carriage turned on to what she recognised as the lane leading to their estate. Soon they would be home and she'd be glad of it, jostled both physically and mentally and ready for a reprieve. Bed was calling and she was more than happy to answer, although another thought occurred to make her hesitate.

Ought she tell Gabriel what was being said of him? He couldn't be aware of the cruel whispers or she was positive he would have told her about them, the accusations too serious to conceal. She wouldn't reveal the maid as her source, but surely it would be best to let him know; while he was oblivious, he couldn't defend himself and such damage to his reputation could not go unchallenged. She would have to be careful how she broached the subject, but broach it she must, the idea of anyone speaking ill of him making her bristle.

*How things change. At one point I couldn't stand the man and now I'd dare anyone to say a single word against him.*

Another yawn, genuine this time, commanded her attention. Now both nauseous and tired, in her current condition she wouldn't be able to do a delicate conversation the justice it required. If she was to speak to Gabriel about what his old neighbours were muttering, then it would be better to do so with a clear head, something she had no hope of claiming as the carriage drew up outside Sisslehurst Manor and rocked to a shuddering halt.

*I'll do it tomorrow.* Glancing across at him, she caught his eye, her heart executing the usual flip at the sight of his weary smile. He didn't deserve the unkind things people apparently saw fit to spread about him and she felt a ripple of protective anger course through her.

*Yes. I'll do it tomorrow when I've slept and am feeling more myself. If I'm to find a way to raise this subject, I'm going to need all my wits.*

In the dim morning light filtering through the drawn hangings of their bed, Gabriel watched as Louisa stirred in her sleep.

He hadn't slept well himself. The previous day's visit to Staffordshire had been unsettling and he'd lain awake for most of the night, unable to quiet the chatter of his thoughts. Returning to the place he'd lived with Frederica had been like stepping back into another life and he had no desire to experience it again, unwanted memories chasing him from room to room as he'd walked through what had once been his home.

It wasn't any longer, however. His place now was with the woman currently sleeping beside him, her flaming hair spread across her pillow and her lips parted on quiet, even breaths. She looked so peaceful and he could have watched her all day, such a beautiful sight that he wanted nothing more than to lie there and drink her in.

She frowned slightly, a tiny cleft appearing between her sandy eyebrows, but to his relief she didn't wake. The longer she slept, the longer he had to enjoy the loveliness of her serene face and the more time he had in which to make up his mind.

Careful not to disturb his wife, he picked up a curl that had snaked on to his side of the bed, wrapping it around his finger in a gleaming copper band. He loved it when she wore her hair loose, but also when it was knotted modestly at the back of her head, just as it had been the morning before when she'd appeared so suddenly at the door of his carriage. He'd been alarmed to see her, but in the end her presence had come as a comfort, not a danger, and now he suspected that had been her intention all along.

He examined the captured curl, admiring the array of different shades of red and brown within it as he tried to decide what to do. Was it not a little too coincidental she'd popped up at the very moment his carriage had been passing by? And that she'd apparently decided spending a day alone at the Manor was too boring to endure when she'd managed to previously? She'd been content enough for him to leave her in the past when he'd had to go into Warwick on other business, never complaining when he was away for hours at a time. The only differences this time had been the reason for his departure and his destination, and he felt the weight of the decision he was trying to reach lift at the thought.

*She knew I didn't want to go back there. She came to support me despite my insistence on going alone and if that doesn't show she cares enough for me to give her my trust, I don't know what will.*

Some last vestiges of wariness lingered at the back of his mind, but he was no longer inclined to listen. For some time, he had questioned whether he could share his secret with her and finally it seemed the answer was *yes*. Louisa had shown what was needed to unlock the door Frederica had made him fasten so tightly, her sweetness and consideration to both Leah and himself proof it was at last safe to let down his guard, and even if the prospect was daunting he had no more doubts that it was the right thing to do.

His heart beat a little faster as he looked again at her sleeping face. Would she wake soon? When she did, he would tell her what he and Miriam had taken such pains to conceal and could only hope it didn't make her perceive Leah any differently. The little girl was still his daughter even if she'd been fathered by another man—something he was now certain Louisa had the compassion to understand.

He paused.

But would he tell her *everything?*

She shifted, burrowing deeper into the blankets, but still she didn't wake. The end of her nose was close enough for him to kiss and he felt temptation rise, although a sharp swell of guilt forced it back.

Louisa deserved to know every detail he'd kept so close to his chest, yet the idea of laying bare what he was suspected of still made him baulk. Even after so much had passed between them there was still a chance she might believe the worst and to see any trace of fear in the face he'd come to care for so deeply would hurt too much to bear.

The loss of her faith in him would be a pain like no other, possibly worse even than when he'd learned Frederica had never loved him after all, and to find that the connection he'd thought they had forged wasn't as strong as he'd imagined would be a devastating blow.

Releasing the ringlet, he rolled on to his back and stared bleakly up at the canopy overhead.

If *he* didn't tell her his old neighbours accused him of indirectly killing his wife, was she likely to hear of it from elsewhere? Louisa was in frequent contact with Eliza, although to his knowledge his cousin was unaware of what was being said of him so many miles away. The only one privy to the full scandal was Miriam and he could rely on her lips remaining sealed, for his sake and that of the little girl she loved as though they were related in truth rather than a pretence sustained to keep Leah safe.

'Good morning.'

A sleepy murmur made him start. Louisa was

watching him from among her nest of blankets, her eyes heavy-lidded but bright with interest. 'You seem far away for such an early hour of the morning. What are you thinking about so intently?'

With unnerving accuracy she'd guessed his current state of mind. 'Nothing of note. I didn't realise you were awake.'

'I know you didn't.'

She stretched, her arms emerging from the covers. For once she was still wearing her nightgown, but all the same she made an inviting sight as she sat up, leaning back against her pillows with the ribbons hanging undone to give a glimpse of her slender collarbone.

'Are you sure there's nothing bothering you?'

Gabriel looked up at her. Clad all in white with her hair falling so prettily around her shoulders, she could have been an angel, sent to free him from the chains he'd bound himself up in and never intended to break. There might never be a better moment to throw caution aside and tell her what had happened three years before and he gathered his nerve, at last prepared to be as honest as he should have been from the start.

Somehow, however, the words wouldn't come.

Shame and frustration ran through him. Why couldn't he spit it out? Louisa was waiting, curious but patient, but his mouth refused to move, any confession he'd wanted to make stalling on its way from his mind to his tongue.

She waited another moment, prolonging his chance to overcome his cowardice, but then her expression changed and he knew the opportunity had gone.

'If you've nothing to say, may *I* speak?'

'Of course.' He tried to sound normal, although it was difficult when internally he was kicking himself hard enough to leave a bruise. 'When have you ever needed my permission?'

Expecting her to smile, he was puzzled when instead she gazed down at her hands.

'Louisa? What is it?'

Her face had tightened. 'I'm not sure how to begin. Perhaps it's best to come straight out with it and hope I can find the right words.'

Gabriel pushed himself up to sit with her against the pillows. 'Ought I be concerned?'

'I have no wish to make you so, although…'

He saw her take a breath before she turned to look at him directly. 'When we were in Staffordshire yesterday, I happened to hear something and I think you should know what it was.'

She slid her wedding ring round her finger, the gold band flashing with each nervous turn. 'Please don't ask me to reveal from whom I learned of it, but apparently… Forgive me. Apparently there's talk you may have played some part in Frederica's death.'

Gabriel felt the blood drain from his face.

'I'm sorry.' Louisa abandoned her fiddling, leaning over to catch one of his suddenly numb hands.

'To upset you is the very last thing I wanted. It just seemed so cruel that people were saying such things behind your back and I thought that as you clearly didn't know about it you weren't able to defend yourself.'

She held his hand in both of hers, her thumbs tracing earnest lines over his knuckles. He wasn't sure when he'd last seen someone look so worried and he wanted to stroke her fretful cheek, although he knew he didn't deserve to do any such thing.

*Well. It seems I left honesty too late.*

Louisa peered at him, her troubled eyes searching his. 'Gabriel? Did you hear me?'

'Yes,' he said hollowly. 'People back in Staffordshire believe I may have hurt my first wife.'

She gazed at him doubtfully, her uncertainty seeming to grow when he didn't say anything more. He knew he should have, but nothing came out, words once again failing him as he tried to resist the urge to bury his head in his palms.

Why hadn't he told her when he had the chance? He could have taken control and given her the truth rather than whatever distorted nonsense she'd been fed by someone else, but now all hope of that was gone. She was sure to be suspicious and he thought he could already see it dawning, her hands still cradling his but their grip looser than before.

'You don't seem surprised.' Her brows drew together, a note of misgiving creeping into her voice. 'Did...did you already know?'

Gabriel's throat felt as though it had been sealed shut. It was a question he would have given anything to avoid answering, but he had no choice, neither willing nor able to look at her and lie.

'Yes.'

To his dismay all the light vanished from her face. Her eyes dimmed, bewilderment robbing them of their usual sparkle. 'But you never said a word. How was it you never mentioned something you must have found so distressing?'

He sat up, trying to reach for her, but she'd already let go of his hand. 'I don't understand. Why would you keep such a terrible thing from me? Did you believe I'd think it was *true*?'

What he saw in her countenance made him feel an avalanche of bitter regret. There was none of the fear he'd been so desperate not to see, only hurt, and somehow that was a hundred times worse.

'Louisa—'

He tried again to reach out for her, but she leaned away. Still there was no fright or even the anger she'd be entitled to feel, just a kind of wounded confusion that cut through him like a knife. Every time he'd imagined how this conversation might unfold he'd pictured her as horrified, but in the face of her disappointment he didn't know what to say. It rendered him mute and raked at his insides, the talons growing sharper when she pulled the sheets higher as if to hide herself from his gaze.

'You didn't trust me. That's why you kept silent, I think.'

It was a statement, not a question. She didn't require him to reply and he knew it, although even if she had wanted him to answer he wasn't sure what he could have said to make things right.

The quiet unhappiness in her voice was the deadliest of weapons. 'I confess I thought we were closer than that. It seems I was wrong.'

'You weren't wrong.' He pushed the bedclothes back so he could turn fully towards her, wishing she'd let him take one of her clenched hands. 'The strength of our connection is something I value more than you know.'

'And yet you kept such a painful secret from me. What good is any connection if honesty doesn't go along with it?' She looked back at him without flinching, although he saw her cheeks were flushed. 'There's nothing I'd seek to conceal from you. I'd thought our marriage might be turning into something more substantial than a forced arrangement, but now—'

Louisa cut off the end of her sentence. The colour in her cheeks deepened as if she was embarrassed for speaking so freely and Gabriel could have roared his frustration aloud.

The legacy of wariness Frederica had left behind had claimed another victim: not just his own happiness but Louisa's, too, and knowing he *still* had one secret left compounded the sensation of darkness spreading through him.

If he told her about Leah now, wouldn't it make an already bad situation even worse?

She would feel the weight of his distrust even more keenly if she knew he'd ever thought he had to protect his daughter from her. It might come as one confession too far—but Louisa's sudden lurch up from the bed pushed the matter aside.

Before he could react, she'd disappeared between the bed's closed hangings, shoving her way through with urgency he didn't understand until he heard her retching into the chamberpot on the other side.

'Louisa? Are you ill?'

Immediately he tore open the curtains, but she waved him back with a feeble hand. The bilious attack subsided as quickly as it had begun and after splashing some cold water from the washbasin on to her face she returned unsteadily to the bed.

'I think I'll lie down for a moment. The room spins every time I move.'

He watched as she flopped down on to the mattress. She looked pale and weak and he felt worry spear through him, the unpleasantness of their interrupted conversation suddenly obscured by concern.

'I don't like the sound of that. With your permission I'll call for Dr Gibson.'

Louisa didn't reply. Her eyes had closed and her

lips pressed together, and with growing unease Gabriel stood up.

Very carefully he drew the blankets up to cover her, tucking them around her to keep out any draughts. The sight of her lying so still and quiet pulled at his already heavy heart and he longed to bend down and drop a gentle kiss on to her forehead, but he found he didn't dare. Such a thing might not be welcome now he'd made her feel as though her trust wasn't returned and so instead he withdrew, trying not to make a noise as he moved to the door and left the room.

Doctor Gibson's hands were cold, making Louisa stiffen as he laid them over her abdomen. She'd pulled a shawl on over her nightgown in an effort to preserve her dignity, but there was little of that to be found as she allowed herself to be poked and prodded all over, staring up at the bed's canopy while she waited for him to tell her what was wrong—or at least, what was wrong *physically*.

She needed no help to understand why her emotions were thrown about like a boat in a storm. The exchange she'd had with Gabriel an hour before had taken an unexpected turn and it was a struggle to keep her face impassive as the doctor did his work. What she wanted was to be alone, to have the chance to privately re-examine the hurtful truths she'd learned, but it seemed her physician had other ideas.

With almost intolerable slowness he carefully

pressed down again. He seemed to be feeling for something, his grey eyebrows knitted together in concentration, until finally he straightened up with a nod.

'I believe I know what ails you, my lady.'

'I'm pleased to hear it. Will you need to bleed me?'

'I think in this instance it would be of little benefit.'

Louisa sat up, pulling her shawl around herself. There was a healthy blaze in the fireplace, but she felt cold none the less, the doctor's chilly touch only partly to blame. Gabriel's confession was the real guilty party, but it appeared she still wasn't yet to be granted time to consider it.

Doctor Gibson was regarding her closely through his round spectacles. 'You said your illness began just over a week ago and is usually at its worst when you wake.'

'That's correct.'

'And you report there are certain foods you can no longer tolerate? Certain smells also?'

'Yes.'

The doctor nodded again. 'I must beg your pardon for an indelicate inquiry, but may I guess that you have missed this month's course?'

Louisa felt herself colour. 'Well, yes.'

'Then I'm certain. Please accept my sincerest congratulations. You are with child.'

He beamed down at her, although Louisa could only stare back.

'I—I'm to have a child?'

The room fell away, the doctor's smiling face all she could see. Shock and amazement almost robbed her of speech, barely able to summon even the shortest of words. 'When?'

'Some time in the summer, perhaps around August. It isn't possible to be any more precise.'

Her jaw had taken it upon itself to slacken, something Doctor Gibson's dry chuckle implied he had noticed. 'You had no suspicions as to your condition?'

Dazed, Louisa shook her head. 'None at all. My mother never explained what signs a woman might look for to indicate such a thing.'

'Quite right. It's far better for a young lady to know too little about the subject than too much.'

She wasn't sure she agreed with his opinion, but in that moment, she wasn't sure of *anything*. That one simple phrase—*you are with child*—made her head spin and she knew she was hardly listening when the doctor went on.

'I'll inform his lordship. It's important he knows you will require special care.'

'No.'

She heard herself speak before she realised she'd opened her mouth. Her instinctive denial came out far too sharply, prompting Doctor Gibson's wiry eyebrows to raise. 'I mean, please don't,' she amended hastily. 'As this is to be my first child, I'd like to tell him myself.'

The doctor frowned. 'As you wish, my lady. But I'd

counsel you not to wait too long to share the happy discovery. You will need advice as to diet and exercise as well as adequate medical attention and I imagine Lord Harnham will want to make arrangements for a nurse as soon as possible.'

Louisa's jaw, previously loosened by astonishment, hardened. *Would* Gabriel think the discovery was a happy one? Until that morning she would have been confident the answer was yes, but now she wasn't so certain. What should have been wonderful news was cast into doubt by what she'd so recently learned about his view of her, her own fledgling happiness overshadowed by his misgivings, and as she tentatively laid a hand over her still-flat middle she felt conflicted delight and despair.

'Shall I ask your maid to bring Lord Harnham to you now?'

'No, thank you.' She attempted a smile, hoping a man so familiar with the human body might still think it was genuine. 'I think I need to compose myself first. I may take a few minutes alone.'

'Very good. It's of vital importance that you don't over-excite yourself. What you need now is rest and lots of it, and you absolutely *must not* fall off any more horses.'

Doctor Gibson bowed, ready to leave, and Louisa did her best to affect a curtsy while still propped up in bed.

'Thank you for coming, Sir. And please remember: I'd like to tell my husband myself.'

The doctor inclined his head with an air of resigned patience. Evidently he was well used to indulging the whims of his wealthy clients and he made no argument as he went to the door, turning back to give one last bow before stepping out and closing it behind him.

Louisa lay back, listening to his footsteps retreat down the corridor towards the stairs. With any luck he would be able to escape without meeting Gabriel along the way, leaving her to reveal her condition when she judged the moment was right.

*And when will that be?*

She drew her knees up towards her chest, folding her arms around them despondently. She hadn't expected a baby would come so soon, but she'd allowed herself to believe her blossoming connection with its father would mean he'd be pleased when the time came, yet that belief had been suddenly undermined.

He didn't trust her in the same way she did him. That was what their earlier conversation boiled down to and the knowledge stung like a paper cut doused in salt. She'd been ready to offer support and comfort in the face of his unhappiness, but he'd already known the rumours and hadn't said a word, keeping them to himself as if she couldn't be relied on to see them for the nonsense they were.

She didn't believe a single syllable of his old neighbours' whispering, but that wasn't the point. By keeping such a secret from her he had driven a wedge between them, pulling away when she'd thought they were growing closer by the day, and it made her wonder whether his regard for her had ever been real at all.

'Perhaps he never had room for me in his heart after all. What if I was deceiving myself that after the loss of Frederica, he would ever let anyone in again?'

The empty room gave no reply. The fire danced in the grate, throwing a warm light over the crumpled sheets, but Louisa felt as though she was a block of ice. With her hand still lying protectively over her midriff she pulled the blankets up higher, wishing she could wrap herself and her baby up and shut out the rest of the world. There was too much confusion, elation and excitement mixed up with pain, and despite the doctor's warning she didn't think she could bring herself to take Gabriel into her confidence as soon as she might have before.

## Chapter Eleven

*Dearest Gabriel,*
*I hope this letter finds you well. Some time has passed since I last had the pleasure of receiving a reply from you, and so I*

Without reading the rest of the letter Gabriel scrunched it into a ball and tossed it into his study's fireplace. It burned up immediately, reducing whatever Frederica's mother had written to ash, but that didn't stop him from knowing exactly what it had said.

'More requests for money, more pleading for influential introductions and more demands to see Leah; none of which I'm any more likely to grant since the last time that woman asked for kindnesses she doesn't deserve.'

He dropped heavily into the chair behind his desk. His mood had not been good even before the early post had arrived and now it was even worse, his relationship with his wife—both past and present—at the forefront of his mind.

Sighing, he rubbed the stubble on his chin. He hadn't had the patience to sit and be shaved that morning and he imagined Louisa would have noticed the prickly shadow at once had she looked at him across the breakfast table.

She hadn't, however, all her attention fixed on Leah instead, and he sighed again as he acknowledged he'd been a fool. If he'd been honest about Frederica from the beginning, Louisa wouldn't now be wondering whether their connection was a fraud and she wouldn't have withdrawn from him as if they barely knew each other at all.

In any other person he might have interpreted her reticence as sulking, but it was clear as day that her new distance from him was something else entirely. She didn't seem angry, only unhappy, and he knew better than most what it looked like when someone retreated into themself to avoid further pain. It was exactly what he'd done after Frederica's betrayal—except his caution had rebounded into causing suffering for someone else and he couldn't blame Louisa for now being reluctant to meet his eye, let alone speak to him in any length.

'I've barely had ten words from her these past two days,' he told a portrait of his father that hung above the mantlepiece. 'I don't even really know what Dr

Gibson said relating to her illness and I'm worried that she doesn't appear to be getting any better.'

The previous Lord Harnham didn't seem to have any advice. He gazed back at his son sympathetically but silently and Gabriel leaned back in his chair, looking around the study as if he might find inspiration elsewhere.

Louisa was still pale and wan and he was beginning to grow concerned. She'd been vague as to what the doctor had told her, only that his recommendation was she take plenty of rest, and it seemed that was all the prompting she'd needed to move into the bedchamber adjoining the one they'd previously shared.

Separate beds were no way to fix a marriage in Gabriel's opinion, but her health was more important than his feelings and so he'd raised no objection, although waking up alone for the past two mornings was not something he'd enjoyed.

'I only have myself to blame for that, however, as I'm sure you'd agree.'

Once again, his father merely watched him from a gilded frame. His mother's portrait didn't have much to say either, although Gabriel could have sworn he saw a trace of censure in her painted eye.

'Don't look at me like that, Mother. I don't need anyone to remind me what a mess I've made.'

His glancing around the room led him towards the fireplace. The brazen letter Frederica's mother had sent him was now nothing more than a smudge of soot, but even so he got up and reached for the poker, stirring up the embers until not a trace of paper remained.

How was it the ghastly woman still expected him to grant her favours after she had torn his reputation to shreds, or even bother to reply to her near-unceasing letters? The last time he'd seen his former parents-in-law had been a few days after Frederica's funeral and heaven knew they hadn't parted on good terms.

They had been far less upset at the death of their daughter than losing their stream of income, he recalled, and far too quick to 'offer' to take Leah off his hands despite never having shown an ounce of interest in her before. His refusal had caused a storm of false tears, but by then he'd known the truth, more likely to agree to surrender himself into their care than force such a fate on his child.

*Although she's not my natural child, is she? And I need to find a way to tell Louisa that without pushing her further away.*

He gave the fire one last poke, probably more savagely than was necessary. The conversation he needed to have was too important to delay, yet the thought of her drawn, pallid face held him back.

Perhaps it would be better to wait until she had recovered from whatever was ailing her before he shocked her once again? She'd been sick again that morning, as he'd overheard through the wall between their rooms, and at breakfast she'd looked as though she ought to return to bed. He had no right to invade her privacy with demands for an explanation, but his concern continued to rise, his mouth turning down at the corners as he replaced the poker and paced uncertainly into the centre of the room.

'I could consult Dr Gibson myself, but I don't think Louisa would appreciate me prying. If she wanted me to know the details of her illness, she would have told me herself and, since she has not, I can only assume she prefers me to remain in the dark.'

With his hands clasped behind his back he took another slow turn about the room. Louisa had been feeling nauseous for over a week, although she'd managed to keep it from him until the morning he'd seen the evidence for himself. She'd looked tired and pale, causing the doctor to recommend she rest, and he'd noticed himself that she now barely ate breakfast or many of the dishes she'd previously professed to like…

He stopped dead in his tracks.

Hadn't he seen those symptoms once before? The patient he'd known then had taken pains to hide them, just as Louisa had more recently, but the similarities were too great to conceal. Frederica had experienced exactly the same things when expecting Leah and all at once Gabriel felt the stuck key of his confusion turn in its lock.

*You idiot.*

Amazed at his own stupidity, he stood still, allowing the realisation to settle. How could he have taken so long to realise? It was true Frederica had hidden the worst of her sickness and fatigue from him, hoping not to draw attention to the child she carried that she knew might not be his, but all the same he should have been much quicker to guess the truth. All of Louisa's behaviour suddenly made sense and a great rush of excitement welled up inside him like water breaking through a dam, rising to wash away his unease of moments before—

Or at least, it tried to.

With alarming speed his excitement stuttered and fell away, a change of direction so abrupt it was like being yanked backwards by some invisible force.

He trusted Louisa, even if she thought he didn't. There was no chance whatsoever that if she was indeed in the family way anyone but he could have fathered her child, yet to his shame he felt doubt creep up from his core.

Horrified by the direction of his thoughts, he resumed his mindless striding about the room, but the notion would not be outrun. With every step it snatched at him, trying to trip him up, and despite his revulsion he found he couldn't shake it off.

'The very idea is absurd.'

A mirror hung on the wall between the portraits of his late parents and he glared into it, daring his reflection to disagree. 'She is *nothing* like Frederica. To think otherwise is an insult to Louisa and not something I'm willing to entertain.'

His mirror-image glowered back at him, its face a veneer of defiance. There was no softness to be found in the tight set of its lips, but to his dismay he caught a glimmer of fear in the dark eyes.

Louisa *had* favoured Sir Christopher before she'd married, hoping to become Lady Stanhope rather than Harnham. Was it possible she'd continued to care for the young knight even after she'd wed, in the same way Frederica had pined for Sir Cecil Allenby? He'd never imagined his first wife was capable of betraying him until it had happened and against every instinct to the contrary he couldn't help but wonder if Louisa could do the same.

Since he had learned the truth of Leah's paternity the idea of an expectant wife went hand in hand with infidelity and grief, an association he knew was unfair but persisted none the less, and although Louisa had done nothing to rouse his suspicions, he felt them stir all the same.

Bile rose at the back of his throat. Why hadn't she told him she was with child? Was it because he had upset her by keeping unsavoury secrets, or was it because she had something to hide? As much as he was disgusted with himself for asking the question it refused to be dismissed, echoes from years past ringing as loudly as if they'd been founded only days before.

Resting his fists on the fire's mantlepiece, he stared down into the flames.

Surely he was being ridiculous. He ought to be delighted, not afraid, but he knew why his fear loomed so large. His only experience of fatherhood had been tainted by the realisation Frederica had wanted another man. If it turned out Louisa felt a similar way, he didn't think he would ever be the same again.

*Because I love her.*

The thought was stark yet undeniable. Until that moment he hadn't wanted to look it in the eye, but there was no evading the truth. If the history that had destroyed his life was set on repeating itself then it would tear him to shreds, the heart Louisa had somehow repaired in danger of being broken once again. She'd overcome every obstacle he'd placed between her and his real self and now he cared for her with every fibre of his being, his feelings for her running deeper even than those he'd held for Frederica before her life had been cut short.

He took a long breath, holding it until his chest ached before he exhaled.

*Stop. You need to be calm.*

With difficulty Gabriel brought himself back under control. He was getting carried away. His desire for Louisa to feel the same things for him as he felt for her was so strong it made his mind race and with that conclusions could be jumped to that had no basis in the truth. The thing to do was speak to her rather than wound himself with assumptions and with another shuddering breath he stood up straight.

'I might be torturing myself for no reason,' he told

his parents as they gazed down at him from the walls. 'She may not even be with child at all, but either way the time has come to tell her how I feel. So much could have been avoided if I'd been honest from the beginning, but right now is the second-best time to start.'

Louisa felt like death.

Her stomach churned as she sat by the fire in her parlour, her sewing lying neglected in her lap. Her mouth held a strange metallic tang that didn't help with her nausea and even her breasts hurt as they pressed against her stays, another delightful symptom of her condition that nobody had seen to fit to warn her about. Under other circumstances she would have written to her mama for advice as to how to bear it, but of course she couldn't yet. She still hadn't told Gabriel his family was set to increase and the longer she waited the harder the task seemed, her worries growing until she didn't know which way to turn.

'Are you still feeling unwell?'

A voice from near her feet broke into her fretting. Leah had been reading so quietly Louisa had almost forgotten the girl was sitting on a cushion beside her chair and she quickly found a smile when a small blonde head appeared from behind the arm.

'A little. I'm certain it'll pass soon.'

To her surprise Leah leaped up. 'Wait a moment.

I have something to make you feel better. Let me fetch it.'

She scurried from the room. Left alone, Louisa took the opportunity to press her fingers against her tired eyes, the pressure behind them building with every sleepless night. Bathing them in warm water might bring some relief, but Leah returned before she could ring for a maid, the little girl standing in front of her with one hand behind her back.

'Here. These are for you.'

With endearing shyness Leah brought out a small bunch of wildflowers untidily tied with twine. 'I picked them myself from the gardens. I thought they might cheer you.'

Touched, Louisa took the posy and brought it up to her nose. The mild scent didn't go straight to her stomach as some other smells currently did and for that she was grateful, perhaps able to keep hold of her breakfast for a while longer.

'They're lovely. They certainly do cheer me, but not as much as your thoughtfulness does.' She cupped Leah's pink cheek. 'Thank you, dearest. You are the best medicine.'

The little girl looked delighted and Louisa felt her eyes prickle. The smallest thing was enough to make her tearful these days and Leah's sweet gesture was no exception, a tiny kindness coming at the very moment she needed it the most.

Sitting back in her chair, she held the flowers up to

her face again to hide the glitter among her lashes. At least she was confident Leah would be excited about the baby, even if it transpired Gabriel was not. His daughter had shown herself ready to accept the new people her father brought into her life and a sibling was sure to be even more agreeable than a stepmother.

*It would certainly be nice to have someone to share my happiness with*, she thought as she examined a petal. *Carrying my first child should be a joyous time, but how can I fully enjoy it when I don't know how Gabriel will take the news?*

Leah returned to her cushion and took up her book. The top of her head came just below the arm of the chair and Louisa stroked her hair, still holding the posy in one hand but the other gently smoothing the blonde curls.

*I'll need to tell him soon. I can't be upset he kept secrets from me only to do the same thing myself.*

It wasn't quite the same, however. He hadn't told her about the distressing rumours circulating about him because he didn't trust her and it was that lack of trust that caused her to hesitate now. Clearly their connection was not as strong as she'd thought and it made her question whether he would welcome having a child with her, especially since the first time he'd become a father had been as a result of real love.

The stinging behind her eyes intensified. When they had married, she'd known it had been against both of their wishes, and yet so much had changed she could hardly recall what life before Gabriel had been like. He was everything to her now and the knowledge he didn't feel the same sat inside her like a ball of thorns. She had thought he'd come to care for her, but she'd overestimated his regard and now she was lost, her heart at risk of being shattered by the one she'd hoped would keep it safe.

Her stomach took her despondency as a cue to lurch menacingly and, quickly placing the posy in her lap, she laid her hand over her middle. It was surely too early for it to be the baby she could feel moving about, but the thought of one day having a bump there to cradle came as a pinprick of sunlight among the dark clouds of her unhappiness—clouds that did not disperse when she heard a knock at the parlour door.

'May I come in?'

The anonymous knock had done nothing, but Gabriel's voice sent a thrill right through her. She'd hardly seen him for the past two days, keeping a careful distance while she tried to unscramble the chaos inside her head and despite her sorrow something within her leapt to know he was only on the other side of the door.

'You may.'

The door opened and Gabriel stepped into the room. Immediately her body wanted to lean towards him, but she made herself keep her seat as he threw her a swift nod.

'So this is where you've been,' he said to Leah,

looking down at her curled on her cushion on the floor. 'I thought the house seemed suspiciously quiet.'

He spoke lightly, but his tone didn't match his face. There was a curious rigidity in his features and Louisa's instinctive pleasure at seeing him changed swiftly into unease.

*What's the matter now?*

Fortunately, Leah didn't seem to have noticed her father's smile only touched the bottom half of his face. 'Yes, Papa. I've been keeping Louisa company as she's not feeling well.'

'Ah.' Gabriel flashed Louisa a brief glance. 'Still no improvement?'

'Not as yet.'

'I see. I'm sorry to hear that.'

There was a pause. It felt loaded, but Louisa wasn't sure what with, only that her apprehension was beginning to gain ground. Gabriel must have sought her out for a reason, but he didn't seem to know what to do now he was before her, hesitating with an uncertainty she didn't understand.

His eye fell on the posy in her lap. 'What is that?'

'I made it,' Leah answered proudly. 'To take Louisa's mind off her illness.'

Louisa nodded, glad of anything to break the awkward spell. 'It was an extremely kind thought. I don't think even Dr Gibson could have recommended a better remedy.'

Gabriel gave another unconvincing smile. His attention lingered on the little bunch of flowers and then Louisa saw something flit over his countenance.

'You know, Leah, when it comes to bouquets, I don't think a patient can have too many. May I task you with the responsibility of making a few more?'

Leah sat up. 'Could I use flowers from the hothouse?'

'Yes. I give you permission to pick as many as you like.'

There was no chance the girl could resist. 'I believe the gardener is outside now,' he went on invitingly. 'Why don't you go to speak to him? There's no time like the present.'

As predicted, Leah was on her feet at once. 'Don't worry, Louisa. I'll go now and I won't come back until I've made the prettiest bouquet you've ever seen.'

She patted Louisa's hand with precocious reassurance. The call of the usually forbidden hothouse was too seductive to ignore and she disappeared, banging the door shut behind her in her haste to get away before her father changed his mind.

Louisa braced herself as the slam rattled the delicate ornaments on her mantelpiece. The fine china figurines tinkled threateningly, but it was Gabriel's ambiguous presence that commanded her focus.

'Why do I have the feeling you sent her away deliberately?'

'Because I did. I'd like to speak to you without being overheard.'

She stiffened. 'What about?'

'I think you may already have an inkling.'

Gabriel turned away to stand in front of the fire. She could only see him from behind, but the tension in his shoulders set alarm bells shrilling, her anxiety peaking sharply as he dropped four soft words.

'Are you with child?'

Her breath caught. For a moment she couldn't reply and at her silence he looked back at her as if hoping to capture some tacit response.

It didn't cross her mind to feign ignorance. It was clear he already knew her secret and with her heart in her mouth she felt herself nod.

'Yes.'

Gabriel's face changed. For a split second, Louisa thought his clear apprehension had given way to delight, but then her heart came crashing down again as she realised she was wrong.

He seemed to grow still, his eyes the only thing that moved as they locked on to hers, and in them she saw confirmation of her very worst fears. He didn't smile or laugh or spring forward to catch her up in his arms; he just stared at her with an expression she couldn't name, only certain that it was not one of unbridled joy.

It was the reaction she'd expected, but prayed wouldn't come, and her unhappiness surged, almost stopping her lips from moving.

'I see the news is unwelcome.'

'Unwelcome? You think I'm not pleased?'

'I can see that you are not. Please don't try to pretend otherwise.'

'That isn't... '

Gabriel took a step towards her. His hands twitched forward as if he wanted to reach for her, but instead he balled them into fists at his sides. 'It isn't what you think.'

'No?' Louisa looked up at him, willing herself to keep hold of what little composure she had left. The tears that her condition ensured were never far away had begun to gather again and she stubbornly forced them back. 'I imagine most men would smile at the thought of having a child, not look as though they're being forced to the edge of a cliff.'

'I'm sorry. That isn't at all what I meant.'

He passed a hand over his face, the very image of a man trapped in a situation he desperately wanted to avoid. He looked like a living parcel of regret, and despite her own suffering Louisa couldn't help but want to ease his.

'You don't need to apologise to me,' she said quietly. 'I understand. I shouldn't have hoped for you to be as excited at the prospect of having another child as you were when Frederica was expecting. It was unfair for me to make any kind of comparison.'

The sound Gabriel made startled her. It was almost a growl and when she peered up at him she saw pure frustration written over his handsome features.

'No!'

He spread his hands, transforming them from fists to incredulously flat palms. The source of his frustration didn't appear to be her, however—it was himself he seemed to be rebuking as he paced away, only to immediately come circling back.

'I've allowed this misunderstanding to go on for too long,' he bit out. 'With your permission I'll explain why I struggle at the prospect of another child. Although I fear it may upset you to hear the reason, I still think it's your right to know.'

Louisa blinked up at him, incomprehension drying the tears trying to bead her lashes. 'What do you mean? What misunderstanding?'

The change in his manner was disorienting. One moment he had looked as though he wanted to walk away and the next that he might burst if she didn't hear him out, such a rapid change it made it hard to keep up. 'And why would your explanation upset me?'

Gabriel's mouth twisted. 'The truth walks side by side with a lie. I have made you unhappy once before by not being honest and I'm afraid in telling you what I've concealed I must do the same thing again.'

A sensation of dread mixed with powerful curiosity needled her. She had no idea what he was speaking of but she suddenly wanted to know more than anything, both for her own understanding and to stop Gabriel from seeming as though he might combust on the spot.

Carefully she got to her feet. The room moved as

she did, but she pushed through the unpleasant feeling to stand in front of him.

'Speak plainly. No matter how terrible you think it, I prefer that to a lie.'

She saw his throat contract. 'I believe you,' he muttered, his voice so low it was almost a hoarse breath. 'I believe, finally, that the past has no place in the present. Although it grieves me more than I can put into words, I have to tell you the truth…'

He paused.

'And that truth is, Leah is not my child.'

## Chapter Twelve

'What?'

Louisa stared at Gabriel, sure she must have misheard. 'What do you mean?'

'Just as I say. I will always consider Leah my daughter, but I am not her natural father.'

'But—'

Dazed, she tried to make sense of what he was saying. The little girl was the lasting legacy of his first marriage, conceived in wedlock between a husband and wife who had loved each other, and for Gabriel to suggest any different had to be some kind of horrible joke. If Leah wasn't his child, then she had to be someone else's, and for that to be the case his beloved Frederica would have needed to betray him with another man...

Dim realisation tried to break through the fog. It was almost too shocking to allow, but she knew Gabriel had sensed it.

'Yes. I think you're starting to understand.' His

expression held a combination of anxiety and relief. 'Will you walk with me? There's much more to say, but not here. If Leah has taught me anything, it's how much children like to listen at keyholes.'

Louisa knew she must have nodded as he began to lead her towards the door, although she couldn't recall having moved her head. It was too full of bewilderment to register anything else and she hardly noticed where she was being taken as he guided her to the front door and out into the cool, crisp air.

A shadow had fallen over Gabriel's face and he didn't look down as they crossed the lawn, only stopping once he had drawn them to shelter beneath a vast, spreading tree. A bench sat among the tangled roots and Louisa was glad to drop on to it, his confession and her own delicate condition joining forces to make her legs feel weak.

He didn't sit down beside her. A kind of nervous energy seemed to have taken hold of him and he couldn't keep still, instead pacing a few steps with his hands clasped behind his back. He might have been wondering where to begin with whatever else he had to say, but Louisa couldn't help him, only able to sit and watch as she waited for him to start making sense.

How long had he known he wasn't Leah's father? Did he know who *was*? And why had he decided to tell her this now, when he'd had countless other opportunities?

Question after question passed through her mind,

but none made it out of her mouth. Mute confusion was apparently something she and Gabriel had in common, but he managed to overcome his first.

'I'm sorry. I have so much to say to you, but now I find I don't know how to start.'

His restless striding was making her dizzy. Her nausea had been beaten back by amazement, but it threatened to return as he swung round again and the desire to avoid being reacquainted with her breakfast forced her to speak.

'Begin with Leah. Above all else, that's what I want to understand.'

Mercifully he stopped. 'Of course. You ought to know everything, but the only way for that is if I go back to before she was even born.'

'Then do.'

Gabriel rubbed his chin. It didn't look as though he'd shaved and the dusting of stubble enhanced the firm line, already clenched tight with strain. He obviously didn't want to start, but Louisa wasn't inclined to give him any choice, waiting in taut silence until he began.

'You need to realise that I met Frederica just after my father had passed,' he said with quiet regret. 'If circumstances had been different, I might have had more sense, but in my desire to escape my grief I seized on what I took to be love. I thought she was enchanting and although her place in society was far below mine it didn't stop me from wanting to make her my wife. She gave every indication that she returned my feelings and we were wed within weeks, the marriage hastened by her parents who insisted there was no reason to delay.'

He looked at her, no doubt wondering how his stilted speech was being received. 'Did you want me to carry on?'

'Yes. I'm listening.'

He gave her another hesitant glance, but then the pacing resumed.

'I believed we were happy together,' he continued reluctantly. 'She was everything I thought I wanted and she gave me no cause to doubt she felt the same. Her parents' manner was the only complaint I could have made: they were intensely overbearing and called constantly, forever asking for money and introductions to those they deemed influential, and although my regard for Frederica made me tolerant their greed soon wore thin. For my wife's sake, however, I never spoke a word against them and I forgot even that small irritation when she told me she was with child.'

He sighed. 'Looking back, I should have seen the signs. Frederica was vague as to when she would be confined and she tried to hide her symptoms as if to stop me from knowing too much about it. In hindsight I understand why.'

Louisa steadied herself against the back of the bench. Frederica had attempted to conceal her condition, just as she herself had for the past two days?

The pieces of the puzzle were beginning to fit together, but she didn't interrupt.

'The day Leah was born was one of the happiest of my life. She was so lovely to me, even when pink and wrinkled, although as the months passed and her features grew more distinct, I could see no resemblance between us. Her only likeness was to her mother, but as I had no reason to think anything was amiss I assumed Leah merely favoured Frederica more than me—a belief I held for three years.'

Gabriel paused again. 'It was Miriam who discovered the truth. She and my nieces had come to stay with us for the Season and one day she saw Frederica in a carriage kissing another man.'

Louisa stifled a gasp. She'd suspected what must have been coming, but all the same it dealt a sharp blow, compassion sweeping over her as she saw pain flit through Gabriel's eyes.

'At first, I didn't want to believe her. I thought there must have been some mistake, that Miriam had misunderstood, but my sister's no fool. She was certain of what she'd seen and so although I doubted her, I resolved to ask Frederica for the truth, not expecting she would crumble almost at once.'

'You confronted her?'

'That very night. I was gentle, still believing in her innocence, but I'd barely raised the subject before she confessed.'

Gabriel's voice grew low. 'She was relieved she

needn't hide her real feelings any longer. It seemed she had been in love with a man I knew vaguely named Sir Cecil Allenby when we met and had never stopped, even when she became my wife. She had never wanted to marry me and had only accepted at the insistence of her parents, who threatened to turn her out on to the street if she refused. My money was the only thing they valued—certainly more than their own daughter's happiness, which to them meant nothing at all. She had been schooled to acquire a wealthy husband to help elevate the family from their modest beginnings and when her parents saw she might become a baroness nothing would stand in their way.'

He lapsed into silence. His gaze was fixed on the Manor behind them, but Louisa had the impression he didn't see the red brick walls. He'd gone somewhere she couldn't follow and her own dread made her shy away from trying, fresh understanding bringing the truth home with terrible clarity.

'She told you all of this on the night of the storm? The same storm…?'

'That caused her to fall from her horse. Yes.'

Gabriel's expression was as bleak as a cold winter night. He seemed far away, untouchable as he retreated into the past and the memories that still had the power to wound.

'When she confessed Leah wasn't mine it felt as though she'd shot me through the heart. I'd loved that little girl for three years and to find out I had no claim to her was the most painful thing I'd ever experienced. I could have borne Frederica's infidelity, but snatching my child away from me was just too much...although her revelation that she intended to leave not only me, but Leah, too, was somehow even worse.'

Louisa started. 'What? She meant to abandon her own daughter?'

'Oh, yes.'

Gabriel laughed hollowly, although Louisa didn't think she'd ever heard anything less funny. 'Allenby enjoys the making of children, but not the raising of them, yet she chose to cleave to him instead of the innocent they had created together. Even the violence of the storm wasn't enough to make her delay going off to find him and she rode away while Leah was sleeping without even waiting to say goodbye.'

He shrugged. 'I should have stopped her,' he said frankly. 'I could have prevented her from having the accident, but in truth I couldn't bear for her to stay. If she was cruel enough to leave our daughter without a backwards glance, then I didn't want her to be near Leah any longer. I allowed Frederica to push past me to the door and I've known I bear some responsibility for her death ever since.'

He stopped talking. He seemed to have finished his tale and in the silence that followed it Louisa found she didn't know what to say.

It was a horrible story. Gabriel looked wretched as

he stood alone beneath the tree and sympathy washed over her more powerful than any before.

The woman he'd loved had preferred another and discovering it had made him want to shut himself off from the world. He hadn't been mourning all those years, still pining for the wife he'd lost—he'd been protecting himself from being hurt again, as well as battling with his guilt, and the desire to show him he didn't need to any longer was so strong it would have knocked her off her feet if she hadn't been all but frozen on the bench. She ached to comfort him—but there was still much more she needed to know, confusion as well as her own unhappiness still sitting over her heart.

Doubtless it was difficult for him to speak of what had happened…although that didn't explain why he had waited so long to tell her the truth.

'But… I don't understand. Why were people so certain you'd harmed Frederica? And if you already knew what they were saying, the things you declined to share with me, why didn't you defend yourself?'

She saw him brace himself against the direct hit, clearly not requiring any reminder of his deception.

'The storm that raged on the night she died was the worst we'd had in years,' he murmured. 'Only a madwoman would have gone out in it, so nobody could comprehend why she hadn't stayed safe at home. My neighbours assumed she must have had a good reason to venture out—a reason her parents were more than happy to invent.'

His lip curled. 'At the funeral Frederica's father openly asked me what financial settlement I meant to offer them since their daughter was no longer alive to connect us. He told me of his role in forcing her to marry me as though I should have considered myself in his debt instead of appalled by his cruelty. For my part I told him he and his wife would never see another penny of my money and in their desire to punish me for cutting them they made up the lie that I had been so abusive that Frederica had been fleeing from me when she died.'

The air was chill, but it was the quiet horror in her husband's eyes that turned Louisa's bones to ice, their darkness taking on a haunted look that cut her to the quick.

'But you didn't deny it? Surely your neighbours would have believed you?'

He shook his head. 'If I'd explained why Frederica had really been leaving me when she went out in the squall it would have exposed Leah's illegitimacy. I would *never* shame her so, especially when her real father was known as a notorious rake.'

Gabriel's face darkened. 'As I told you before: she may not be mine by blood, but I will always think of her as my daughter. Allenby has other children he doesn't claim and I resolved Leah would never be one of his cast-offs, even if it meant my name was dragged through the mud to protect hers. I refused to explain the accident and so my neighbours assumed the rumours of my brutality—and Frederica's desperation to escape it—must be true.'

Louisa sat for a moment, trying to process what she had heard. She realised she'd barely been breathing as she'd listened and her chest felt tight, her brow similarly contracting as she followed his reasoning to its conclusion. 'So that's why you didn't tell me Leah wasn't yours? You were worried I might tell someone and that because of my idle chatter Leah would be disgraced before she was even old enough to understand why?'

Gabriel looked pained, but he didn't turn away. 'I won't try to deny it. Her disgrace was certainly one thing I wanted to avoid, although Frederica's parents coming to claim her was another.'

He must have seen how she stiffened. With a handful of words, he had thrown her character into question and it was clear he'd realised it as he came closer to the bench.

'They used their daughter to their advantage,' he went on hurriedly. 'They never once thought of her happiness or what she might have wanted from her life. Their only goal was to push her into a marriage that would benefit them and as such began training her as bait when she was just a child. I couldn't let them do the same to Leah. I'm certain they didn't know about Frederica's infidelity—she wouldn't have wanted to risk their anger—and if they *had* known Leah wasn't mine, they would have tried to take her long before now.'

Louisa nodded slowly. The air seemed suddenly more bitter than ever and she pulled her shawl more tightly around her, although somehow it didn't help her to feel any warmer.

His argument made sense, but it hurt all the same, his lack of faith in her biting too hard and too deep to immediately forgive.

Of course Gabriel wanted to protect his child. For him Leah's safety came first and she wouldn't dream of reproaching him for it. The little girl's well-being was too precious to risk, but the fact he had ever thought *she* might be the one to risk it shone a damning light on how he saw her. It was the final proof that any hope she'd had that they had been drawing closer together had been false, her dreams so utterly and completely shattered that when Gabriel reached for her hand she couldn't stop herself from pulling away.

The power of Gabriel's dismay almost felled him where he stood.

Louisa was looking at him, but there was no light in her eyes. When he'd tried to touch her, she'd shied back as though he would have stung her, the hand he'd hoped to take hold of now bundled in her lap.

'I would never do anything to harm Leah,' she said softly. 'I thought you knew that.'

'Now I do, of course, but not at first. We were strangers when we wed and—'

'We haven't been strangers for *months*,' Louisa interjected, an edge creeping into her voice. 'You could have told me the truth long ago, but you chose not to. For all this time I thought we were making progress, that perhaps we were building something worthwhile, but in reality you've been hiding all along.'

She ended unsteadily and he saw her bite her lip as if to stop it from shaking. In the wintry sun she was more beautiful than ever, but sadder, too, and internally Gabriel cursed himself with every swearword he knew.

This was what he'd been afraid of. In explaining himself he'd been forced to admit how much Frederica had damaged his ability to trust and it was no wonder Louisa took it as an attack. He was making accusations she didn't deserve and he was just racking his brain for how he was supposed to make things right when she spoke again.

'Would you even have told me *now* if I hadn't been with child? You said you wanted me to understand everything, but—'

She stopped abruptly, drawing in a snatched breath. 'Oh. Of course.'

To his alarm she stood up far too quickly. The movement seemed to make her dizzy, but she twisted away when he tried to steady her, that fleeting rejection like an arrow to his heart.

'That's why you didn't seem pleased to learn I was expecting, wasn't it?' she demanded, her face blanched the colour of cream. 'That's what you meant when you said the reason might upset me. You thought perhaps I had done the same thing as Frederica and that the child I carry might not be yours?'

The bottom fell out of Gabriel's stomach.

He could have lied. He could have tried to soften the blow, but dishonesty was how they had come to such a pass and any further bending of the truth would only make things worse.

'For a moment. Yes.'

Louisa's lips parted on a gasp. They looked pale, as if shock had drained them of blood, and it occurred to him with a thud of despair that he would probably never be allowed to kiss them again.

'How could you?' she asked hoarsely. 'How could you doubt me like that? Doubt *our* child?'

She wavered and again he tried to support her, but she shook herself free, retreating to stare back at him from behind the bench. It was a flimsy construction and he could have easily set it aside, but he didn't try to approach her again, even though every inch of him longed to catch her up in his arms.

'It was never my intention to wound you. Please try to understand.'

Louisa clutched the back of the bench, her bare hands gleaming white. 'I am trying. I'm truly sorry for how much you've suffered. You've been through such torment and I wish it wasn't so. If I could take some of the pain from you, I would—but how can you expect me to forget what you thought I was capable of, just like that, when I've never given you reason to doubt?'

The tremor in her voice was more pronounced. It suggested tears might be brewing, but if so, she did well to hold them back, her eyes clear as they fixed on him.

'Who did you think the man was? Who did you think I'd be willing to betray you for, that could tempt me to do something so abhorrent?'

Gabriel couldn't remember ever having been asked a question he wanted to answer less. Louisa's unhappiness and his shame at having caused it seized him in a punishing grip, however, squeezing the truth from him regardless of his reluctance.

'Sir Christopher Stanhope.'

*'Christopher?'*

She stared at him incredulously. 'What I felt for him was so childish and fleeting it doesn't bear remembering. Since you and I wed he's hardly crossed my mind, any thoughts of him replaced completely by...'

'By what?'

'Nothing. It doesn't matter now.'

She seemed to withdraw into herself. Whatever she'd been about to say had been tossed aside and Gabriel burned to know what it was, wondering with a sinking feeling whether he had just made her claw back something he would very much like to have heard.

He wanted to step forward, but that damned bench was still in the way. Louisa stood behind it as though it could protect her from any further hurtful words and he couldn't bring himself to breach her defences, the pain he had caused her written clear on her pale countenance.

'Even if I had retained some feelings for him, I wouldn't have acted on them,' she asserted, her voice now determinedly controlled. 'I am your wife and you are my husband, and there has never been room in my marriage for anyone else.'

The breeze lifted a copper curl and she brushed it back behind her ear, a quick movement, but one that showed her hands were not as steady as her tone, and he felt a sharp stab of concern alongside the other emotions writhing inside him. It was a bad idea for a woman in Louisa's condition to be outside, cold and upset. As he was the one who had caused her to be in such a state it seemed unlikely she'd listen to his advice, but nevertheless he had to try.

'Perhaps we should continue this discussion inside. This wind is increasing and you ought to keep warm.'

As predicted, she shook her head. 'I don't think there's much left to discuss. I might return to the house, but there's no cause for you to accompany me.'

He tried to summon some argument before she could turn away—although what it would have been he didn't know—but she spoke again before he could open his mouth.

'There *is* one important thing I'd ask while we can't be overheard. What of Leah? She matters more than either of us. Do you intend to tell her the truth, or will you keep her in the dark, too?'

Desperation rising, Gabriel pushed a hand through his hair. Everything was falling apart, but even so Louisa still considered his daughter before herself, once again showing the kind-heartedness his stupidity had let slip through his fingers. 'Not yet. I'll say nothing until she's old enough to understand. All she needs to know for now is that she's loved.'

'On that at least we can agree.' Louisa didn't loosen her hold on the bench, using it to help her stand motionless against the wind. 'You may not believe it, but I have only ever wanted her happiness. I confess I can't see how telling a six-year-old child she was unwanted by both of her natural parents will in any way enhance it.'

At last surrendering her vice-like grip on the wooden rail, she stood back. Gabriel felt his muscles twitch with the urge to move towards her, but he made himself keep still, forcing himself to obey the very clear signs that she didn't want his touch. For his part he craved nothing more than to feel her hands on him again, yet such a thing seemed suddenly impossible, the woman he loved now looking at him as though he was someone she barely knew.

'I suppose you did warn me,' she murmured, hardly loud enough for him to hear. 'You said the truth was upsetting and I wanted it none the less. Perhaps it's still better I know where I really stand rather than living a lie.'

She paused to pull her shawl closer about her shoulders. Her body was shaking now as well as her hands and he could hardly bear to watch, horribly afraid it wasn't just because of the cold.

'I knew you didn't marry me because you wanted to. You made your feelings on that account quite clear and I never resented you for it. I had hoped, however, that at the very least you might have more respect for me than to confuse me with your first wife.'

'Louisa. I—'

At his fraught lurch forward she held up a hand, sidestepping any attempt he might have made to reach out for her. 'Leave me be, Gabriel. I need some time to come to terms with what you've told me…and how I now know you truly feel.'

## Chapter Thirteen

Christmas came and went, and still nothing was as it had been before.

For Leah's sake they had gone on with the festivities, pushing through so she didn't miss out, but Gabriel knew it had been a trial for Louisa as well as himself. Every time he looked at her, she'd seemed far away, only snapping to attention when Leah was close by, and she hadn't moved back into their bedroom since she'd vacated it after Dr Gibson had recommended she take plenty of rest.

She might pretend she was following medical advice, but they both knew the truth: she could hardly bring herself to be in the same room as him, let alone the same bed, and as the days passed Gabriel despaired more and more. They were civil to each other, but nothing deeper than that, anything he'd dared dream was blossoming between them now pulled out by its roots.

*That wasn't what I meant to happen. I meant to re-*

*move any obstacles that might be standing between us—but how can I tell her how I feel about her now, when I've been such a fool?*

Sitting on the edge of his lonely bed, he rubbed his aching eyes. Sleep was something he'd been getting far too little of since Louisa had withdrawn from him, his nights haunted by thoughts of his own stupidity and regret at the pain it had caused.

If he had handled the situation better, he could have confessed what was in his heart and she might even have been pleased to hear it, but surely she wouldn't welcome a declaration from a man who had called her principles into question in at least two different ways. Every time he recalled her expression when she'd realised what he'd suspected her of he recoiled inside, unable to bear the image of such unhappiness on the face of the woman he loved, yet at a loss as to how to fix what he'd broken.

A low, familiar noise caught his ear.

Louisa's bedroom was next to his. They were linked by an adjoining door that she kept firmly locked, but that didn't stop her voice from drifting beneath it and he stilled to listen to the sweet tone. More than anything he wanted to hear it at closer quarters, but as it was his fault she no longer spoke more than a few words in his presence he would have to be grateful for what little he could get.

Still listening, he heard another voice join the first. Evidently Leah was in there with her, although that was hardly a surprise. Since they had told her she was to have a brother or sister she'd barely left Louisa's side, apparently considering herself both guard and nurse, and it was a comfort of sorts to know there was at least one person at Sisslehurst who wasn't currently miserable. Leah was delighted by the news and had thrown herself into helping with the preparations—which, given what was to happen that day, could only be a good thing.

With a hint of foreboding, he stood up from the bed. Perhaps it had been a mistake to allow Louisa's mother to organise a gathering in honour of the forthcoming baby? She—and Louisa, he supposed, although it was clear the scheme was Mrs Burcombe's idea—had asked his permission to hold the event at Sisslehurst and of course he'd agreed, but he'd been unable to tell whether Louisa actually *wanted* to host an at home when she felt so little like celebrating. If he'd refused it would have given her an excuse to dodge the obligation, but she hadn't given him any clues and now it was too late to change his mind.

He sighed. A husband shouldn't have to gather his nerve before he went to speak to his wife, but as he crossed to the door that led on to the landing he realised he was doing exactly that. He was expected in Warwick that afternoon for a meeting with his bookkeeper and wanted to check on Louisa before he went, although he doubted his attentions would be received with much enthusiasm.

Stepping out on to the landing, he took the two paces needed to bring him to her door and knocked gently.

'Louisa. May I come in?'

The hum of voices coming from inside stopped abruptly. There was a short pause and then, after one last murmur, the door swung open.

Leah stood on the threshold. 'You may enter, Papa, but I'm afraid I can't stay. I'm going down to the drawing room. I must make sure everything is ready before the guests arrive.'

She spoke with such an air of solemn importance that he almost smiled. Clearly she believed herself to be hostess-in-chief and he stood smartly aside to let her pass.

'Of course. Don't let me delay you.'

His daughter swept away as if on pressing business and, with a mixture of anticipation as well as reluctance, he entered the bedroom.

Louisa looked up as he came through the door, her face reflected in her dressing-table mirror. She was sitting before the glass adjusting a couple of loose curls, her back turned to him, but even without the mirror he thought he could have guessed her state solely from the stiffness of her spine.

'Good morning.'

She nodded in response to his bow. 'Good morning. Did you wish to speak to me?'

'Not about anything important. I just wanted to let you know I was leaving for Warwick shortly.'

She nodded again. Her gaze had switched to the clusters of ringlets by her ears and she didn't seem inclined to look at him, her eyes turned determinedly forward as he stood just inside the door. 'Very good. Thank you for keeping me informed.'

Louisa might not want to glance at him, but that didn't stop Gabriel from having a good view of her. Her copper hair was pinned up in a stylish knot, leaving the nape of her neck exposed, and he had to clasp his hands behind his back to help restrain the urge to cross the room and run a finger over that delicate curve.

The skin there would be warm and he knew it was soft from the hours he'd spent exploring her body when she'd been happy to lie in his arms, an occurrence he acknowledged with a pang was unlikely to be repeated. It was a particular kind of torture to be mere feet away, but not allowed to get any closer, relieved to be in her orbit, but at the same time reminded of what had been lost…

With a slight suggestion of self-consciousness, she stood up. When she turned to the side the outline of a small bump was *just* visible beneath her skirts and Gabriel had to twine his hands together more tightly to control the desire to cup it with his palm. He was tempted every time he saw it, excited for what he knew was growing inside even if Louisa thought otherwise, although of course the desire to touch his wife was nothing new.

He watched as she pushed her hands into the small of her back and stretched. She was still a little pale, but for the most part she seemed better than she'd been previously—or, at least, better physically. She rested in the afternoons and took care not to overexert herself, although that didn't prevent the hesitation that still lurked in the back of his mind.

'Are you sure you won't find it too taxing to host today? I can always stay if you'd prefer.'

At last, she spared him a glance. 'I'm fine. It's kind of you to offer, but I imagine you'd rather boil your own head than attend an afternoon at home with so many of our female acquaintance.'

It wasn't a very tactful way of putting it, but Gabriel couldn't argue. It was true that attending a women's tea party didn't rank particularly highly with him as an enjoyable way to spend an afternoon. The occasion was meant to be a gathering of their female family and friends and he had to admit listening in to a roomful of chatter about labour and difficult births was not his idea of a good time.

However, he merely shrugged. 'I won't pretend I have any opinion as to fashionable nightgowns, but none the less I'd be happy to stay if you needed me.'

He paused, leaving space for her to respond. Part

of him hoped she'd say yes, extending an invite to spend time with her he knew he didn't deserve, but the greater, more rational part of him wasn't surprised when she shook her head.

'No, thank you. As I said—I'm certain I'll be fine.'

She still stood in front of her dressing table. She hadn't come towards him: she kept her distance, one hand now placed protectively over her subtle bump, and it stung him to wonder whether she kept her distance just for herself or also to safeguard their child. It should have been a joyous time for her, but he had soured it with his insistence on dragging his past along with him, and he was almost glad when she turned away again and he was spared the sight of her drawn, careworn face.

Louisa opened her jewellery box and he decided it was time to leave. If he stayed much longer, he'd have to watch her hold one glittering necklace up to her throat after another, trying to decide from her reflection which one to choose, and to have his attention drawn to the tempting dip between her collarbones wouldn't help him to drag himself away.

'I'm leaving now. I hope you enjoy yourself later.'

'Thank you.'

She didn't look round again. Bent over the jewellery box, she gave the impression she was waiting for him to go and, although his arms felt heavy with dismay, he made himself push the door open and leave her in peace.

\* \* \*

Settling back against the cushions of the sofa, Louisa finished yet another cup of tea she hadn't had to pour. Apparently even lifting a teapot was considered too much exertion for someone in her condition and it was slightly alarming to be surrounded by a roomful of ladies so concerned with her every move.

Aunt Eliza had arrived with a jug of nourishing calf's foot jelly. Another aunt, on Gabriel's side this time, had brought a recipe for a tisane certain to ward off fever after the birth. Her closest friend in the neighbourhood had tasked herself with passing pieces of cake whenever she suspected Louisa might be feeling faint and Mama had plumped the sofa cushions so vigorously it felt like sitting on a cloud. The parlour was abuzz with the swapping of advice and sometimes frightening stories of childbed stretching back many years, the room growing warmer as so many well-meaning bodies crowded around their overwhelmed hostess.

If she was honest, presiding over a gathering was the very last thing she felt like doing. For the last few weeks every day when she woke from her fitful sleep it was with a weight on her chest and an empty pillow next to her, both caused by the chasm that had opened between her and Gabriel, and that morning hadn't been any different.

She missed him: his warmth beside her in bed and the way he made her heart skip with the power of a single glance, the gleam in his dark eyes sometimes so wicked it made her blush. There was none of that now, however, only unhappiness and the distance she was trying to keep to spare herself more hurt, essential since she'd learned for certain her feelings were not returned.

That day beneath the tree had wrenched the scales from her eyes and there could be no going back. Before then she'd harboured hopes their marriage might be turning into something real, but Gabriel had torn that dream apart, exposing exactly how badly she had been wrong. If he truly cared for her, there was no way he could have thought her capable of the same betrayal as Frederica and the fact he drew any similarities between his two wives told her all she needed to know.

Aware the false smile she wore was in danger of slipping, Louisa pulled it back into place. It wouldn't do for her guests to suspect she was anything other than delighted to be in their company and she kept the upward tick of her mouth even as her cheeks began to ache.

He had hurt her, humiliated her, made her wonder how she could have been so blind—and yet, despite it all, the well of her compassion refused to run dry. The reason Gabriel didn't trust her was because he'd been taught such a harsh lesson three years before and even amid her own suffering she still hated to think of his.

To find out Leah wasn't his natural daughter must

have been an unendurable agony and she could understand why he feared the same thing happening again…but understanding and accepting were two very different beasts and just because she saw his reasoning didn't lessen the pain it had caused.

Leah was perched beside her on the arm of the sofa and, without prompting, she produced a fan from somewhere among the folds of her skirt.

'Are you too hot, Louisa? Let me.'

She flapped it in front of Louisa's face with more enthusiasm than skill, but her thoughtfulness was appreciated all the same.

'Thank you, dearest. As always, you're very considerate.'

Blinking a little more rapidly than normal from the sheer force of the breeze being directed into her eyes, Louisa squeezed the girl's knee. Her feelings towards her stepdaughter hadn't changed one bit on learning there was no blood tie to Gabriel, no matter what he might have imagined. Leah was the innocent victim of others' choices and deserved to be protected from their consequences for as long as possible, although of course that couldn't be for ever.

She would have to be told of her true parentage eventually, when she was old enough to understand, but until that day Louisa was resolved the child would never have reason to suspect she had ever been unwanted by the people who should have cherished her the most.

She looked around the room, trying to stop her eyes from watering from the little girl's energetic assistance. A gaggle of her mother's friends were swapping tales of wet nurses nearby while Mama herself stood surveying the scene with obvious satisfaction. The gathering had been her idea: all of her friends had to be made suitably jealous now her once-overlooked daughter was luxuriously installed as a wealthy baroness, neatly ignoring the fact that for most of Louisa's life it had been Mrs Burcombe herself doing much of the overlooking. It had proved impossible to find a reason to refuse that didn't reference the cracks in her marriage and so Louisa had relented, although she found she was regretting it more and more as the minutes ticked by.

*A tea party to celebrate my first child should be pleasant, but how can I fully enjoy anything to do with the baby when its father has cast such a damning cloud?*

Suddenly desperate for space in which to breathe, Louisa set down her empty teacup. 'Would you excuse me a moment, dearest? I think I'd like to stretch my legs.'

She made to stand up. Immediately a number of hands shot out to steady her, but she politely waved them away, determined to stand on her own two feet.

'You'll soon change your mind.'

Aunt Eliza had materialised out of the crowd and she shot Louisa a knowing, although not entirely ladylike, grin. 'When you're bigger you'll want all the help you can get.'

'I'm sure you're right. Until then, however, if I can get up unaided, I will.'

With great effort she returned her aunt's smile. Eliza had three children of her own so could be trusted to know what she was joking about, although her face became more serious as she linked Louisa's arm.

'So. Married life is suiting you?' Eliza murmured as together they moved towards a window in search of slightly cooler air. 'I was worried at first, given how you and Gabriel began, but you seem more or less content.'

It was hardly a question Louisa could answer honestly, yet she hesitated to tell an outright lie.

'We muddle along. It seems strange now that I ever thought so poorly of him.'

*That* at least was the truth. She could hardly remember now a time when she hadn't loved him, although of course that love had brought her little joy. It had torn a hole in her heart and she didn't know how to mend it, but she would never admit as much to her aunt. Nobody needed to know of her pain and so she kept it inside, saying nothing as Eliza drew her closer to the cool glass.

Settling herself on the window seat, Louisa sneaked a sideways look at her aunt. Something had been niggling at her and while they were sitting so close together, currently unobserved, it seemed a good time to ask.

'Aunt Eliza… Did you know what was being said about Gabriel in Staffordshire? The whispers that existed before we wed?'

'I'm not sure what you mean. What whispers?'

There was no trace of deception in Eliza's frown. Clearly she had no idea and Louisa sought to backtrack before she gave too much away. 'Nothing of note. Just some silly rumours about his first wife.'

'Hmm.' Eliza's eyes narrowed, but to her credit she didn't try to push for more details. 'No. I didn't and still don't know of any idle talk. People should let the poor woman rest, though, rather than speak of business that isn't their own.'

'I agree.'

Louisa nodded, mildly relieved. It would have been another unpleasant surprise to find her aunt had known of the scandal and decided not to mention it, and there had been quite enough surprises already.

Eliza regarded her closely. 'Is it anything you're worried about?'

Summoning her best impression of uninterest, Louisa lifted one shoulder. She wouldn't have wanted to discuss the terrible gossip even if Eliza *had* known of it—anything that caused her to recall the day her world had fallen apart not a topic on which she wished to dwell. 'No. As with any nonsense, it's not worth giving any thought to.'

A sudden burst of tinkling laughter made both women look across the room. Mrs Burcombe had evidently just said something her friends found excessively witty and Louisa saw her aunt's eyes narrow in response.

'That reminds me. I must speak to your mama. It's Emanuel's birthday next Thursday and I want to invite her and your father—and you and Gabriel, of course—to dine with us. Will you excuse me?'

Eliza rose from the window seat, leaving Louisa alone. It was agreeable to have a moment to herself amid the bustle and noise, the chance to let her lips fall out of their pretended curve; but then she noticed Leah.

Despite an endearing attempt to hide it, the little girl was clearly bored rigid. Her eyes had taken on a vague sheen as she sat quietly on the sofa, surrounded by adults chattering about things she neither understood nor had any interest in, and Louisa felt a stab of sympathy. She could still recall *exactly* how dull it had been to endure her mother's at homes when she'd been around the same age and with a wave to catch her attention she beckoned Leah to her.

'Sweetheart. I need your opinion.'

The little girl's face brightened as she came closer. 'What about?'

'I'm concerned about our guests being hungry. Do you think we have enough cake?'

Louisa bit her lip to hide her first genuine smile

in weeks as Leah eyed the refreshment table guiltily. 'I'm not sure. Someone *has* been eating a lot of it.'

'I think you're right. Could you go down to the kitchen and speak to the cook? I'm sure she must have more in the oven and most likely she'll need someone to sample it before sending it up.'

Louisa waved regretfully at the crowded room. 'I hope you don't mind my asking. I'd go myself, but I ought to stay with our guests.'

Leah's response was immediate. 'I can do that for you. You don't need to worry.'

'Thank you.' Louisa gave a sigh of relief. 'It's certainly useful to have a second hostess. Take as long in the kitchen as you need. We must be sure everything is satisfactory.'

With businesslike swiftness Leah left the room, her delight at having something important to do—and more cake to eat—clear, and Louisa envied her escape. She couldn't abandon her guests, however, and as she looked around the room again, she knew she ought to be more grateful so many ladies had come to wish her well, even if their number had made the parlour increasingly humid. From her perch on the window seat she had a good view of the various groups scattered about, but it was a solitary figure in the far corner that suddenly caught her eye.

The woman wasn't engrossed in conversation with anyone else. She was peering around the parlour as if in search of someone, although the manner in which she was doing so seemed almost furtive. Her face was half-hidden beneath a lace cap, but all the same it was vaguely familiar in a way Louisa couldn't quite place—perhaps she had been at the wedding, a day so dizzying many of her memories of it were now a blur? Certainly the woman wasn't one of her mother's friends, even if she was the right age to be of Mrs Burcombe's social circle. She looked to be in her mid-fifties, attractive and well dressed, and as she craned her neck to see over the heads of those around her something about her profile made Louisa pause.

*I'm certain I've seen her before. She must be from Gabriel's side of the family. Odd that she doesn't seem to have anyone to talk to among her own relations.*

With some reluctance she stood up. If none of the woman's own relatives were in any hurry to converse with her, there was probably a reason for it, although that made no difference. As hostess it was her job to make sure all of her guests enjoyed themselves and even if she had no idea who the woman was, she still couldn't allow her to remain ignored and alone.

Carefully she threaded her way through the throng towards the quiet corner. The woman saw her coming; for one strange moment it struck Louisa that her mystery guest seemed to freeze, but when she smiled the other woman replied—slightly hesitantly—in kind.

'Good afternoon,' Louisa said with forced brightness. 'I'm so sorry we haven't spoken until now. It was very good of you to come.'

She curtsied, praying the stranger would drop some hint as to her name. It was highly embarrassing to have someone in her house whose identity was a complete unknown, but it seemed she wasn't to be given any clues.

The woman offered a curtsy of her own, although her lips remained sealed. Other than a swift glance towards the door, she didn't give anything away, but Louisa was not to be deterred.

She tried again. 'I hope your journey here was tolerable. It's a pleasure to see you again.'

Thankfully her guest seemed to recover her tongue. 'Again, ma'am? I don't believe we've met before.'

'Oh.'

Confused and more than a little discomfited Louisa quickly headed off a frown. If they had never met, how was it the woman's face was so familiar? 'My apologies. I was so sure we had. You *are* a relation of Gabriel's, though?'

'In a manner of speaking.'

Louisa nodded as pleasantly as she could. For some reason, however, unease had begun to take hold and it didn't abate as she looked down into the older woman's uncannily recognisable countenance. She found she instinctively disliked her: the surreptitious way she'd surveyed the parlour was suspicious and her smile didn't give any animation to her cool blue eyes. Something about her was unsettling and Louisa couldn't completely pinpoint what it was, only that she abruptly understood why no one had seemed to want to draw the woman into a cosy fireside chat.

It was an unforgivable offence for a hostess to feel such aversion to a guest, but it was true none the less, and despite what social etiquette demanded she realised she couldn't wait to walk away.

'Well. I'm sure he'd be glad you're here. Oh—if you'll excuse me, I must just speak with my cousin.'

Fortunately, Uncle Emmanuel's eldest daughter passed by at exactly the right moment. In linking her arm Louisa was able to escape to the other side of the room and although she had to suffer a harrowing account of a dishonest servant as they walked, she considered it a small price to pay. The unknown woman watched her go with her cold eyes and Louisa had the disagreeable sensation they were boring into her back as she moved away.

Once ensconced on a sofa again, however, and her cousin disappeared into the crowd, she shook her head at her folly. What was wrong with her? The poor woman probably had no idea her manner was so offputting and Louisa felt a pinch of shame. She ought to be hospitable to all of her husband's relatives, not just the amiable ones…although as she saw someone approaching her sofa, she reflected that was not always easy.

Miriam was drifting towards her and Louisa suppressed a groan. It had been kind of her sister-in-law to make the journey to Sisslehurst for the occasion, especially considering how ill riding in a carriage apparently made her, but her presence hardly helped ease Louisa's mind. She was too reminiscent of Gabriel and had shared his suspicions as to his new wife's trustworthiness, an insult it was difficult for Louisa to ignore. Her attendance at the Manor suggested a desire to make amends, however, and when Miriam was close enough to hear a mutter Louisa put her to good use.

'Miriam. That lady over there. Who is she? A relation of yours, I know, but what's her name?'

Turning slightly, Miriam squinted over the back of the sofa. 'Which lady?'

'The one in the corner, standing alone. I could have sworn I'd met her before, but she says not.'

She didn't want to seem as though she was staring at her anonymous guest, so instead Louisa kept her eyes on Miriam as she peered in the direction of Louisa's subtle nod. For a second nothing appeared to register, but then she blanched a stark white.

'What is *she* doing here?'

Her sister-in-law's voice was so harsh Louisa felt a reflexive thrill of fear. 'I've no idea. I didn't invite her. Is something wrong?'

A transformation had come over Miriam's features. Before she had been softer, perhaps intending to make up for her brusqueness the first time they had met, but now her lips were pulled taut and she seemed almost ready to fly across the room.

'That woman is Mrs Maltravers. *Frederica's mother.*'

'*What?*' Disbelief launched Louisa to her feet. 'Why on earth would Frederica's mother be at Sisslehurst? Surely Gabriel didn't invite her?'

'No.' Miriam ground the single syllable out through her teeth, still staring towards the corner. 'There's no chance he would want her in his house, not even if he lived for a hundred years.'

Louisa spun round to follow Miriam's glare. The woman—Mrs Maltravers—was too busy with another study of the parlour to notice she was being watched and Louisa felt a sickening swoop of dread.

*That* was why she knew her face. Mrs Maltravers looked just like her late daughter, who in turn had passed on her fair prettiness to Leah. There was a strong resemblance between the three generations and Louisa's insides plunged again as she recalled what Gabriel had told her about the older woman's plotting, her callous willingness to use her own family to further her aims the cause of so much of his pain.

'You're right.' Louisa placed a hand on the back of the sofa to steady herself. Confusion still rattled her, but a growing pulse of anger had begun to beat in her veins. 'If Gabriel didn't ask her, how is it she dares to come here?'

'I don't know, but I'm going to find out.'

Miriam surged forward, but Louisa checked her sharply. 'Wait. This is *my* home she's pushed into. If anyone is to confront her, it'll be me.'

Gabriel's sister wore a complicated expression. There was anger in it, obviously directed at Frederica's mother rather than her, but also new respect at Louisa's wrath. 'Very well. But be careful. Don't do anything to risk your child.'

Miriam stood aside and Louisa swept past her, her heart thumping. The last thing she wanted was to cause a stir, drawing attention to things she knew Gabriel wanted to keep behind a veil, and with untold difficulty she managed to move through the crowd with her bland hostess's smile stapled firmly in place.

Only when she reached the intruder's corner did she let it drop. 'Mrs Maltravers. I don't believe you were invited here. I must politely ask you to leave.'

For the span of one blink the older woman looked afraid. She faltered, shrinking from Louisa's icy civility, but then she gathered her nerve.

'I want to speak to Gabriel. Once I've spoken to him I'll be more than happy to go.'

'He isn't here. If you've anything to say to him, perhaps you could write.'

'I do write!' Mrs Maltravers's indignation was shrill and indiscreetly loud. 'He never replies! If he won't reply to my letters, what choice do I have but to come and seek him face to face?'

Louisa took a step forward, lowering her voice even more in the hopes her unwanted visitor would do the same. 'If he doesn't answer your letters, then he must not want to engage with you. Coming to his home isn't likely to make him change his mind.'

'You know nothing about it. How long have you been married to him? Five minutes? Ten?' Frederica's mother drew herself up importantly, her tone dripping scorn. 'He was wed to my daughter for three years. You'll never take her place.'

At one time her barb would have hurt. It was certainly flung with the intent to wound, but such spite had lost its power. Louisa knew Gabriel didn't look back on his first marriage with longing and she almost felt pity for the woman in front of her whose bitterness made her want to cause harm.

'I wouldn't try to take Frederica's place,' she said coolly. 'It has never been my intention to supplant your daughter or attempt to erase her as Leah's mother.'

Mrs Maltravers scowled up at her. Her pale eyes radiated loathing and Louisa wondered if she was about to make a scene—but then her manner changed.

'It was Leah I wished to speak to Gabriel about, although now I consider...' Frederica's mother gave a smile that made the hairs on the backs of Louisa's arms bristle warningly. 'Men are so stupid about anything to do with children. It would be much better if we decided matters between us—you and I.'

'What matters?'

Not in the least bit cowed by Louisa's obvious wariness Mrs Maltravers gestured to the slight bump beneath her skirts. 'I wasn't aware you were expecting a child of your own until I arrived here and saw the evidence. Such a special time. You must be so excited.'

Her wheedling was almost as unpleasant as her spite had been. It made Louisa want to walk away, perhaps leaving Mrs Maltravers to suffer Miriam's fury, but with all her other guests in earshot there was little she could do but stay and listen.

'With that said,' Frederica's mother went on, 'you must want to devote your full attention to your baby and for Gabriel to devote all of *his* attention to it, too. How can that happen with Leah in the house, constantly getting in the way with her demands? It would be much better for everyone if you gave her into my keeping rather than have her here getting under your feet. Wouldn't you prefer to have your husband all to yourself, concentrating on his new child instead of having to carry the burden of the previous one?'

She stopped expectantly, her head on an encouraging tilt, and Louisa had to remind herself she was in a room full of witnesses.

Mrs Maltravers's argument flew straight to the very centre of her sadness and lodged there like a splinter digging down into flesh. The subject of Gabriel and his feelings towards their baby was an open wound and Frederica's mother had unwittingly twisted a knife into it, slicing far too close to the bone. It was entirely the wrong angle to approach from if she'd meant to be persuasive, but her tactlessness wasn't the only reason Louisa felt her blood begin to burn.

She was overwhelmingly glad she'd sent Leah down to the kitchens. The idea of the little girl overhearing herself spoken about in such terms was maddening and Mrs Maltravers would never know how lucky she was that Louisa's procession of childhood nursemaids had taught her how to behave properly in public. If there had been no one around to watch, she wasn't sure she'd have been able to contain herself, disgust and anger making it difficult to remain calm.

'No,' she bit out. 'I do not consider Leah a *burden*. The fact that you do only makes me even less inclined to let you take her—not that I ever would have considered it, even for a moment.'

Mrs Maltravers opened her mouth, but it snapped shut again when Louisa advanced another step and leaned down to mutter into the other woman's ear.

'Please leave. You may do so quietly and with dignity or be removed by a manservant, but either way you are leaving this house at once.'

The glare Frederica's mother gave her would have soured milk. It contained all the ugliness of a selfish heart and Louisa only just managed to stop her own lip from curling as she gazed back. She could feel her hands shaking. Usually she avoided confrontation, but for Leah's sake she would have wrestled Mrs Maltravers from the room herself if the woman hadn't stormed away of her own accord, pushing her way to the door without a word of apology to the ladies she shoved aside in her haste.

When the door closed again Louisa gulped a breath. Had that truly just happened? With unsteady fingers she smoothed down her bodice, trying to compose herself before anyone noticed her agitation. Fortunately, nobody seemed to have observed the unpleasant exchange, although when someone touched her arm she couldn't help but flinch.

'What did she say?'

Turning, she saw Miriam stood close by. She must have been watching from across the room and it was a relief to have someone to lean on as her legs felt suddenly weak. 'Give me a moment. I need to collect myself.'

'Of course. Come and sit down.'

She allowed her sister-in-law to steer her over to a chair almost completely concealed behind a curtain. It was the perfect place to recover without being seen and no sooner had Louisa sat down she covered her face with her hands.

'My head's spinning. The *nerve* of the woman…'

Miriam crouched down beside her. 'I watched you speaking to her. I was ready to intervene, but you looked as though you were managing perfectly well on your own.'

Louisa exhaled a mirthless laugh. She still felt as though she was swimming against a strong tide, but the admiration in Miriam's voice was almost worth the effort. 'I'm not sure about that. All I knew was that I had to make her leave.'

She lowered her hands to her lap, laying them flat and straightening her fingers. They hadn't stopped shaking yet and she imagined it would be quite some time before they did.

'Frederica's mother wanted Leah. She made it sound as though she'd be doing me a favour by taking her, but we both know her real plan. She'd have taken Leah and either used her to extract money from Gabriel, or else begun training her up as the next pretty young woman to be sold for her own gain.'

Louisa thought she sensed Miriam's temper rise. Her already dark eyes, so like Gabriel's, seemed to darken even more and it was Louisa's turn to shudder as she wondered how much more ferocious his reaction would be even than his sister's.

For the time being, however, she tried to set thoughts of Gabriel aside. There were more urgent matters to attend to and she rose determinedly from her chair, shaking her head at Miriam's attempt to make her sit down again.

'Leah's in the kitchen. I must just check she didn't hear anything untoward. I doubt she was aware her grandmother was even here, but I must be sure.'

Her sister-in-law nodded. 'Yes. That's a good idea. Have your cook make you a cup of broth while you're there, though. You've had a shock and need to regain your strength.'

Louisa slipped away, more by chance than skill, managing to leave the room without being waylaid.

The danger had passed, but she knew she wouldn't feel truly easy until she was certain Leah hadn't been swept up in what had unfolded, her legs still trembling as she moved through the house towards the kitchen stairs.

'Leah?' she called out as she wobbled downwards. 'Leah, where are you?'

There was no answer. A couple of maids fluttered out of the scullery as she passed, nervously straightening their aprons, but there was no sign of the little girl and with a stab of unease Louisa lengthened her uneven stride.

'Leah?'

The kitchen lay at the end of the corridor. The door was ajar and she tried to suppress a nagging disquiet as she reached it and put her head round the frame. The delicious smell of freshly baked cakes rose to greet her—but a child did not, and fighting down sudden instinctive fear she addressed the cook. 'Mrs Cannock, where's Leah? Is she still with you?'

'No, my lady. She left a few minutes ago.'

Louisa gripped the door handle so hard it hurt her palm. 'Left?'

'Yes, ma'am.' The cook peered up from kneading a great mound of dough, a dusting of flour on her cheery, trusting face. 'Her grandmother came to fetch her. They've gone out for a ride.'

## Chapter Fourteen

Maids leapt out of Louisa's way as she tore towards the servants' entrance, her skirts flying as she went. She ripped the door open so forcefully it squealed on its hinges, but she had no time to care. Leah was in danger and until she was back where she belonged she couldn't pause for even one snatched second, her chest heaving as she stumbled into the cobbled courtyard behind the kitchen and sucked in a lungful of freezing winter air.

It burned all the way down her windpipe and she couldn't tell whether it was the pain or her failure to keep Leah safe that brought tears to her eyes.

*I should have known what that woman was planning. How could I be so stupid as to think she'd leave that easily?*

She slid to a halt, cold water seeping through the flimsy silk of her slippers. Which way would they have gone? There was no doubt Mrs Maltravers had slipped away through the kitchens but once outside she'd have a choice of escapes. It would waste precious time if Louisa went in the wrong direction and she cast about wildly, desperate for any clue. The stables were closest and with her heart in her mouth she turned for them, praying she was right.

'Conway!'

The groom looked up as she barrelled towards him. 'Have you seen a woman come by here? With Leah?

To her combined horror and relief Conway nodded. 'Yes, my lady. She took her out of the side gate. Miss Leah didn't seem very happy about going with her but I thought—' He wavered, obviously noticing she'd paled. 'Is something amiss?'

Louisa shook her head. It would take too long to explain. She had to go after Leah *now* and, ignoring the fear welling within her, she caught the groom's arm.

'Are any of the horses saddled?'

'Yes, my lady. Nutmeg was about to go out.'

Her agitation seemed to worry him. He looked from her hand on his sleeve to the Manor behind them, perhaps wondering if someone might be coming to help, but of course no one did. With Gabriel away from home Louisa was in charge and she knew it was her responsibility to rescue Leah, every second that elapsed another second in which the girl was afraid.

'Nutmeg will do. Please bring her at once.'

'But, my lady, it isn't a side-saddle—'

'At once. Please.'

Fresh fear tried to rise, but she kicked it away, determined the groom wouldn't see it. The thought of riding again made her throat contract, yet what choice did she have? If she had to get back on a horse for Leah then that was what she would do, and with a firm nod to Conway she climbed the mounting block.

The groom looked decidedly unhappy as he brought the horse forward and Louisa herself had to curb a sharp breath when Nutmeg stopped in front of the block. The mare was taller than she remembered, but she made herself scramble up on to her back, the saddle forcing her to sit uncomfortably astride. She hadn't even stopped to snatch up a cloak when she'd fled the house, let alone change into something more suitable for riding, and she shivered with cold as well as dread as the skirts of her thin day dress rose up above her knees.

With her head bare and her silk slippers reduced to wet ruins she didn't look much like an elegant baroness, but that was the very last thing on her mind as she gathered the reins, turned Nutmeg's head towards the open side gate and tapped her heels smartly against her flanks.

Gabriel was not in a good mood.

His afternoon in Warwick hadn't been enjoyable. His bookkeeper was a dependable man, but not an interesting one, and as he'd droned on about cash flow and depreciation Gabriel hadn't been able to stop his mind from wandering. He'd hoped the meeting might provide some distraction from the thoughts of Louisa that plagued him day and night, but if anything boredom had made them worse, his wife's face flickering constantly before him as he'd fought not to close his eyes, and now as he rode back towards the Manor images of copper hair and petal-soft lips chased him every inch of the way.

He rolled his shoulders, feeling the tightness in his muscles. He was tired, but he knew already he wouldn't be able to sleep. Lying there knowing Louisa was on the other side of his bedroom wall, so close but not able to touch her, wasn't something he was looking forward to, but, as always, he was torn. To be near his wife was a pleasure as well as a torment, even if they didn't speak, and the prospect of seeing her still made him urge Juniper into a longer stride.

She cantered towards a gate set into one of the hedgerows. It was a shortcut they often used, the lane leading up to Sisslehurst's long drive lying just beyond, and with his thoughts still on Louisa Gabriel let his horse carry him along the familiar track, hardly paying any attention to his surroundings until a sudden flurry of movement made him sit up in the saddle.

A horse had gone flying past the gate he was riding towards, appearing and vanishing again before he could blink. It was heading down the lane away from the Manor, and although he'd barely caught a glimpse of the rider something inside him knew who it was.

*Louisa?*

It was the strangest feeling, but he didn't stop to question it. He'd know her anywhere, no matter how fast she was going or how unlikely the circumstances, and with a sickening lurch of his insides he realised something was wrong.

The slightest touch of his crop was enough to put Juniper into a full gallop and she jumped the gate with ease. Habit made her turn towards the Manor, but Gabriel pulled her back, wheeling her round to follow Louisa's fleeing back.

Hunching low in the saddle, he pressed his horse on faster, his hands locked tight on the reins. He could see Louisa's hair streaming out behind her and a flash of white where her stockings showed beneath her hitched-up skirts, her inadequate dress a sure sign she'd left in a hurry.

But why? And what was she doing riding so fast in her condition?

His heart shuddered to a momentary halt.

What did Louisa think she was doing, getting back on a horse when he knew the prospect frightened her? If she lost her nerve and fell, it could kill her and the child she carried and any lingering confusion turned to icy fear as Gabriel saw the worst flash before his eyes.

He couldn't allow that to happen. Frederica had been lost in that very way and for such a tragedy to claim Louisa as well would be beyond all endurance. A life without her in it would hardly be any life at all, for him or for Leah now they had both come to love her, and lowering his head almost on to Juniper's neck he drove the horse on faster than he'd ever ridden before.

The wind lashed at him, chilling his already cold skin. He felt its bite even through his warm clothes, so he could only imagine how Louisa must have been suffering in nothing but a thin dress, his fear for her redoubling as with a thundering of hooves he finally drew alongside.

She turned her head towards him, hardly able to see through the loose hair rippling around her. He tried to call out to her, but the words died in his mouth as he saw the ivory mask of her face, so set and strained he hoped he'd never see the like again.

'She's taken Leah,' Louisa shouted above the rushing of the wind and clatter of iron shoes. 'Mrs Maltravers. She came to the house.'

It was like a blow to the back of the head. For a moment he didn't understand—surely she was wrong?—but the terrible intensity in her eyes pushed all doubt aside.

Gabriel swayed in the saddle, almost losing his seat. Juniper was galloping, but time seemed to have slowed, each second stretching out agonisingly as he struggled to speak.

'Where?'

He managed one harsh rasp. His mouth was too dry for anything else, but Louisa understood.

'Just up ahead. A hired chaise.'

He whipped round. In the distance a cloud of dust was rising from the wheels of a small open-topped carriage, moving away at speed. There were three people inside: one driving, one passenger facing forward and another that seemed to be looking back, too far away for their expression to be clear, but their mouth open in what might have been a scream—

Gabriel gripped the reins so tightly he could have torn the leather in two.

'Stay here.'

He had to bellow to make himself heard over the sound of the horses and the clamour of blood in his ears. Rage had begun to roar up to displace some of his fear and he harnessed its power, using it to spur himself on.

'Leave this to me. And for heaven's sake, *get off that horse*!'

Throwing Louisa one last burning look, he bent over Juniper's neck once more, pushing her onwards. The horse was running flat out, blowing hard with each breath, and her efforts weren't in vain. Out of the corner of his eye Gabriel saw Nutmeg and Louisa drop back and he felt fleeting relief that she'd be safe, still horrified she'd been so reckless in the first place but also—conflictingly—admiring her nerve. She hadn't hesitated to act when she knew Leah was in danger and he was passionately grateful for it, although the knowledge of what could have happened as a result made his fury deepen.

If Louisa or her unborn child had been hurt while trying to rescue Leah from the Maltravers, he would have hunted them to the ends of the earth.

With grim determination he muttered encouragement to his horse, her ears flicking backwards at his voice. They were gaining on the carriage speeding ahead, the figures inside it growing more distinct the closer he drew. Mrs Maltravers was sitting beside the driver—he could see her peering over her shoulder, her face white with what he hoped was fright, although she was still trying to restrain Leah as the girl struggled and kicked.

'Papa!'

Leah's cry pierced Gabriel's soul. She'd seen him: she threw herself against the open back of the chaise, reaching out for him with both hands, and with a last desperate surge he forced Juniper alongside.

The driver tried to swerve as Gabriel cut across his path, but his horse had other ideas. It shied away from Juniper, stopping abruptly as it tried to rear, and the moment of delay was long enough for Gabriel to leap from the saddle.

He wrenched open the door of the chaise while it was still rocking to a standstill and tore Leah from Mrs Maltravers's arms. She tried to cling on, but one savage look sent her flinching back as his daughter collapsed against him, tears coursing down her face.

'Papa…'

He held Leah to him, rocking her without a word. His heart was hammering against his breastbone and he couldn't speak, closing his eyes for a brief second as he rubbed his face in her hair. Every emotion overcame him—relief, thankfulness, the sheer wonder of breathing in her familiar scent—and he allowed them all, standing on the chaise's step as the world righted itself around him.

'Gabriel?'

His eyes snapped open.

Frederica's mother was watching him like a mouse might regard a cat. She was pressed into a corner, half-hiding behind the driver, and it took Gabriel a second look to recognise the other man. Mrs Maltravers looked the same as she had last time he'd seen her, but her husband had aged ten years in three, now far more frail than he'd been at his daughter's funeral, and he deliberately avoided meeting his former son-in-law's gaze as Gabriel stared him down.

Mrs Maltravers licked her dry lips. Her eyes darted to the chaise's horse, but as Juniper was still standing in front of it there was no hope of escape. 'Now, Gabriel. We were doing you a favour. With the new child coming, I thought—'

'Do not.'

The words couldn't have been colder if they had been carved from ice. With Leah cradled against him he had to maintain his composure for her sake, but with white-hot rage boiling it was not an easy fight to win.

'You were acting in your own interests, just as you always have. Don't try to pretend you were thinking of anyone but yourselves.'

With either bravery or foolishness it seemed as though Frederica's mother was about to argue, although she hesitated when another horse halted a few yards away from the carriage.

Evidently his command to stay back had fallen on deaf ears. Louisa slid to the ground with far more agility than he might have expected from someone in her condition and then she was beside him, pale and out of breath, but looking so fierce he felt a sharp stab of admiration along with his concern.

Silently he passed Leah to her. The little girl went willingly, tucking herself beneath Louisa's chin, and he saw his wife sag as some of the tension left her. Nothing needed to be said: with a single glance Louisa withdrew, retreating to where Nutmeg stood over them like a towering guard.

Mrs Maltravers stood up. 'Don't give Leah to *her*!' she shrilled indignantly, causing her husband to shrivel in his seat. 'She's nothing but—'

'But what?' Still standing on the chaise's step, Gabriel glared down at the woman in front of him. 'Somebody who cares more about Leah's happiness than her own kin does? The person who has gone to the trouble of getting to know my child as an individual, instead of trying to use her as a pawn in a game of greed?'

Frederica's mother retreated from the whip of his anger. She didn't sit down again, but she did draw back, although some last dregs of her foolish courage survived.

'She's our granddaughter. You have no right to keep her from us!'

Gabriel held his breath. It was a trick his governess had taught him when he was a young boy, struggling to keep his temper, and he called on it now to stop himself from losing all control. Leah and Louisa were only a short distance away and he didn't wish them to see him in an unchecked fury, even if the Maltravers deserved nothing less.

Leaning down, he lowered his voice to a guttural murmur. 'You dare to speak of rights? You two sold your own daughter into a life she never wanted. I'd die before I let you do the same thing to mine.'

He saw Mrs Maltravers seize her husband's sleeve. She seemed to want him to say something, but of course Frederica's father had only ever been able to intimidate vulnerable young women. Against a fair opponent he was just as cowardly as any other bully and Gabriel felt a bitter swell of triumph as Mr Maltravers merely pulled his sleeve free, much preferring to save his own skin than defend his wife.

Gabriel stepped down from the chaise. 'Never come here again,' he said simply as he stood back away from the wheels. 'Never write to me or Leah or make any attempts to see her. This is the last time I'll be gracious. If you try me again, you'll wish you had not.'

With deliberate strides he walked to the front of the carriage and took hold of Juniper's bridle. She moved out of the way of the other horse and immediately Mr Maltravers shook the reins, driving the chaise forward while his wife still stood wordlessly staring at Gabriel as if she couldn't believe he was sincere.

He didn't bother to watch them go. He heard the crunch of the wheels as they rolled away over dried mud, but he didn't turn, his eyes instead fixed on Louisa as she came towards him.

She bent to lower Leah to the ground and his daughter ran to him, a lump rising in his throat as she flung her arms around his waist.

'Who was that lady?' she demanded, her face pressed against his coat. 'I didn't know her. She said she was my grandmother, but how could she be if I'd never seen her before?'

His breath coming in shaky bursts, Gabriel shook his head. Didn't that tell him everything? Leah had no recollection of her own grandparents, their lack of interest in her while Frederica had been alive meaning they were strangers to her now. She must have been terrified beyond belief to have been snatched away by people she didn't know and he held her closer, wrapping his arms around her as Louisa laid a hand on the top of the little girl's head.

'Don't worry,' she said gently. 'You're safe now. You never have to see those people again.'

Gabriel released a shuddering sigh. While chasing down the carriage he'd been fuelled by wrath, but now it was beginning to ebb and he realised the full extent of how afraid he had been. Leah could have been taken and Louisa could have been hurt, and with a glance at his shivering wife he unclasped one hand from around his daughter.

He half-expected Louisa to back away, but to his amazement she allowed him to draw her closer. Leah didn't seem too cold, but Louisa's lips were almost blue and, hardly daring to believe his good fortune that she was letting him touch her, he gathered her firmly beneath his arm.

'You're freezing.' He frowned down at her, longing to chase away the blue tinge with a kiss, but aware it would undoubtedly be a liberty too far. 'You shouldn't have come out without a cloak and you *definitely* shouldn't have been on Nutmeg. You could have been killed if you'd fallen. You and our child.'

Louisa looked him straight in the eye, making his heart turn over. '*Our* child?'

The emphasis she placed on the first word was telling. Clearly even the dreadful events of that afternoon hadn't made her forget how stupid he'd been, but then a trace of colour crept into her pale cheeks.

'But isn't Leah our child, too?' she asked softly. 'I promised you I'd always do my best for her. It wasn't a lie.'

She said it so simply and he knew she meant every word. Her devotion to his daughter was absolute and his trust wouldn't be broken, hard for him to bestow but now more than justly earned. For him all that remained was to convince Louisa of it, but while the three of them stood shivering in the middle of a freezing lane was hardly the time.

When they got back to the Manor, he would have to throw himself on her mercy and pray she might forgive him, and as he shepherded his wife and daughter towards Juniper for the first time he allowed himself to wonder if there might yet be some hope.

'Is Leah asleep?'

'At last, yes. I'm half-expecting her to wake again, though. What happened to her today was enough to give anyone nightmares.'

Gabriel didn't fully close the parlour door behind him. He needed to be able to hear Leah if she cried out, although he didn't like the cold draught that followed him inside. After dispatching her curious guests, he had settled Louisa beside the hearth with a blanket thrown around her shoulders, but all the same he was tempted to throw another log on to the already roaring fire.

'How are you feeling? Are you warm enough? No sign of a chill?'

The colour had returned to her lips and he thought he saw them lift slightly at his barrage of concern. 'No. I feel perfectly well, if not still a little shaken.'

Gabriel nodded distractedly. It was the closest thing she'd given him to a smile in weeks and it made his determination to speak the truth surge like water pressing against a dam.

Surely nobody could have withstood such force. The desire to make amends was too powerful to resist and he had no choice but to obey. Gathering his courage, he cleared his suddenly parched throat.

'I'm sorry. Given what happened this afternoon I can't keep quiet any longer.'

Louisa looked up at him. There was wariness in her face that he knew he deserved and it made it even harder to meet her eye, but there was nothing else to be done. She had to see how much he meant what he was about to tell her and so he couldn't turn away—laying himself bare before her the very least she was owed.

'If any harm had befallen you today, I don't know what I would have done. Before you came into my life I was miserable, stumbling along with no direction, but you brought a light that chased away the darkness.' He paused to wet his dry lips. 'Please let me confess: I love you.'

The last three words slipped out more easily than

he'd imagined they ever could. There was something liberating about telling the whole truth when it had been hidden for so long and he found he couldn't stop, not even when he saw Louisa's eyes had flown wide.

'When I saw you tear past on that horse... The idea of you being hurt frightened me to my bones. You and Leah are more precious to me than I can express and it only seems right that you know it.'

Curiously breathless, he tried to read some reaction in her stunned face. She couldn't seem to move—but Gabriel could and, without stopping to consider his dignity, he dropped to his knees.

'I'm sorry for all the things I've said that have made you unhappy,' he rushed on, well past the point of no return. 'I don't expect you to feel the same things for me, only to know that I intend to right every one of the wrongs I've done you, starting with making you feel that I didn't want the child you carry. I should never have allowed Frederica's conduct to make me question yours and I apologise for letting fear overtake what I knew to be true.'

He stumbled to a halt, finishing his garbled declaration with his heart in his mouth. Louisa still hadn't moved, sitting on her sofa like a beautiful statue, and as silence fell he wondered desperately if he had given enough.

She stared at him, the green scrutiny that had such power to unman him fixed on his upturned face.

No spotlight could be more searching. Her wide eyes missed nothing as they took in his sincerity, roaming from his earnest gaze to his now fully honest mouth. Louisa didn't stir and neither did he, the two locked together in wordless tension as she decided his fate.

The clock on the mantelpiece ticked away a full ten seconds before she broke the spell.

When her hand slipped into his it was like the sensation of having had too much to drink, although infinitely more agreeable. His head felt light, all the blood in his body rushing to where Louisa's slender fingers lay in his grasp, and he hardly heard her above the pounding of his heart.

'Come. Sit here.'

With unthinking obedience, he rose from the carpet to sit beside her. The sofa was small, forcing his leg against hers, but she moved closer rather away.

'Look at me.' Still holding his hand, Louisa drew it against her, laying his palm flat against the fabric beneath her bodice and pressing it firmly into place. 'This is *our* baby. Yours and mine. You've shown a child doesn't need to be of your blood in order to be loved, but I can assure you that in this instance that needn't cross your mind. There is nobody for me but you and whatever fears you hold can be laid to rest.'

She was blushing, but she didn't look away. 'Do you

understand that now? You needn't carry that burden. Set yourself free.'

He could feel the warmth of her body beneath his palm, but it was her words that lit a taper in his soul.

*Nobody for me but you.*

A burst of delirious happiness welled inside him. It seemed too good to be true—but wasn't the truth exactly what they had just committed to sharing, no matter how vulnerable it made them to reveal?

He looked back at her, seeing the utter lack of guile on the features he'd come to adore. For the first time since they'd met nothing stood between them: no secrets or uncertainties or lingering misgivings as to whether they both felt the same way. As much as guilt for Frederica's death would probably always live within him, some other part felt lighter than it had done in years and, as he bent his head to seek out Louisa's lips, he knew who he had to thank for his release.

She melted into his arms, blessedly allowing him to kiss her mouth and nose and the lids of her suddenly damp eyes. He tasted the salt and knew she was fighting back tears, but they dried when he held her against him, lifting her into his lap so she could fit beneath his chin. Holding her again was like taking a gasp of air after being under water and he buried his face in her curls, surrounding himself with their softness and never wanting to let go.

'I'm sorry I ever doubted you. I was a fool.'

'Yes, you were. But you don't need to keep apologising.' Louisa's voice was muffled, her face against his shirt. 'Even if the road here was bumpy, we can put it behind us now. I don't want to keep looking back.'

Gabriel tightened his arms around her. Some superstitious corner of his mind was afraid to surrender her, frightened she might slip away at the very moment their happiness was complete, but newfound confidence brushed the thought aside. She wouldn't leave him and he'd never leave her, and the knowledge would have kept him warm even without the fire blazing in the hearth, content now to sit in joyful silence with his wife tucked securely where she belonged.

One of her hands had sneaked up to cup the back of his neck and he abandoned himself to the pleasure of feeling her fingertips trace lightly over his skin. If she kept up the teasing caress, he would have to find a way to make her pay for it, but luckily for her she interrupted his train of thought.

'The only man I've ever loved is you,' she murmured, somehow both shy and decided at the same time. 'I suppose I ought to be grateful for how badly Uncle Emanuel trains his dogs seeing as it was Comet who put you in my way.'

Gabriel laughed, his mouth pressed to her hair. It gleamed prettily in the firelight, glowing like polished bronze, and he wasn't *quite* able to believe he'd be the one fortunate enough to see it spread out across his pillows once again—hopefully very soon.

'That damned dog. Next time we visit Cressex Hall I feel I ought to reward him for doing me such a good turn.'

# *Epilogue*

*Eight months later*

Carefully, quietly, taking great pains not to wake any of the three people asleep on the sofa, Louisa drew a blanket up over Gabriel's legs.

He lay back against the cushions, his chest rising and falling on steady breaths. One arm was curled around Leah as she snuggled close to him and the other cradled his son against his shirt, a tiny head on his shoulder with a pair of large eyes at last firmly shut.

Tentatively she stood back to admire the scene, hardly daring to move. It was a picture of serenity, baby Jonathan at last having fallen into an exhausted sleep after fighting it for an hour, and she smiled as she watched Leah unconsciously nestle closer to her father's side. The little girl had weathered her brother's crying with admirable patience; not once had she grown annoyed with the noise or at having to share

Gabriel's attention, and as she returned to her own chair beside the fire Louisa felt another wave of the gratitude that was never far away.

Gabriel was just as handsome when he was sleeping as when he was awake, although it wasn't *just* his face she'd come to love. The disagreeable man he'd been when they had first met had been replaced by one much better and it gave her great satisfaction to know his former neighbours had at last realised his true merit—just as she had. Never had she been so glad that servants had such a notorious penchant for gossip: news of the Maltravers' abduction of Leah had spread like wildfire, decimating the reputation they had been so determined to advance.

Such bizarre behaviour made their acquaintances question where the blame for Frederica's death ought really to lie and it hadn't taken long for them to decide that perhaps Gabriel might not be the villain his former parents-in-law had claimed. He didn't need Society's approval, but it was gratifying to know he'd been acquitted, ironically due to the very people who had hoped to hurt him with their lies, and although he had no plans to move his growing family back to Staffordshire, it was good to know he could have done so with his head held high.

Jonathan squirmed in his wrappings and Louisa half-rose from her chair, but he didn't wake. The eyes that had been so reluctant to close were currently blue, but Aunt Eliza was certain they would darken to mimic Gabriel's rich brown, although even if the baby ended up looking nothing like his father Louisa knew there would be no suspicion now.

She sat back in her chair, still watching the sleeping faces on the other side of the fireplace. Frederica and her unhappy legacy of mistrust had finally been laid to rest. Her memory would live on, but only in the best of ways, through the daughter she'd left far too soon rather than a reminder of past pain. The shadow she'd cast over Gabriel had lifted and Louisa bore her no ill will, instead able to feel compassion for a woman backed into a corner with no way of escape.

Her own eyes were beginning to feel heavy. To the astonishment of her mama she had declined a wet nurse, insisting on feeding Jonathan herself, and the interrupted nights were taking their toll. If there had been room on the sofa, she would have joined her husband and children for a well-deserved rest—but they were far too comfortable to be disturbed and, with one last look at the three people she loved more than she'd known possible, she closed her eyes and fell sound asleep in her chair.

\* \* \* \* \*

*If you enjoyed this story, why not check out one of Joanna Johnson's previous captivating reads*

The Officer's Convenient Proposal
Her Grace's Daring Proposal
Their Inconvenient Yuletide Wedding
A Marriage to Shock Society
'Their Yuletide Reunion'
*in Regency Family Christmas*

# MILLS & BOON®

Coming next month

### RESCUED BY THE RAKISH LORD
Sarah Mallory

'It is a rather delicate matter. It concerns Lord Graddon's guest, the one with the roguish epithet Devil Blackbourne.' Lady Kenton declared. 'You will recall we all thought he had quit Graddon Hall.'

'But he has returned?' Selina replied cautiously.

Lady Kenton nodded.

'And now, I suppose, it is all over the town and all the poor mamas are once again anxious for their chicks. But is this all, ma'am?' Selina asked, still anxious. 'I cannot think it warrants you driving here especially to tell me.'

'You are quite correct, if it was only the rake's return I would have left it until we met, or you heard it from one of your other friends. As it is, Sir Alfred came home today with the most alarming report and as soon as I heard it, I came to warn you.'

Selina was now thoroughly alarmed. Was news of her masquerading as a serving maid all over Torrisford now? She waited anxiously while Lady Kenton tapped her fan against her palm, clearly struggling to find the right words to express herself.

'Oh, my dear Selina,' she exclaimed at last, 'The rogue has made you the subject of the most outrageous wager!'

*Continue reading*

**RESCUED BY THE RAKISH LORD**
Sarah Mallory

*Available next month*
millsandboon.co.uk

Copyright © 2026 Sarah Mallory

# COMING SOON!

We really hope you enjoyed reading this book. If you're looking for more romance be sure to head to the shops when new books are available on

# Thursday 23rd April

To see which titles are coming soon, please visit
**millsandboon.co.uk/nextmonth**

MILLS & BOON

# TWO BRAND NEW BOOKS FROM
# Love Always

Be prepared to be swept away to incredible worldwide destinations along with our strong, relatable heroines and intensely desirable heroes.

## OUT NOW

Four Love Always stories published every month, find them all at:

**millsandboon.co.uk**

# FOUR BRAND NEW BOOKS FROM
# MILLS & BOON MODERN

Indulge in desire, drama, and breathtaking romance – where passion knows no bounds!

## OUT NOW

Eight Modern stories published every month, find them all at:

### millsandboon.co.uk

# LET'S TALK
## *Romance*

For exclusive extracts, competitions and special offers, find us online:

- **f** MillsandBoon
- **X** @MillsandBoon
- **◉** @MillsandBoonUK
- **♪** @MillsandBoonUK

Get in touch on 01413 063 232

For all the latest titles coming soon, visit
millsandboon.co.uk/nextmonth